THE BURNING OF HER SIN

A Novel

By

Patty G. Henderson

Published By
Barclay Books, LLC

St. Petersburg, Florida
www.barclaybooks.com

PUBLISHED BY BARCLAY BOOKS, LLC
6161 51ST STREET SOUTH
ST. PETERSBURG, FLORIDA 33715
www.barclaybooks.com

Copyright © 2002 by Patty Henderson

Printed and bound in the United States of America

ISBN: 1-931402-26-4

"To my mother, Blanche; not just the best mom in the world, but my best friend too."

Also By Patty Henderson

BLOOD SCENT

Prologue

Port of Tampa, Florida, 1926

The wallpaper was melting. The flames had engulfed everything in their path. When Carlotta opened her mouth to scream, the smoke and heat she swallowed seared her tongue and burned her chest like a fireball hurled down her throat.

Angelique was dead. He had killed her instantly. The blood from the wound to her head had made a large, spreading puddle on the floor before the fire lapped it up and made it black and bubbly. Angelique's body seemed to quiver in the embrace of the flames before the smoke mercifully draped a curtain of darkness over the entire room. But the smell! It lingered enough to make Carlotta vomit uncontrollably.

She had to get out. Find an exit. She wasn't going to die here like Angelique. She had stopped screaming his name for help when she realized he meant for her to die in the inferno as well. Confused and dazed, she had fallen easily into his trap.

She coughed, and what she spit out was as black as the smoke surrounding her. The window! It was the only way out! She knew this room like the back of her hand. Pushing through the roiling wall of smoke, she ran wildly toward where she hoped the window would be.

When she placed one hand out to balance herself, whatever she touched was so hot it bit into her skin. She screamed in pain, jerked back, and continued to run. The fire licked at her arms and face and finally caught hold of her dress, hungrily working it's way up. Pain shot through her legs and thighs. This couldn't stop her. She wouldn't let the fear tearing through her stomach drag her down into the raging inferno.

Putting both arms up in front of her face as a shield, she threw herself into the blackened glare of the first story window. It shattered like paper. Shards of hot glass stuck to her flesh as she landed awkwardly on the grass outside.

She couldn't feel her legs. They had buckled underneath her. Her whole body felt like a piece of lead. She rolled quickly on the grass, extinguishing the fire in her dress. She wiped at her face in panic, aware of excruciating pain. It felt raw, blistered. Her arms and hands were black; she didn't know if this was from the smoke or whether they were burned of all the flesh. She didn't care. She couldn't think.

She looked back at the house. Orange, angry flames were leaping out of the servants' quarter room, blackening the outside wall. Then she saw the figure approaching from the front of the house. He was angry. Screaming. And he was running towards her. She tried to get up, but her legs wouldn't move. Even if she dragged herself on her arms, she couldn't get away. He was going to kill her. There was no one to help her. No one to hear her.

Chapter 1

Brenda practically ran out of the shower, towel dried in record time, and picked out a black suit and white shirt. She was later than usual. The big case on her desk was hers and hers alone. She couldn't screw this up. She had clawed and growled for this one. It was January 2001. Collins, Davis and Associates were ready to add a Junior Partner to their lineup and she wanted the job.

She'd had it up to her blonde bangs with domestic violence, divorces, and vanilla cases. Any new lawyer fresh out of college and hungry for recognition could ace those. She needed more. Thirty-two wasn't fresh faced anymore and her college days were mercifully behind her.

She adjusted the double-breasted jacket, made sure her hair fell just right behind her ears, and grabbed the briefcase. Her eyes fell on the newspaper left open and folded to the classified ads. She smiled and thought of Tina. Every morning now for the past three months, Brenda circled the summer house of her dreams and left the ads on the table for Tina to find when she got home from the art institute.

Almost since the beginning of their five years together, she and Tina had dreamed and flirted seriously about finding a summer home away from the gray, heavy reality of life in Newark. New Jersey wasn't exactly paradise for the soul. Hell, it wasn't even an island. Still, Tina would calmly count down her levelheaded reasons against a summer house and that would be the end of it.

Brenda had to practically tip toe through some areas of their loft for fear of brushing against Tina's sculptures. They were everywhere. On tables. On the floor. In the bathroom. The upper floor of Taggert's Sewing Machine Company had been the perfect place for them. It was a red brick building built in the 1920's and completely renovated for the upwardly mobile, and convenient to downtown where Brenda worked. That was four years ago. Tina had almost outgrown it. Half the place was now Tina's work area.

Brenda closed the door behind her and headed for the lift. She felt lucky today. Even the air smelled good for once.

* * *

The new millennium had come in with a whimper for Danny Crane. He couldn't care less what year this was. Things hadn't changed much. There was no hope for him. He lifted the sawed-off shotgun gingerly with one hand and placed it like a fragile child in the stained, denim duffel bag. With a grim smile, he reached for the semi-automatic on the bed. Fingering the barrel, he let the bitterness, the anger, and the sadness converge into one thought. The memory of his wife handing him the duffel bag ten Christmases ago was somehow muted by the hate he fueled now.

She had taken everything from him. The court divorce had been messy. The faces of his daughters remained with him always. They had given his wife custody of their two girls, Sara and Michelle. The house was hers. The car. The bank account. They had given her everything.

He shoved the gun into his pants and grabbed the dirty jacket he had worn for over two months. Making sure the shotgun was out of sight in the bag, he left the dump he had called home since the divorce and headed for Collins, Davis and Associates. Their fancy lawyers had paved the way to his downfall. They would pay for the misery in his world. Someone had to pay.

* * *

The information receptionist didn't even give the dingy man with the salt and pepper beard a second look when he asked about the stairs. Nowadays, there seemed to be increased demand for the stairwell as an alternative to elevators. Health nuts had multiplied.

Danny Crane worked his way purposefully up the green and white stairs. Collins, Davis and Associates were on the 7th floor. Heaving up seven flights of stairs wasn't going to stop him. He would just stop if he got tired, rest, and then be on his way again.

Abruptly, he stopped when the door to Floor 3 opened and two men brushed by him. Engaged in conversation, they didn't even glance at him. Danny uttered a noise more like a growl and spat out the yellow phlegm that had built up in his throat.

"Fucking suits."

He continued, hugging the duffel bag close to his chest, paranoid that someone might bump into him or cast a look too close his way. It would have been so easy to just blow them away. Blow them all away.

Halfway before the 5th Floor, he had to stop. His breath was short and his lungs felt tight. His legs felt like old rubber bands. Holding on to the handrail, he cast a hurried look toward the empty stairwell above and below him. He was still alone.

Danny Crane shoved the door open on the 7th Floor and let it slam behind him. He knew where he was going. The glass double doors with the gold and black names of Collins, Davis and Associates were directly across the deep, blue, carpeted hall. With a bounce in his steps, he walked. Adrenaline pumped into his blood like a drug he didn't know how to handle. His head pounding, he couldn't hear the world around him. He could only see pictures. Pictures his brain wouldn't let him forget. The shotgun in the bag was screaming his name.

As Danny Crane burst through the glass doors, he flung the empty duffle bag at the young receptionist sitting behind the front desk. He lifted the shotgun, pumped once, and fired. Her body fell behind the desk. Blood and flecks of brain matter formed a pattern of death on the wall nearby.

Screams erupted beyond the reception area. Crane ran quickly to the left, into the main office. People scattered as fear turned into hysterics and pleas for God. Papers flew in Crane's face. He caught only passing images of frantic eyes. Mouths contorted. He smiled, feeling the thrill course through his body. Yeah. They would all pay.

Pointing the shotgun out, he fired without caring. Without guilt. Wood splintered and glass shattered as screams hammered the air. Danny Crane dropped the shotgun and pulled the semi-automatic from his belt. To his right, a door opened and a handful of men and women peered out.

"You fucking cowards!" Danny Crane's angry growl echoed as he fired the handgun.

"Close the door!" a woman yelled from inside. They couldn't close the door in time. Bodies fell as the door split into pieces.

Eyes glazed, Crane turned his head back to the office. "Mother fuckers, come up where I can see you!"

Hate was running rampant in Danny Crane's mind, and the lust for blood hadn't yet been sated. Holding the gun with both hands, he walked in quick steps through the office, kicking paper baskets, computers, and anything he could find. Women began to sob. He could hear them, but couldn't see them. *Damn it*! They were all hiding behind their desks. This made him angrier. If they wouldn't come out for him, he would find them.

Danny Crane walked through Collins, Davis and Associates and emptied his entire round into innocent, frightened workers. People he didn't know. Each one pleaded for life. Called to

God. *He isn't here.* Danny Crane would laugh. On this Monday morning, Danny Crane loaded his semi-automatic one more time and murdered again and again.

* * *

Brenda Strange would never forget the look on Peter Collins' face when the gunshots began. They were sitting in the conference room and the senior partner had just fulfilled her lifelong dream. A goal she had pursued doggedly. She was a new junior partner in Collins, Davis and Associates.

Brenda Strange was now one of them. Then the gunshots came. Those sitting around her scrambled under the large conference table and cried. Some prayed. Someone was dialing a cell phone. She froze.

She was aware that Peter and two others were crawling on the floor towards the door, intending to open it. She could do nothing to stop them. She was paralyzed. Then the screams stuck her brain like a sharp pin. She saw the door opening. Getting up faster than she thought she could ever move, she pushed toward the group at the door, fear pounding in her head. Her heart was beating so hard, she thought it would stop.

Peter Collins and three others were crouched almost on their knees. Peter opened the door as Brenda lunged from behind to push it shut. Angry words roared their way as the man with the gun spotted them. Too late. He screamed again and pointed. She heard the shots first. Then the splinters from the door flew into her face. A burning pain pierced her stomach and again through her chest. Something warm splashed over her neck. Beneath her lay Peter Collins' body, face torn open, distorted by the bullets.

Brenda's world began fading into silence. Like a record player slowly winding down. The gray in front of her eyes clouded the room. Her heart couldn't keep up with her thoughts. She was dying, falling slowly as if in a slow motion movie. Then the black came flooding in, taking her away from conscious thought. Taking her away from the madness of death outside.

And then Brenda Strange woke up. To blackness. She felt a heavy pressure in her chest and stomach. A feeling of emptiness seized her and she panicked. Until she moved and literally lifted herself up! Her body felt light.

Like a helium balloon, she went higher and higher, until the darkness began to fade. Suddenly, she saw everything around her. She was suspended in the air looking down at herself on an operating table! Figures in green masks and scrubs probed and cut into her body. Tubes connected her to machines that heaved and pumped life into her. Brenda smiled. She thought she looked very peaceful lying there. She realized she was dead or dying and this was the way to the afterlife. She was already on her way.

A pang of deep regret clouded her thoughts and she suddenly found she couldn't move. She started to scream, except the voices stopped her. Muffled, garbled, and distorted, they distracted her. She had to find them, whoever they were.

She thought she heard Aunt Lydia. But no, that couldn't be. Aunt Lydia had died in a head on collision fifteen years ago. Without warning, Brenda was suddenly pulled away and swept into a dark vacuum. She was moving so fast in the dark tunnel that she couldn't see anything around her. She couldn't even open her mouth to scream. Brenda was frightened. Where was she going? What was happening to her? Was this the way to heaven or hell?

Like a roller coaster ride, she began to slow down until she finally just stopped. Suspended in complete darkness. Darkness so suffocating she gasped for air even though she didn't need to. After all, she was already dead! Then she saw the light. Its delicate glow touched her head, illuminated her face, and consumed her entire body.

She was suddenly filled with joy. An inner peace. As if she had gorged herself full of love. She reached out toward the light but found it impossible to touch. The light was everywhere. Everything. Above her. Behind her. Surrounding her. Caressing her body. Then something touched her. Even though it startled her, she wasn't afraid. It felt like a baby's hand. Soft, pudgy, and small.

"Timmy?" She spoke his name in her head. Her little baby brother was here. Other hands then began to stroke her. She knew them all. And then she heard a voice. A real voice. Not just in her head.

"Brenda, don't leave me. I don't know what to do. I don't even know how to pray."

It was Tina's voice. Small, lost, distant. It was calling her back. Loving hands were suddenly replaced by strong, insistent hands that grabbed her gently and began to pull her away.

"No," she tried to resist. The light began to shrink. Her body felt cold, alone. Back through the black tunnel, she was being pulled. Faster and faster until she just closed her eyes and stopped. Melting into nothingness, only a tiny, far away voice faded with her, insistent on its message.

"Go back."

Chapter 2

Recuperation. That was what the doctors said she needed. And a whole lot of patience and understanding too. Brenda couldn't quite get a handle on what they wanted from her.

She had knocked on Death's door, put one foot inside, and was sent back, packing. NDE or "near death experience" is what all the books called it. She wanted to talk about the experience. That was what she felt she needed. To talk. But she never said a word. Not even to Tina. The therapists and the psychologists thought her withdrawal had to do with her ordeal. The trauma of it all and the hours of plastic surgery she endured to reconstruct her cheek. They were wrong.

It was enough that Tina shouldered the hardships of Brenda's recovery. The strain was already starting to show. Brenda would watch her as she moved about the loft. Digging into her lumps of clay. Gently caressing nothing into works of art. Cooking. Paying the bills. Worrying. Brenda had always been best at these things. Things she should be doing.

Tina had lost too much weight. She looked anorexic and she was too pale for all her black hair. The worst thing about it was that Brenda couldn't help her. Since the day she left the hospital, Brenda Strange ceased to exist. Someone new had taken her place.

Brenda never went back to the law firm. Not that it mattered. Collins, Davis and Associates had dissolved. Both Peter Collins and Ted Davis had died that fateful morning. So had Danny Crane. A SWAT team put a bullet through his head. After months of legal wrestling, Brenda and other survivors of Danny Crane's massacre received permanent, lifetime compensations. All of Collins, Davis and Associates assets were liquidated. She and Tina didn't have to worry about money.

Brenda didn't even care. Her visit to the other side of life and death consumed her waking and sleeping hours. She was morose. Such behavior, she knew, was causing a rift between Tina and her, yet she felt so helpless. If only she could reach out. Explain to Tina that what she wanted now was to help others. To share her discoveries.

Fear held her back. What if Tina thought her mad? As it was, Tina couldn't understand why Brenda wouldn't go back to work. There were lucrative offers bouncing her way almost monthly. Instead, Brenda sat in front of their large window watching the giant billboard atop the apartment building across them change advertising every month. Cell phones. Milk. Whiskey. Underwear. They all vied for her attention.

Today was different. She'd had her morning appointment with the therapist who continued to persuade her to take up some sort of hobby or check into a new career change. Brenda had actually listened to most of the shrink's suggestions.

Brenda began to make teddy bears. Not just ordinary bears. Miniature bears. She spent hours pouring through *Teddy Bear and Friends* magazine, craft books, and sent away for upholstery fabrics. Tina just shook her head and indulged her in this new, unexplored side of Brenda Strange.

Brenda's first tiny teddy didn't turn out all that bad. She named it *Tina* and it sat on Tina's worktable. As for career changes, she flirted with getting into the private eye business. She had a New Jersey PI license that she was able to get by working closely with the firm's personal PI, Kevin O'Brady.

She worked so many divorce cases with Kevin that he persuaded her to get her own PI license. But, for the moment, the flirtation was just that.

* * *

Brenda came home from a therapy session just before lunch, picked up the mail, and sat back down in front of the double windows, disappointed that the new upholstery fabric she'd ordered hadn't arrived. That was when Tina walked in the door. She very rarely came home for lunch.

"Hey baby," Tina said as she disappeared into the kitchen. "How did it go with the therapist?"

Brenda couldn't see her. The kitchen was a center island in the middle of the huge floor. Brenda heard some papers rustling.

"You know, the same. What brings you home for lunch?

"Had to do something here."

Tina reappeared from the kitchen, came over to Brenda, wrapped her arms around her, and plopped a folded newspaper on the small table next to her.

"Your turn, honey." After she kissed Brenda on top of her head, Tina sat down on the chair opposite Brenda and propped one leg over the arm of the chair. "You've always marked mostly Florida property, so I concentrated on Florida real estate." Tina could barely conceal the smile on her lips.

It was the Real Estate section. Several ads had been circled in bright red.

"Are we really going this time?" Brenda had to fight the tears pooling in her eyes. "Honey, are you serious about this?"

"I've already asked for a leave at the Institute. We can leave whenever you want."

Tina got up and worked herself onto Brenda's lap. She was as light as a feather. Brenda felt a tinge of sadness, brushed it aside, and held on to Tina tightly. Tina brushed a stray hair from Brenda's eyes.

"I want you to be happy, Princess Di. If it means finding some beautiful, perfect summer house in Florida, then we're doing it," Tina said as she looked down into Brenda's face. Brenda eyed her intently.

"You think I still look like Princess Di? I mean, is my cheek really even with the other?" Tina had jokingly referred to her as "Princess Di" when they started going out. She insisted that Brenda was the spitting image of the deceased icon. Brenda was embarrassed by it, but secretly liked the attention. Besides, others had remarked on the same thing.

"I think you're even more beautiful than Princess Di." Tina reached over and picked up the teddy bear magazine on the table.

"Tell me one thing though, Brenda. Why teddy bears?" She leafed through the colorful pages of the magazine.

"They remind me of Timmy."

* * *

The flight to Tampa, Florida wasn't near as long as Brenda feared. They arrived near dusk, on time at 8:35 PM. Because of daylight savings time, they were able to catch the picture postcard sunset promised by all the brochures. The orange glow of the setting sun painted the sky in watercolor strokes of orange, purples, pinks, and pale blue, reflected in darker hues on the rippling water of the bay. The Tampa skyline was not the cluttered giant of Newark, but smaller, more intimate.

Neither Brenda nor Tina had ever been to Florida. The only memories Brenda could connect to the Sunshine State were those silly souvenirs her parents always brought back for her. She always laughed and called them "coconut people." They were these horrendous little dioramas of Florida coconuts decked out with tacky clothes, hair, and bouncing little eyes. There were glue spots where some underpaid, overworked production worker had carelessly applied cheap, tiny seashells. And aside from the media overexposure of Key West, Florida remained an exotic, beckoning lover. Tina was a born and bred Bronx native. Brenda didn't even think Florida existed for Tina. All her dreams had been hatched and fulfilled in the world of New York.

The real estate agent had booked them at the Wyndam Hotel. Located near Tampa International Airport on the corner of Westshore Boulevard and Kennedy, it was a beautiful hotel at a very busy intersection. There was an upscale mall across the street called Westshore Plaza with a Sak's in plain view.

Cindy Taylor of Tampa Sun Realty was set to pick them up at 10:00 in the morning for a walk through of the two properties in Tampa that she had listed. She had also mentioned some choice waterfront homes in Sarasota.

Brenda had her eye on the older house in Palmetto Beach, an area of the Port of Tampa. A large, sprawling house built in the late 1800's, the Malfour House needed cosmetic care and painting. But the price was definitely right. Cindy had faxed them a complete description before they'd left Newark.

Situated smack in the middle of The Tides of Palmetto, a new, upper class community off 22nd Causeway, the Malfour House was the first property Brenda wanted to see. The house was sticking in her thoughts.

However, it was obvious Cindy wasn't trying very hard to sell them the Malfour House. She downplayed the value, resale potential, and location. Instead, she focused Brenda and Tina toward the properties in Sarasota even after Brenda insisted on seeing the Malfour House first. "It would require too much work," Cindy persisted, eventually admitting that Tampa Sun Realty hadn't had much luck with this particular property.

Well, Brenda thought. *I'll see about that.*

Chapter 3

Cindy Taylor picked them up promptly at 10 AM. She was in a white and charcoal Lexus SUV. A short, round woman with smiling brown eyes, her deep, throaty voice didn't fit her look.

Brenda didn't have to bring up Malfour House. Cindy exited the parking garage of the Wyndam Hotel and glided smoothly into the heavy traffic.

"The Malfour property is first on our list this morning. We'll be taking the Selmon Express Way to Port of Tampa and then crossing the 22nd Causeway Bridge into Palmetto." She looked briefly at Brenda beside her. "Not exactly the scenic route, but we'll be able to make more time. We have more properties to get to this morning, ladies." She smiled back at Tina in the rear.

She's rushing us through the Malfour House, thought Brenda. *Well, I just might take my sweet time. Throw a serious kink into Cindy Taylor's well-orchestrated time management.*

Don't be so mean, a tiny voice inside her head said. *Too small to listen to.*

Brenda settled back into the soft, gray leather seat and watched Cindy pass out some color brochures to Tina as she drove with one hand. Tina flipped one on Brenda's lap. It was a showcase of some of the available Tampa Sun Realty properties. Brenda couldn't find much of interest.

Tina had some general questions regarding real estate in Florida. Thankfully, this kept Cindy well occupied for most of the trip. Brenda merely wanted to soak in the new Tampa environment.

After getting onto a fairly deserted Interstate (well, in comparison to New Jersey, anyway) and paying several tolls, they approached the downtown area of Tampa.

Downtown Tampa was indeed very small and spread out. Brenda liked the open feeling. Those towering, claustrophobic, shoulder-to-shoulder buildings of the mega cities always bothered her.

There was little to see as they sped by downtown. Cindy pointed out the Channel Drive district, where development was running rampant. Coffee shops, restaurants, theaters, art galleries, hotels, and money, money, money were all expected to take shop along the water.

Brenda wasn't listening. She was mesmerized by the large, rusting ships docked right along the channel below them. Cindy took an exit, paid another toll and veered right.

"Port of Tampa was one of the first settlements here. Tampa was the premier port in the South during the eighteen hundreds," Cindy said as they turned onto a two-lane road.

Port of Tampa was a quaint part of the city. The houses Brenda saw were small frame houses, most of which needed painting. Broken down cars and trucks littered the sandy lots around the homes. Grocery stores, gas stations, and grimy neighborhood-type restaurants dotted the tight road. No McDonald's here.

"Ybor City is a few miles behind us. It's a real hot night spot in Tampa," Cindy added.

They sped past a large, multi-storied red brick building with a green metal sign posted outside. Brenda could only catch some of the lettering. It was a cigar factory. Brenda had read about them in a booklet about the history of Tampa. There was a banner across the face of the building. Artist's Hub of Tampa

Bay, it had read.

The tight two-lane road gave way to an intersection where a small, red brick wall read *Welcome to Port of Tampa*. They went over the bridge and Brenda could see what looked like a fleet of shrimp boats the whole length of the Bayway. Tall holding tanks pierced the sky, and large, flat buildings dotted the channel.

"Shrimp capital of the world, huh?" Tina joked.

"You can really get a feel for the shrimping industry here in Port of Tampa. This is the heart of the shipping industry in Tampa," Cindy said.

"I like it," Brenda added, not taking her eyes off the surrounding area.

"You have a great view of downtown Tampa if you look behind you," Cindy added.

Both Brenda and Tina turned their heads to see the Tampa skyline behind them. Once over the short bridge, the road continued as a four lane with a grassy median. They passed a restaurant to their right, sitting on the water's edge.

"That's The Gulfbreeze. Been here since the early 20's. Best seafood in town," Cindy said. Food must have been good; Brenda noticed the number of cars in the parking lot. She made a mental note to come back here. She loved fresh seafood.

About half a mile past the Gulfbreeze, Cindy turned left through a recently paved road. Two red brick signs with aqua script lettering welcomed them to The Tides of Palmetto. The landscaping was beautiful, with fresh, deep green grass, a myriad of pansies in bright colors and small, round palm trees.

Past the entrance signs, the road went on for about another half mile before they came to a small guardhouse with an electric gate. As they pulled to a stop, a heavy woman in a khaki uniform came to the window. Cindy pulled a card out of her bag and handed it to the guard.

Just beyond the gate, Brenda could see the rippling water of a wide inlet and a long, narrow two-lane bridge stretching across to what presumably was The Tides of Palmetto. The gate opened and they drove onto the bridge.

"Hey Princess, isn't this exciting?" Tina was sitting up close behind Brenda.

"I'm already in love."

"I'm jealous."

"Well, at least you know the mistress."

They both laughed and ignored Cindy Taylor's tight smile. Brenda tried to control her excitement. Malfour House lay beyond. Waiting. Would it be all she thought?

"The developers of the Tides had to put in the guardhouse." Cindy broke Brenda's inner musings. "As you can see," she continued, "the security is max. There's a camera that takes photos of every car's tag that goes through the main gate."

This was probably an important selling point for some buyers, but Brenda had made a living sticking her face into crime. And if someone really wanted to, they could find a way to get around the guard and the camera.

They went over the short, two-lane bridge and then they were on a long road lined with palm trees and bright flowering bushes in bursts of pinks, whites, and purple. The palm trees swayed to the gentle fingers of the gulf breeze. Brenda had never seen so many different kinds of palm trees. It was love at first sight.

Cindy took a sharp right turn onto a less well-maintained road, the grass and shrubs growing wild and untrimmed.

"You can see the Malfour House up ahead," Cindy said, an anxious smile on her lips.

When Brenda first caught sight of the house, her heart skipped a beat. Even from a distance, Malfour House was huge. She craned her neck to get a better look. They finally reached the clearing and the Malfour House grounds spread out before them. The house was a large, Victorian. Larger than Brenda imagined. It almost appeared to swallow everything around it. Sky, land, air.

Cindy followed the circular drive up into the covered porch and stopped the car. Malfour House was surrounded by palm trees with beautiful white and pink azaleas surrounding the house. The house itself was medium beige with borders and trim a dusky rose. A one hundred percent Florida wood frame antique. Here and there, Brenda noticed smaller trim in jade as well. Brenda had to bend her head back to look up at the uppermost roof. There was a row of wooden gingerbread along the roofline with little round notches in clusters of three, painted jade.

Like the scales of a dragon, she thought.

The warm air brought with it the scent of Tampa Bay.

"Wow, is it always this strong?" Tina's nose wrinkled in disgust.

"Oh, that's the bay at low tide. It can get pretty strong at times," Cindy said, "but you get used to it."

"It's beautiful," Brenda said, not taking her eyes off Malfour House. She noticed that the landscaping and the grounds were well kept.

"Is there someone who keeps up with the grounds, Cindy?"

"Oh yes, the owner takes care of it. Since the restaurant moved out, Peter Cuenca hired a professional lawn care business. They're out here regularly."

"I don't think you said, but is Mr. Cuenca local?"

"No, the Cuencas live in Key West."

"Why wouldn't they want to live here?"

Cindy Taylor smiled and motioned toward the house. "The Cuencas inherited this house. They already had their home in Key West." She talked as they walked up the porch, going under an arched roof. "I was told some of Mr. Cuenca's children did live here some years ago, before the restaurant, but for some reason, didn't stay."

Brenda noticed the large floor-to-ceiling windows downstairs and upstairs. Like staring sentinels. The door was a dark, cherry wood with two beautiful, oval, stained glass panels. Brenda could make out flowers, leaves, and other designs. When they stepped inside, Brenda took a deep breath. An empty house always smelled of sadness. Something solid, wanting attention. The Malfour House was virtually screaming, *"Look at me. Look at me."*

Inside, the sun coming through the multitude of windows warmed everything it touched. Brenda exhaled. Tina beside her was casting her logical eye at Cindy.

"This place been closed for long?" Tina asked her.

"The restaurant closed up a little less than a year ago. As you can see, they made some rather unique modifications," Cindy answered.

No kidding, thought Brenda. They were standing in the Main Hall and the restaurant owners had put in metal railings similar to those found on old ships, like the Titanic, running along the walls of the room. There was a flight of stairs to their right, a lonely waiting bench left behind to gather dust sitting below it.

"This was the restaurant's reception area," Cindy continued, "and straight ahead is the original drawing room or library. To our left is a sitting room and here to our right is the original dining room of the house."

Brenda noticed Cindy looking at a plan of Malfour House she was holding in her note pad.

"Of course, the restaurant used all of these rooms as individual dining areas. The kitchen is behind the dining room and adjacent to that is what was called the servants' quarters in the late 1800's, but the restaurant remodeled it for storage area."

"This is so big," whispered Tina, leaning towards Brenda.

"You don't have to whisper, dear," Brenda smiled.

"I'm afraid if I speak any louder, it'll echo through the whole damned house."

"And who do you think will hear you? The ghosts?" teased Brenda. Tina just arched one dark eyebrow at her. That was when Brenda smelled it. She turned to Cindy.

"What's that smell? Is someone burning wood around here? A barbecue maybe?" She put her nose up in the air. Both Tina and Cindy did the same. The smell was very strong.

"I don't smell anything," Cindy finally said, looking at Tina for confirmation.

"I don't smell it either," Tina agreed, both of them looking back at Brenda.

"It smells like something burning." *What's wrong with them? Why can't they smell it?* thought Brenda. It was all around them. She walked toward the stairwell and peeked into the dining room. It was even stronger there.

"I think it's coming from here."

She heard Cindy's heels following her.

"Maybe one of the neighbors is doing a barbecue," Tina said behind her.

"Well, your closest neighbor would be the Davis' about one block down to your right," Cindy added. "Does it smell electrical?"

But then it was gone. Like it was never there. Brenda tried to catch the scent again. She shook her head.

"Never mind. Maybe it was my imagination," she let the words trail.

"If you'd like, I can have the house re-inspected as soon as possible," Cindy added quickly.

"No, it's okay," Brenda smiled. "Maybe it was just something carried in the air." She fought hard to hold the smile. Tina had that concerned look on her face. She was being foolish. They should just finish the tour of the house.

Cindy took them through the rest of the first floor. The house was actually in better shape than they had first suspected. The kitchen area in the back was the worst for wear and the area originally intended as a servants' quarter had been sectioned off into smaller storage rooms, but all in all, nothing too traumatic.

Brenda noticed the beautiful garden through the dining room windows. Bursts of colorful plants crowded the garden, with a short path winding down to a grassy area that looked out into the inlet circling behind and around Malfour House. A small bench sat looking out to the waterway.

Upstairs, Brenda and Tina only fell more in love with the house. The large, upstairs room with the circular wall of windows was especially breathtaking. Brenda looked at Tina, whose face was glowing like the sun bathing the magnificent room. She could bet what Tina was thinking, *My studio. My studio.* Brenda was thinking more like, *Our bedroom. Our bedroom.*

"There's a large attic upstairs. It's still got some boxes, I'm afraid. I apologize, but we haven't had the chance to go through any of it," Cindy was saying. "If you want, we can have someone come in and haul it out."

"No," Brenda blurted out. "We can do that ourselves." What was she thinking? "I mean . . . if we decide to buy Malfour House, I'd like to go through those things myself. I'm a sucker for old trunks and junk in attics." Her smile was nervous. Tina was pretending not to listen.

Cindy stuffed the map of Malfour House into her bag and smiled back at Brenda. "Well ladies, this is Malfour House. Now, are we ready to continue on to our other properties?"

"I think we want to talk about this house first." Brenda glanced briefly at Tina. "I mean, Tina and I need to discuss it. We can decide on the Sarasota properties tomorrow, if you don't mind?"

Tina was quiet. Her eyes told Brenda she would play along.

"Certainly. However you want to do it," Cindy said. "Just call me later this evening." She dug in her bag and pulled out a card. "My cell phone number is listed as well. Just give me the word and I can be ready." She handed it to Brenda. "I have to be honest though, Peter Cuenca has been a tough cookie to break. Doesn't seem to want to budge on the selling price of the house. His son Louis is in charge of negotiations and even he's had trouble communicating with his father."

"May I call him? Do you have his number?" Brenda wouldn't let the seller's stubbornness deter her.

"Sure. It couldn't hurt. But let me check and make sure that's okay with them. I'll let you know." Cindy added the Cuenca's number on the back of her business card.

* * *

"Honey, don't you think we should look into this house before deciding to buy it?" Tina was asking as they unlocked the door to their hotel room. "Or at the very least, look at the other properties Cindy has?"

Tina's rational, logical nature was kicking in. Brenda knew Tina had loved Malfour House as much as she had, but had she listened to the walls? They had spoken to Brenda. Whispered through the wallpaper, the floors, and the peeling paint. Malfour House had secrets. Something that old was drowning in them.

Brenda threw her bag on the king-size bed and took off her shoes. She noticed how wrinkled her linen blouse and pants were. She loved the cool elegance of the fabric, but hated the way it creased so easily.

"C'mon, Tina. You loved the house. I saw it on your face."

"Yeah, baby, but it's just the first house we've looked at." She shook her head slowly, brows furrowed. "I don't know."

Brenda unexpectedly went over and kissed her lightly. "Why don't we talk it out over lunch?"

"Downstairs at the very expensive restaurant?"

Brenda laughed as she slipped into her shoes again. "C'mon dearie. I'm buying."

Chapter 4

The following morning had brought them no closer to a decision on Malfour House. The day before, after a long and expensive lunch, they had toured Westshore Plaza across the street, leased a loaded Jeep Grand Cherokee, and tossed the choice of their future summer house back and forth like a beach ball.

Brenda was brushing her teeth in the bathroom when she heard the television over the running water.

"Hey Princess, come look at this."

"It better be good," Brenda gurgled, fighting to keep toothpaste from dribbling down her chin.

Tina was sitting at the edge of the bed, mesmerized by the pictures on the screen. "It appears, sweetheart, that Tampa is a hot bed of intrigue."

"Turn it up and scoot over." Brenda snuggled next to Tina.

"A woman's body washed ashore at PicNic Island early this morning and was found by two men getting an early start on a fishing trip. Early indications are that it was a diving accident and the police at this time are not treating it as a homicide until further investigations are conducted. The body of the woman has not been identified. If anyone has any information, they are

being asked to call the Tampa Police Dept."
"Feel like home?" Tina teased.
"C'mon, we're wasting time. Turn that off."
Brenda had already made up her mind. Malfour House could be a new, unspoiled page for the two of them. A chance to start fresh. She wanted to call it *home.* She hoped Tina would agree.
"Tina, I'm going to call Louis Cuenca. They have to sell Malfour House to us."
Tina turned the TV off quickly and turned around, surprised.
"Whoa. I think the house has lots of potential too, but once again, are we ready? Shouldn't we look at those other properties?"
"No Tina, this is it. I know it. I feel it. Don't you? Please Tina, say you feel it too?" Brenda sat back down next to Tina and took her hand, giving her her best puppy dog look.
Tina looked deeply into Brenda's eyes. Brenda knew she would eventually agree. This was the same back and forth ritual they indulged in. And besides, she knew Tina couldn't argue with the fact that the Malfour House was magnificent. More beautiful than anything they thought they could ever afford.
"What makes it so special to you, Princess? I mean, to be honest, it's got class, yeah, but it's going to need an awful lot of TLC like Cindy said."
"It doesn't matter. I'll get the best contractors money can buy. I want Malfour House to shine like it did when it was built."
Tina whistled and shook her head. "You're talking one helluva restoration, baby. Furniture, structure work, paint. Need I go on?"
"Tina, I know. But just think. When you build and create something yourself, it means so much more. You should know this. Sure, we could go and settle on some fancy, showpiece home with all the trimmings already added, but it would be someone else's idea of home."
Tina looked at her a moment longer, then broke out in a wide grin. "I have to tell you one thing, I wouldn't want to be Louis

Cuenca when his phone rings."

* * *

And his phone did ring, persistently. Brenda heard a small voice answer.

"Hello?" It sounded like a child.

"Hi, can I speak with Mr. Louis Cuenca, please?"

"Ummm, I don't know."

Now, Brenda was sure it was a child. "Hi honey, can I talk to your dad?" Brenda suddenly heard the hard knock of the phone dropping and waited. There was a TV in the background.

"Quen es?"

Oh great. Spanish. "Hello, I'm Brenda Strange. I'm trying to reach Mr. Louis Cuenca."

"Oh, hees not here." Her voice was very loud.

"Do you know where I can reach him? It's about the Malfour House property in Tampa."

Silence.

"Un momento, por favor."

Brenda heard the phone put down again.

"I can geeve you his work number."

"Yes, that would be fine."

Brenda hung up and dialed the new number quickly. She got a hold of a moped rental store, and after minutes on the phone, finally spoke with Louis Cuenca. She explained her reason for calling and made it clear she was willing to go the extra mile for Malfour House.

"I appreciate your calling Ms Strange, but my hands are tied," he said.

"Don't you hold the deed?" This was getting confusing. "Cindy Taylor suggested I call you."

There was a short pause, then a half-hearted chuckle.

"I appreciate Tampa Sun Realty trying so hard to sell the property, but it all boils down to my father having the final say. He's the owner and holder of the deed. I'm just the go between."

Okay, this was getting more complicated. And frustrating.

"Look Mr. Cuenca, my partner and I are interested in buying your house. We have the finances but we're short on time. We're here from New Jersey and can't stay forever in a hotel while your father decides. How can I speak to your father directly?"

"My father?"

What was so difficult to understand? "Is he alive?"

"Oh yes. My father is 92 years old, but very alive."

"How can I get a hold of him then?"

Louis Cuenca chuckled again on the other end of the line. Brenda was starting to lose her patience.

"I have to warn you, it won't do you any good. Two others have tried to purchase the house. We've tried everything to persuade my father to sell."

"Well, maybe I'm the lucky one," Brenda just blurted out. She couldn't understand why a man could be so attached to a property he never lived in.

"My father lives with us, Ms Strange," Louis was saying. "He should be home if you want to talk to him. Good luck."

"Thank you, Mr. Cuenca." Brenda didn't even wait. She hung up and immediately rang the Cuenca residence again.

"Ola." It was the same woman.

Brenda tried to remember some of her college Spanish.

"Senor Cuenca. Pedro Cuenca, por favor."

"See, un momento."

Bingo. Off the woman went. It seemed like forever before anyone picked up the phone.

"Deime." It was a raspy, harsh voice, like a car slowly going over gravel.

"Mr. Peter Cuenca?"

There was a long pause. "Yes, this is Peter Cuenca. Who are you?" It was not a friendly question and he struggled with his words.

"My name is Brenda Strange and I hope I'm not disturbing

you. I'm calling from Tampa. Cindy Taylor at Tampa Sun Realty gave me your number. Mr. Cuenca, we're interested in buying the Malfour House."

"You want my son."

"I've already spoken to your son. As I told him, we've got the money, Mr. Cuenca and we would like to close quickly." Brenda heard a loud intake of breath. She needed to remind herself how old this man was.

"The agent gave you a price?"

"Yes, she did, but that's what I wanted to talk to you about. I'm sure you know the house needs repair, inside and out. I'm willing to get a contractor out to give us an estimate and then work out a deal for the asking price. I want the house, Mr. Cuenca. I would be willing to work out a deal favorable to you."

"The house goes for the asking price, no less."

Okay, this was going to be more difficult than she thought. Peter Cuenca was obviously very attached to his property. Perhaps he too could understand the magic of Malfour House.

"Mr. Cuenca, I can't fully explain this to you and I hope I don't come off sounding like some flake, but the house just seems . . ." She paused for a moment, trying to find the right word, but couldn't. "It just feels right, Mr. Cuenca. It's almost like it needs me."

The silence on the other end of the line was so deep, so long, she was afraid she'd said something wrong.

"Mr. Cuenca?"

"I have never heard anyone put it quite that way." His voice was softer.

"Mr. Cuenca, the house needs attention. It's dying." It was only after she said it, that she realized how stupid it sounded. But Peter Cuenca was quick with his answer.

"Have Ms Taylor call me after you get your contractor. We will talk." The line went dead.

Brenda let go of the breath she'd been holding.

"Oh my God," she said out loud as she hung up the phone.

"What happened? Did he agree?" Tina asked from the bed.

Brenda nodded in a daze. "I think we just bought ourselves Malfour House."

Chapter 5

Not only did Peter Cuenca agree to the sale of Malfour House, he accepted Brenda and Tina's first bid. Brenda was beside herself.

She and Tina rented an apartment on Harbour Island. The apartment was a property Cindy had available and she offered them an open lease until they could move into their new home.

Cindy Taylor promised to follow through on her promise to make a quick closing. The Cuenca family provided all the necessary papers and signatures. It would be a done deal in less than four weeks.

Brenda busied herself with every detail of the house. She located an interior decorator specializing in Victorian decor. He and Brenda pored through heaps of books and catalogs. Everything from furniture to the wallpaper was selected and ordered. Already, a contractor recommended by Cindy had started work on the house itself.

In the meantime, Brenda found a shopping heaven in a place called Hyde Park Village. Not only did she love the exclusive shops and the shady, tree-lined location, she could shop for all the linen clothes she could ever want! But, what topped it all off was the discovery of Teddies in the Park, an honest to goodness teddy bear collectibles shop.

She met Felice Putnam, who owned and operated the old house turned teddy bear heaven and immediately took a liking to her. Brenda even talked Felice into consigning some of her own miniature bears and offered to bring in some samples. Now, she was beginning to feel like she'd finally be able to get a new start in Tampa.

When she got home from the teddy bear shop, excited to share her new find with Tina, she found Tina packing.

"Tina, what's going on?" The surprise echoed in her voice.

"Gotta get back to the Institute, Princess. Final Exams before summer break have to be done." Tina didn't look up, but continued to pack.

Brenda walked up and sat on the bed next to the suitcase, looking for something in Tina's eyes. "I wish you didn't have to go. When will you get back? I mean . . . will you be able to be here by July 1st? That's when we can move into Malfour House. The bed arrives then and I thought we could set it up ourselves." She was smiling, but the sadness inside cut it short.

Brenda stood up and put her arms around Tina's waist, pulling her away from the packing. "Sweetheart, I want you here to spend the first night in the house. Our house."

"Honey, I want to be here with you too, but you knew this was going to be a summer house. I'm a teacher, remember?" Tina held on a second longer to Brenda's hands, then pulled away and began to pack again.

Brenda really *did* understand. Teaching was Tina's passion just as law had been hers. But suddenly, all that seemed so far away. *Lawyer.* She let the word trickle slowly away, fading in the blinding reality of Malfour House.

"Princess, why don't you come back home with me?" Tina interrupted her thoughts, "We can both be back here when my classes are done."

A certain sense of panic struck Brenda like lightning. Leave the house? No, she couldn't. Not now. There was so much still left to do. She didn't want to leave. That sobering thought rushed through her, leaving her speechless. She looked up at Tina, her eyes saying what she couldn't.

Tina stood for a moment, a tight smile forming, then fading. She resumed packing. "No . . . I didn't think so."

* * *

The small, wood frame house on Chestnut was much like all the other homes on this old Tampa street. This neighborhood had seen it's glory days and since, waved them a sad goodbye. Run down homes and mostly vacant lots, the once thriving Cuban population had dwindled to only a few of the oldsters who either insisted on staying or couldn't afford to go elsewhere.

The house popularly referred to as "La casa de los gallos," was a very small bungalow style home in need of paint. And electricity. But Papa Chucho didn't need a fancy house. And the only light he needed he got from the candles that flickered like tiny stars in every room of the house.

The faint breeze whispering through the steamy June night pulled at the burning candles and played on the tattered curtains that barely covered the windows. Most who came to this house came in search of something. Riches. Good health. Power. Love. Tonight, others' desires would be saved for the later hours. The hours just before the rooster warned the world of the coming daylight, the impending reality of another day. Tonight belonged to the initiates.

The man who got out of the black Toyota carried a small box delicately in his hands. Papa Chucho knew him. He'd been welcomed in this house before. He had come to Papa Chucho for Ebos before. After all, Papa Chucho was a favored priest of the Orishas. Among Tampa Santeros, he was one of the most powerful Santeria practitioners.

In the backyard of the "house of the roosters," a small circle of men and women moved in rhythm to the low, persistent beat of drums. A small row of candles glowed around a collection of large platters piled with an assortment of fruit, meats, vegetables, and herbs.

Papa Chucho greeted the man with the box in the living room, in front of a large altar littered with food and figurines, surrounded by at least a hundred votive candles. There was another younger man dressed in a white shirt and red scarf, who stood protectively beside Papa Chucho.

"Chango loves you and looks for your offerings." Papa Chucho smiled and revealed a mouth of broken and missing teeth. He was a small, dark withered man with a head of bushy white hair. "Do you have what is needed?"

The visitor said nothing, only handed him the box. Papa Chucho took the box greedily and opened the flap. He looked up at the man, his grin wide like a hungry ghoul. "I did not think you could do it, muchacho. Dog shit and cat shit was easy, but the eyelashes and whiskers . . ." He let the sentence die as he spotted the smaller, black box on the bottom. His eyes locked on the other man's and his smile faded. "And the scorpion . . . I will not even ask how you managed." Papa Chucho handed the box to his assistant who disappeared into another room.

The drums outside began to beat stronger, with persistent passion. A potent, pungent smell invaded the house. Papa Chucho had not removed his eyes from the man who stood before him. "You know the Oshiras require much blood for what you ask. They get very hungry doing the curses. Did you bring the four roosters?"

"They're in the car," the man finally spoke. "I bring them in offering. To add strength to the curse."

"Are you fully protected, my son? You will need much purification and protection. If those you curse find you out, they can turn it against you."

A cold, cruel laughter shattered the flickering silence.

"Those two fools will never know what's happening until it's too late. They'll run so fast and so far that not even Chango will be able to find them. That is, if they survive."

His laughter turned into a manic cackle as the drums outside echoed the darkness in his voice.

Chapter 6

The call came too early in the morning. She was still half asleep when she finally hung up with the contractor. Ed Banners wanted her to come down to the house this morning. No real emergency, just something he thought she should see.

Brenda had already learned her way around the general vicinity of downtown Tampa, Hyde Park, and some of South Tampa. She could get to Malfour House blindfolded. This morning, she decided to stop at The Gulfbreeze before heading out to the house. She'd been so busy, she hadn't gotten a chance to check it out.

As she rolled into the gravel parking lot, she noticed there weren't many cars this early in the morning, even though a big, bold sign outside the restaurant boasted their $3.50 breakfast: two eggs, ham, bacon or sausage, and hash browns or grits with coffee or OJ.

When Brenda walked in the door, what she found was a narrow waiting parlor, lined with chairs and a large dining area beyond, surrounded by floor-to-ceiling windows. To her right were a bar and several tables. Everything was paneled in a rich varnished oak.

It seemed that every bit of wall space was occupied by

paintings depicting boats, lighthouses or somber portraits of long dead, sea captains. Here and there fishing nets with shells and starfish clinging for dear life were draped over some windows.

Amusingly tacky, thought Brenda.

"Breakfast for one?" An older woman wearing a bright pink dress came up to greet her. She led Brenda to a booth with a relaxing view of the shrimp boats moored in the bay and the downtown Tampa skyline beyond.

"Cubbie will be with you shortly." She smiled, dropped a menu into Brenda's hand, and walked away.

Brenda let her thoughts drift to Malfour House. What could Ed Banners possibly want her to see so early in the morning? She was missing Tina badly. They talked almost every night. As soon as Tina's classes closed, she would make arrangements to drive down in Brenda's XKE. The 1963 Jaguar E convertible was Brenda's pride and joy. It had been a gift from her dad when she graduated from law school. Raymond Strange collected cars like most people collected dolls or cards. The Jag had been in the Strange family since her grandfather bought it new off the Jaguar car lot. A beautiful creamy, pale yellow color with black leather seats and black top, Brenda didn't get much of a chance to enjoy it in Newark. She kept it under lock and key. But now here in Florida, she could drive it everyday. Tampa was definitely convertible friendly.

"Decided what you're havin', sweetie?"

Brenda hadn't even heard the woman come up to the table. She was as round as she was short, with big dimples in a heart-shaped face, copper-colored hair, and sparkling blue eyes, dressed in black pants and white shirt. She smiled patiently down at Brenda.

"Just coffee and a bagel. Lightly buttered, please." Brenda smiled and handed her the menu. She was aware of the waitress's eyes studying her.

"Light eater, huh?" She scribbled quickly on her order pad. "My name is Cubbie. If you need anything, just holler."

Brenda stopped her before she left. "Oh, Cubbie, can you bring me some water, please?"

Cubbie smiled, winked, and walked away, moving quicker than Brenda thought someone her size could. Within seconds, she was back with the water. "There you go darlin'." She wiped her hands on her apron and smiled a crooked smile at Brenda. "Hope you don't mind my askin', but do people ever tell you you look just like . . ."

"Princess Diana," Brenda interrupted her.

"Yeah." Cubbie laughed heartily.

"All the time," Brenda laughed with her.

"Is this your first time to The Gulfbreeze?" Cubbie spoke with a heavy Southern accent.

Brenda found her warm and friendly. "Yes, actually. My partner and I bought the Malfour House in the Tides of Palmetto." She pointed out the door. "Just down the street from here."

Cubbie's eyes widened and her mouth opened into the letter O. "The Malfour House? Boy that there house has some history round these parts. Welcome to Tampa, hon. I'll be right back with your bagel."

Before Brenda could stop her, she was walking away towards the kitchen area. Here was a woman who obviously knew something about Malfour House. She had to talk to her.

Cubbie was back fairly quick with the bagel and steaming mug of coffee. "Here you go darlin'." She arranged the small plate and mug neatly in front of Brenda.

"Thank you," Brenda said, taking a gulp of the black coffee. "Listen, Cubbie, I wanted to ask you about the Malfour House. Have you heard anything about it?"

Cubbie chuckled and flung a hand up in the air. "Oh honey, I was born and raised in Tampa. Still live up the street just off 50th. I've picked up all kinds of stories about that house." She leaned down closer to Brenda. "Used to know Sandra Stone. She waitressed at The Palmetto Seafood Company. That was the restaurant that took up at your house. Well honey, she swore up and down the place was haunted. Said customers complained about the cold. No matter how they adjusted the air conditioning, it was still cold. She even told me cups and plates would fly off tables without anyone touchin' 'em."

Brenda let it all sink in. Of course old houses would have their ghost stories. What respectable Victorian wouldn't? "How about the Cuenca family? Didn't they live there at one time?"

"Yeah," Cubbie searched her memory. "There were some young folks livin' there years back. Nice folks. Had some kids with them, I think. Came in often. Didn't say much, just spoke to each other in Spanish."

Someone tapped a bell in the kitchen and a man yelled "Cubbie. Order up."

"Cubbie scribbled quickly on her order pad and stripped off the check, laying it under the creamer. She smiled big and wide at Brenda. "You come back, honey. We can talk more."

Brenda finished her bagel, savored the last drop of coffee, and picked up the check on the table. She smiled as she took a look at it. Cubbie had written *No Charge. On the House.*

* * *

When Brenda rolled to a stop in front of the carriage porch, the first thing she noticed was the absence of work trucks. When last she'd been here, it seemed that the entire grounds were littered with trucks of every kind, from pickups to large, heavy load trucks overflowing with lumber, cans of paint, and assorted machinery. That was three weeks ago.

There were only 3 pick up trucks parked toward the side of the house. Then she noticed the house itself. Malfour House was a queen showing her royal clothes again. They'd done quick work on the outside. Rotted columns, balustrades, lattice work, and window trim were proudly wearing their new paint job. Same colors, just sparkling.

She decided to circle to the side and around the back to check on the two chimneys. The house had two fireplaces, one in the kitchen and the other in the large, circular drawing room overlooking the bay inlet. The terra cotta on both chimneys had chipped and fallen off in places. They too had been refinished in record time.

She circled back around the front door, not able to suppress a smile of satisfaction. When she walked into the house, she held her breath. The hall, the drawing room directly ahead of her, everything was beautiful! The wallpaper was up, the floor had been buffed, the wood waxed and the marble set. She exhaled and took in another deep breath. She could smell the fresh paint, wallpaper adhesive, and wax.

Brenda wanted nothing more than to take a good, long look around her house, but the sound of workers back in the kitchen area sent her in search of Ed Banners. As she rounded the stair landing into the dining room, she thought she caught a whiff of that same burning smell. But no, there was nothing there. Just her overactive imagination.

When she walked into the kitchen, she was astonished to find everything practically gleaming. This was the one area of the house she wanted updated. Stainless steel and black ceramic was her choice of kitchen decor. It was all in place, the floor a coffee color ceramic tile. Ed Banners was standing with one other workman in what had once been a servants' quarter but sectioned off into separate storage rooms by the restaurant.

"Hey Ed." Brenda waved as she worked her way among piles of splintered wood and sheet rock.

"Ms Strange, come on over here," he motioned her over. He wore a white hard hat, orange tee shirt, and jeans.

Brenda gingerly stepped over some sort of heavy machinery with hoses attached to it. Looking around, she noticed the gapping hole in what once had been a wall.

"Sorry I called so early," Banners said, "but I thought you needed to see what we got here before we go any further." He held plans of Malfour House in his hands.

Brenda kept her eye on the gutted wall. Somehow, this room made her feel uncomfortable. Not only was it stuffy, but there was debris, scaffolding, and drop clothes covering the floor. She tried to convince herself that it was just the unfinished state of the room that was creating this mood for her. But the wall . . . the hole in the wall was like a sore in the face of the house.

"Ms Strange?

Brenda shook her head to tear herself from the dark thoughts. She looked at Ed Banners who was eyeing her closely.

"Ms Strange, there appears to be two walls behind those added by the restaurant." He shuffled some of the pages of the house plans and folded one flat for Brenda. "Here, let me show you."

She listened intently, sometimes looking toward the three other workmen who were deliberately pounding the old wall down, piece by piece.

"I believe it's the original wall behind the second one." Banners pointed to the dingy, shadowed wall peeking out through the growing hole.

"Now let me get this straight," Brenda said, "The partitions that the restaurant added were actually the third additions to this room? You think there might be a hidden wall or something?"

"We won't know for sure until we get these completely down and can tear into some of the next one, but yeah, I believe that's what we've got." He kept pointing to the plans in his hand. "You see . . . there is some major square footage missing from this original floor plan. It has to be somewhere."

Brenda had not done well with the real estate part of her law major. She really didn't need to look at the floor plans. She wouldn't understand them anyway.

"We just needed your go ahead before we could continue."

"Oh, sure. Of course." Brenda couldn't keep her eyes off the old wall peeking through. Like a ghost trying to come out of the dark. "Do whatever it takes." She started to walk away. "Oh, by the way, I'm going to go through the attic, so if you need me, just come up."

Chapter 7

Everything was finished upstairs. She'd selected lighter shades of wallpaper for the second floor and the mahogany gleamed in the morning sun that poured through the bare windows. All her dream house needed was the furniture. That was still set for a July 1st delivery.

The attic stairs were tucked behind the main stairwell on the second floor. Brenda opened the narrow door and was immediately hit with suffocating heat. Air conditioning stopped here. As she worked her way up, the creaking of the stairs didn't bother her as much as the musty, humid smell.

The attic was huge. Brenda stepped on the wooden floors and scattered dust into the air. The beams on the roof criss-crossed above her. She watched tiny particles of dirt float up, sucked into the spaces between the beams. There was a pair of windows in the center of the room. Grime and dust had blurred the windowpanes, but the sun still peeked through. As she looked around her, Brenda couldn't help but feel disappointed. There wasn't much here. Some old tables with empty flower pots. An old wooden chair with several legs broken, sat forlornly in one corner. Then she saw the box hidden in the dark recesses of the right corner, far away from the light of the sun.

It was a large cardboard box. Shoving aside her fear of spiders and other critters that might lurk in the dark, she walked carefully to the corner. She couldn't resist looking out the grimy windows. She must have been up at the highest part of the house, everything looked so small. She could see the rippling water of the bay and the palm trees that swayed in the breeze. The garden and garage were on the right. Immediately she noticed the stillness. And quiet. She couldn't even hear the workers pounding the walls away downstairs.

When she reached the box, she shivered involuntarily. It was much colder in this corner. The box was unlabeled, and judging by the dust it had accumulated, it was pretty old. Brenda took her hand and wiped off the thick layer, waving away the floating particles around her. She kept thinking of what some people had found in their attics. Valuable antiques, clothing, and jewelry. Old stock certificates, rare baseball cards.

Carefully, she pried open the flaps. Peering inside, she eyed some clothing and papers. It was too dark for her to see more. Making sure the box wasn't too heavy, she dragged it out toward the windows.

She pulled out the old shoes first. They were men's shoes, the type with the tiny holes that made an intricate design on the top. They were worn, musty, and smelly. Brenda wrinkled her nose and put the shoes down. There was a shirt, yellow with age, an old *Arrow* label still on the inside collar. Beneath it was a pair of what might have been tweed pants at one time. Now they appeared to be covered in some kind of mildew or mold— some black stuff—and they too smelled funny. Who did they belong to, she wondered? She made a pile of the clothes on the floor.

There wasn't much left in the box. What appeared to be papers, lay scattered on the bottom. They had really gotten wet. She pried some of the papers on the very top carefully. They had stuck together with age and were now mottled with dark, spreading spots.

As she fumbled with the collection of the papers in her hand, she noticed that pieces of the pages were missing. They looked like someone had cut or poked holes in them. Brenda gathered all the pages together and plopped down next to the smelly clothes. Okay, so she hadn't found any valuable treasures, but she could amuse herself by reading whatever these notes were.

She crossed her legs Indian style and randomly picked out a page. The writing was in an elegant hand. Feminine, she thought.

Her eyes fell on a single sentence.

I can do nothing but think of you.

My God, they were love letters! Excited, she started from the top.

Tuesday, November 11th, 1924

My Darling _____,

I don't know how much longer I will be able to keep this masquerade. My dearest _____, my days are filled with thoughts of you and only you. When shall I be able to touch you again? Your hair, the scent of your perfume? And yes, dare I speak it in this letter, kiss your sweet, sweet lips? Darling _____, I can do nothing but think of you.

What shall we do?

Carlotta

Brenda lifted her eyes from the letter and realized her hand was shaking. She shivered again and looked around, thinking there might be a draft. But of course there wasn't. This was June in Florida. And there was no air conditioning up here.

She was perplexed at the parts of the letter that had been purposefully and carefully cut out. As she stared at the water-stained letter, she thought about the name that was missing. But why? And who was Carlotta?

"I can do nothing but think of you."

Someone was whispering. In her ear.

"What shall we do?" Again. *"I can do nothing but think of you."*

Brenda listened intently. She wasn't afraid, even though the words were whispered softly, ever so softly, in her ear. Suddenly, there was an icy touch across her cheek. Brenda startled, then moved backward, waving a hand across her face. She couldn't explain it, let alone understand, but she knew without a doubt that someone was trying to communicate with her. A woman. But who? Carlotta?

She looked at the letter in her hand.

"Ms Strange?"

Brenda couldn't take her eyes off the page in front of her.

"Ms Strange?"

This time, the booming voice broke through the trance she'd been lost in. Ed Banners came up through the attic opening. "Ms Strange, I think you better come downstairs. We found something."

Brenda had to shake the cobwebs in her brain, find her voice again. She almost forced herself to focus on Banners. He couldn't have picked a worse time to drag her away.

"I'm sorry, Ed. I didn't hear you calling. I'll be right down." She couldn't find a smile.

He nodded, then disappeared back down the steps. Brenda gathered up all the pages and put them inside her Fendi bag. Never mind that the pages smelled awful and she would probably have to throw out the bag. She had to read more. She piled the musty clothes back into the box and shoved it into the same darkened corner.

Downstairs, she found Ed Banners huddled in conversation with two other men. When Banners saw her, he walked away from the men, then toward her as she approached.

"Ms Strange, we got a mighty interesting discovery here." He was excited as he guided her towards the wall they'd been working on.

Brenda was surprised by the progress they'd made. There was very little of the dingy second wall left and only a blackened, barren stone wall peeked through.

The back of the fireplace chimney? wondered Brenda.

"We've taken down two walls." Banners pointed toward the men still working. "What you see here is the structure's original wall. A red brick wall at one time. But, as you can see, there must have been a fire at one time." He motioned for Brenda to step forward.

She started to follow, but stopped dead in her tracks. The burning smell was back. Strong. Maybe it had originated from here all along? But it shouldn't be this strong. This wall was over a century old!

"Ed, the smell is pretty strong still. Is that normal?" When she looked at his face, she was suddenly sorry she'd said anything. He didn't smell it.

"Oh no, Ms Strange," he half chuckled, "there was a mighty big fire here, but that must've been a long time ago." He completely ignored her and put a hand on the blackened brick. "And it was a big fire to cause this much damage." He leaned back and pointed up for Brenda to follow. "If you notice, the fire burned all the way up." The bricks were indeed singed all the way to the ceiling.

"So when do you think this fire happened?" Brenda asked. It was all she could do to keep from gagging. Why couldn't anyone else smell the fire? Why was she the only one? Was she losing her grip on reality? Maybe she needed to get back to the therapist's chair.

"Oh, my guess is at least seventy years or so. Hard to tell. Now my concern is whether the room above suffered any damage as well. Gonna have to check the measurements upstairs."

"That would be one of the bedrooms, right?" Brenda was trying to remember the room layout on the second floor.

"Yes ma'am . . . the bedroom overlooking the front lawn."

"Will that mean a delay?"

"Oh yeah."

"Leave it alone, then." Brenda was quick with her answer, surprising herself.

Banners nodded with a short smile. "Yes ma'am. You're the boss." He dismissed it easily. It wasn't his house. What did he care? "Oh, before I forget . . ." Banners walked away to a small table full of papers, rulers, and coffee cups. He came back with a small metal box in his hand.

"We found this box underneath the floor boards behind the second wall." What he handed Brenda was what appeared to be a metal security box. It too was covered with some sort of black soot.

"Was there a key?" Brenda asked, feeling a sick tightening in her stomach.

"No ma'am. Not sure how you can open that, but maybe a lock shop can do it."

Brenda stood holding the box like a child just given a Christmas gift from a total stranger. What was inside? Why was this small box causing such turmoil in her head?

Without a doubt, she'd been shaken by this morning's discoveries. Maybe it was time to check into some of those psychic organizations she'd read about. Some of the books had said that sometimes, after going through a traumatic near death experience, people picked up residue from the afterlife. Psychic abilities were heightened. Was this what was happening to her? Could she somehow be tuned into Malfour House? Maybe the fire all those decades ago was the trigger?

Chapter 8

Brenda made just one stop before heading back to the apartment. At Mac USA, she purchased a brand new Apple Power Book and the fastest modem available on the market. How could she resist indulging herself in the laptop of her dreams? Besides, with her old computer back in Newark, she'd need one here.

When she got home, there was a message from Tina waiting on the answering machine. She was wrapping up at the Art Institute and would be driving down at the end of the week. And she was bringing Brenda's teddy bear supplies. As many as the Jaguar could hold.

Brenda smiled. The sound of Tina's voice made her quiver inside. And the teddies were coming with her. Icing on the cake. Unfortunately, she hadn't had time to even think of getting into another teddy, but she made a mental note to set enough time aside to get started on her new idea: A line of bears corresponding to the twelve zodiac signs. All this made her even more anxious for Tina. That, and the anticipation of their first night in Malfour House.

She unpacked the PowerBook and modem and connected everything to the surge protector she'd bought. The whole world knew about Florida thunderstorms and Tampa's "lightning capitol of the world" reputation.

Signing onto her AOL account, Brenda headed straight to the web. From the dresser, she dug out the wallet with her old business cards. She remembered writing the web addresses of several psychic and paranormal organizations on the back of one of them.

"Aha," she said out loud as she found her scribbled card. She turned it around and hesitated. There was her name in bold black, raised letters, and on the bottom, Attorney at Law, Collins, Davis & Associates. She turned it quickly over. The memories stabbed her, threatening to come stumbling back inside the wall she'd fought so hard to build.

Brenda shook her head hard, and Danny Crane's angry voice faded away like a shadow running from the sun. She focused on the keyboard and entered the web address for The Psychical Research Foundation of Massachusetts. What came up was a bare bones page with info on the Foundation, history, and current projects. They seemed to be focusing mostly on ESP studies.

Next, she entered the other address. The San Diego Central Register for Paranormal Studies was more up her alley. The website had a handy listing of topics and links. Her eyes immediately locked on the listing *Haunted Houses and Ghosts*. She clicked there and went to an intro page about The Register and the part it played in the investigation of haunted houses. They were adamant in denying connections with "ghost busters" and detailed in depth, the long history of their organization's importance in this field of paranormal studies. They backed this up with a listing of documented cases. Brenda clicked on the highlighted word.

Haunted house cases were listed by States. Brenda scrolled down to Florida and then froze. *Malfour House, Tampa, Florida*. She took her hands off the keyboard and caught her breath. She wasn't expecting this. Cubbie had been right. The house she'd just made a home was haunted. She resisted the urge to chide herself and say *I knew it. I told you so.* Tina would do that for her soon enough.

Tina. What would she do when she found out? Brenda didn't have time to think about that. Brenda was on a high. Her head was spinning. Was this how cocaine addicts felt when that first rush went through their system?

She quickly scanned the page for any more info, but the listing was the only thing available. Scrolling down, she located a name, snail mail address, phone number, and e-mail of a contact for further information on Haunted Houses and the Register. She didn't want to wait for an e-mail response. That could take days. Brenda practically tore at her purse for a pen.

The foul smell hit her hard. The letters from the attic! She'd forgotten all about them. They'd have to wait. Grabbing the pen, she jotted down Mark Demby's name, number, and extension, signed off and picked up the phone.

* * *

"Malfour House?" Mark Demby paused. "Yeah," he finally said. "Can't forget that one. Malfour was one of my first field assignments."

Brenda's heart jumped into her throat. This was getting more incredible by the minute. "You actually had people here?" she asked, wondering why neither Cindy Taylor nor anyone else had mentioned that a real-life ghost hunting had taken place in her house.

"Yeah, several years back. Well, at least 3 or so. It wasn't something we wanted lots of publicity on. When we go in a house, the less distractions, the better."

"Who hired you?"

"If my memory serves me correctly, it was some kind of seafood restaurant there at the time. I'll tell you what, Brenda, I can send you copies of all the transcripts and whatever else we've got on the Malfour House."

Brenda was touched by his offer, but she needed a fix now.

"That's very kind of you Mark. Thank you, but if you don't mind, since I have you on the phone, and you being actually involved with the investigation, may I ask what your personal impressions were of Malfour?"

There was a momentary silence on the other end. Brenda swore she could hear his fingertips tapping on the desk. "Well, if I remember, it was hot. August, I think. There were four of us and we took turns in the different dining areas and storage rooms."

"How about the attic?"

"Hmmm . . . don't remember doing the attic. Maybe someone else did. Don't recall much physical evidence collected, but the truth is Brenda, there was something there."

This time, it was Brenda's line that was silent. *There was something there.* She heard it over and over.

"I think we classified the house as a gray house," Mark continued.

"A gray house?" Brenda broke free of her thoughts.

"Yeah. It relates to gray ladies. Ghosts of women who have died for their love. Sometimes violently. Some believe they remain in the place waiting to be united with the one they loved or for revenge. There have been some cases where these gray ladies make appearances only to avenge a murder."

Brenda found herself gripping the phone so tight, her knuckles were white. "Why are they called gray ladies?"

"When they appear, they're either dressed in grey or appear grey in complexion."

"Did you see a gray lady in Malfour?" It's the question Brenda had to ask. It's what drove her to this conversation. He seemed to take longer than normal to answer, but maybe it was just her hyperactive imagination. Her desperation for an answer.

"No. No, I didn't. I don't think anyone saw anything . . ." he paused. "It was more of a general ill-feeling. And some in our group smelled wood burning. It's all in the transcripts I'm sending you."

So she wasn't the only one who could smell the fire! Mark

Demby only reinforced what she'd been trying so hard to ignore. Somehow, she'd developed some kind of psychic link with Malfour House. Was this psychic ability now a part of her very being? Was it a gift from God or something worse?

"Have you heard the legend about Albert Malfour and the mysterious disappearance of his wife, Carlotta?"

Carlotta. The name stuck like flypaper in Brenda's head. "I really haven't had much time for research. All I know is that Peter Cuenca was the owner of the house when we bought it."

"Yeah, Albert Malfour left the house to him in his will. Malfour was as cold and ruthless as his father. So they say. He was Victor Malfour's only son. Victor wanted to marry his son into money. Carlotta Moreno was the daughter of Alfonso and Christina Moreno, a wealthy Cuban sugar cane farmer. His plantation in Cuba was said to be a palace. Albert and Carlotta met in one of the Malfours many trips there. Albert and Carlotta instantly became puppets manipulated by Victor and Alfonso. It wasn't a marriage of love. Rumor has it that Albert Malfour murdered his wife. They never found a body and she was never heard from again."

Brenda's mind was swimming in questions. So the letters in her bag were from Carlotta Malfour. To her husband? But why the cutouts?

"Did the police ever investigate?"

"They did, but quickly closed the case when Albert flashed his money and some say, stuffed some pockets. Oh, he went through all the channels and filed a missing person report, but later, he offered police information which led them to believe Carlotta ran off with a mysterious Cuban captain which no one could locate. Of course, this is all pure hearsay and historical rumor."

"What about her family? Why didn't they push the search for their daughter?"

"Well, nobody knows for sure. The Tampa Police closed the case. Albert Malfour seems to have led a pretty empty life after that. He had one son out of wedlock. Oscar. The mother was reportedly a prostitute who died from venereal disease. Oscar was killed in World War II. Malfour was penniless when he died. All he had left of any value was Malfour House, which he left to Peter Cuenca."

"That's where I get confused," Brenda said. "Why Peter Cuenca? Were they related?"

"Nope. As far as we can tell, Peter Cuenca and his father, Roberto, were long time employees of Malfour. Caretakers of the estate and more like an extended family. Malfour took to traveling most of the time, rarely spending an entire season at Malfour. He trusted his people to watch over it and take care of everything."

So lost was Brenda in the story, that she hadn't even realized he had stopped talking. How long had it been?

"Brenda?" Mark Demby was still on the phone.

"Yes, Mark, I'm sorry. This is all just . . . too fascinating."

"We can help you, Brenda."

"Excuse me?" She knew what he meant.

"You're psychic. You wouldn't be looking us up if you hadn't had some kind of experience in your house. The restaurant had to close. But you don't have to be alone in this. The Register has resources you can use."

"Well, I . . . I just wanted . . ." Brenda stumbled on the words.

A steady beeping sounded on Mark Demby's line. "Brenda, can I get you to hold a second. I'll be right back." He was gone.

The silence allowed Brenda to sort everything out. Her thoughts were dangerously close to overload. The feeling was exhilarating. It was close to those highs when she was doing undercover investigations for Kevin in Newark for the law firm.

In her bag, she had letters written by Carlotta Malfour. Letters of a passionate nature with mysterious words strategically cut out. A puzzle of the domestic kind with the distinct suspicion of a murder. She never could resist mysteries.

"I'm sorry for the interruption, Brenda."

His voice was an abrupt intrusion into her thoughts. "Oh no, it's okay Mark. Listen, I want to thank you for your time and all that valuable info, but I've already taken up too much of your time."

His laughter was soft and friendly. "Consider it an introduction of sorts. But before I forget, let me give you the name of a book that might be helpful. *The Cigar Kings of Tampa*. Lots of info on the Malfour Family. Listen . . . Brenda, if you should ever decide to pursue your psychic abilities, please contact us. And I'll get these copies out to you today."

* * *

Brenda found the perfect setup for the woman who didn't feel bonded to the kitchen. It was called Dine One One. Participating restaurants delivered their hot, fresh entrees right to your door.

Feeling exotic, she ordered a curried chicken dish from The India Palace. She didn't want to waste any time. Tina would be back in two days and there were still all kinds of little things to do. Tomorrow, she would head out to Malfour again.

Meanwhile, the letters from the attic sat on the bed, their odor overwhelming the apartment. Dumping what she couldn't finish of her dinner, she showered, snuggled into her favorite nightshirt, and plopped on the bed.

There were 6 pages in all and each one appeared to be a letter. Taking the one she'd already read, Brenda put it aside and grabbed the next one.

January 6, 1925

Darling,

Tonight, when the full moon romances the sky, sneak out if you can and meet me in the garden. He will be gone tonight.

How lucky for us, dearest. Make it 9 o'clock, shall we? If you do not show, I will miss you so. My fingers long to run through your hair.

Carlotta

The mystery grew more perplexing. It was a very romantic letter. If Albert and Carlotta had a loveless marriage, who were these letter to? *He will be gone tonight.* Was she talking about Albert? Was the letter to her unknown captain lover? Why were the letters in the house thrown in some box with dirty clothes?

All the puzzle pieces had to fit into a bigger picture. But was it a murder scene or just the story of an unhappy woman running off with the man of her dreams? Brenda strained her eyes, shaking the cobwebs of sleep from her mind. It was late and she'd had a very draining day. But she couldn't stop now. There were too many letters to get to.

Picking up the stack, she briefly glanced through each one, skimming down the delicate writing. All of them echoed the passion and desire of a woman in love, trapped in a relationship she didn't belong in.

Deciding to put them away for the night, she put the two she'd already read in the nightstand drawer, and laid the others neatly next to the lamp on the table.

As Brenda drifted into sleep, the musty smell from the letters blended into the gathering darkness, already part of her fading reality.

Chapter 9

The following morning, Brenda stopped again at The Gulfbreeze for her usual bagel and coffee. She gave Cubbie her new phone number, invited her to Malfour House, and then set out for the final run through of the house. The decorator was supposed to meet her there with the drapes for the upper floor.

When she drove up, she was surprised to see a large pick up truck in the front yard with one of those cages attached to the back, full of lawn equipment. Two men were out and about, one of them sitting on a riding mower.

Brenda stopped her car, got out, and approached the other man who was standing in front of the porch, eyeing the house with great interest.

"I'm Brenda Strange. Can I help you?"

The man appeared startled. Then he turned around and smiled, flashing a mouth of white teeth.

"Hello, Miss Strange, I'm Louis Cuenca." He extended his hand to her.

"Good to meet you, Mr. Cuenca." Brenda took his hand, trying to hide the surprise.

"I hope you don't mind, but Carlos here has been doing the grounds work for us since we've owned the property. I was in town and took the opportunity to come along with Carlos and meet you." He glanced back at the house. He smiled again. "I told Carlos he could keep his job. Hope that's okay with you?"

His Latin good looks and jet-black hair with streaks of grey couldn't distract Brenda from her first impression. Smooth operator. The Sade song had been a favorite of hers. She didn't like being bullied into any situation, but there really wasn't any reason why Carlos shouldn't keep doing the lawn. She just wanted to make that decision herself.

"Carlos has done a great job on the grounds. I would like for him to keep it up, but you really should have called and checked with me."

"My apologies." He kept smiling and pointed to the house. "You've done a beautiful job."

Brenda couldn't help feeling proud. Malfour was magnificent. He obviously thought so too.

"Mr. Cuenca . . ."

"Oh, Louis, please."

Brenda forced a smile. "Louis. Does Carlos have a regular schedule he keeps?"

"Yes. He has a biweekly schedule."

"Does he have his own pass then? For the guard?" Brenda didn't want to have to be here for Carlos to get past the guardhouse.

"Yes, I believe he does."

It was obvious to Brenda that Louis Cuenca still had fond ties to Malfour. She felt bad just leaving him outside. Her decorator was probably waiting for her inside.

"Would you like to come in? Take a look at what's been done?"

His eyes lit up. "Yes, thank you so much. I would love to." He was like an excited child as they stepped onto the porch. "I haven't been inside since my daughter and her family moved out." Brenda remembered some of the stories Cubbie had told her.

"Louis, if you don't mind me asking, why did your daughter

leave? I mean . . . Malfour House is prime property."

They were inside and Louis Cuenca froze as if someone had slapped him. His voice echoed, the awe apparent on his face. "This is amazing. Unbelievable." His eyes took in every detail around him.

Brenda closed the door behind them. "We wanted to capture the look and feel of the original."

She felt like a new parent. It was all hers. But she didn't have all day to stand around with Louis Cuenca. "I have to do a walk through inspection. In fact, my decorator should be here somewhere."

She started to walk to the sitting room to their left. "You're welcome to walk with me."

Even though a part of her felt uncomfortable bringing a total stranger into her house, he followed her through the bottom floor. The decorator had been busy. Drapes were in place in every downstairs window.

"My daughter definitely did not have your designer's eye."

Brenda laughed. "You probably don't want to know how much money we spent on the interior restoration alone."

She couldn't help but admire the choices she and the decorator had made. Burgundy, deep green, taupe, and off-white. She'd never cared much for florals.

Louis only nodded, too absorbed in adoration of the house his father had been quick to sell. Something uncomfortable nibbled at Brenda's thoughts. Had Louis Cuenca been against the sale of Malfour? Why had his own father not passed the house to him?

"Brenda? Is that you?" A voice echoed from upstairs. It was Benny Hafler, the decorator.

"I'm coming up, Benny." Brenda smiled at Louis. "Take a look downstairs if you like. Good to meet you."

Louis took her hand and shook it enthusiastically. "Thank you for allowing me into your home. I hope you and Tina are very happy here."

Somehow, his smile was just a little too strained for Brenda, but she brushed the thought aside and ran up the stairs to meet Benny on the top floor landing. She and Benny went through the whole second floor, making sure everything was where it should be, and every drape, hook, rug, painting, lamp, and shade was the proper choice. Malfour was smiling and showing it's best face. It waited only for the furniture to arrive tomorrow.

* * *

The day had run away from Brenda. By the time Benny had said his goodbye and walked out the door, two hours had passed. Brenda suddenly remembered Louis Cuenca. She looked out the front foyer window and noticed that Carlo's truck was gone. Louis Cuenca had left. When she walked out to the porch, she couldn't help admire how neatly Carlos had trimmed the lawn, hedges, and plants.

Circling to the garden out back, she immediately noticed the fresh, new shrub plants he had planted as well. They were bursting with new, fluffy red flowers. She would have to ask what kind of plant it was. They were almost blood red.

Brenda had one more stop to make before calling it a day. As she pulled out onto the bridge and then past the guardhouse, a thought snuck up on her, unbidden and unwanted. Did Cindy Taylor retrieve any extra keys the Cuencas might have had for Malfour? And had the Cuencas turned in any of the security passes?

These suspicions bothered her. She'd been trained to be suspect of anything and anyone, but these thoughts were unrealistic. Unfounded. Pushing them under the mountain of other, more pressing concerns, she headed for Raven's Books.

* * *

Brenda fell instantly in love with Raven's Books. She took her time in the small, cozy atmosphere. It was stuffed with books.

She wasn't quite done browsing when her cell phone rang. It was Tina. She'd just pulled into Malfour.

Brenda hurriedly paid for *The Cigar Kings of Tampa* and rushed back to the house. Tina was early. One whole day early. She must have broken all kinds of speeding limits. Brenda could never get her to slow down.

She spotted the Jag first as she pulled into view of Malfour. Tina had parked it under the carriage porch. There was a bright red BMW behind it. As Brenda rolled into the garage driveway, she noticed Tina standing on the porch with another woman, talking in her usual animated fashion. She talked with her hands as well as her mouth.

As soon as Tina saw Brenda, she rushed over and hugged her tight.

"I'm so happy to see you."

Brenda smelled the Musk perfume Tina liked to wear. It was good to have her back. Tina let her go and looked back at the thin blonde staring at them with interest.

"Brenda, this is Joan Davis. She and her husband live down the lane. We're neighbors."

"I come bearing gifts." Joan Davis's voice was smooth as expensive brandy and her hair was so long, it almost draped one side of her face like a curtain of yellow silk.

Veronica Lake popped into Brenda's mind. She loved the old Alan Ladd, Veronica Lake films. Veronica handed the basket she'd been holding to Brenda.

"Thank you, Joan." Brenda took it, still mesmerized by Joan Davis's shimmering hair. The basket was full of fresh fruits, nuts, and flowers. Brenda was conscience of Joan's expensive clothes. Everything about her said *money.* "Joan, I would love to invite you in, but we don't even get the furniture until tomorrow."

"Oh, yeah, I'm a day early." Tina looked at Brenda, winked, and smiled.

"Oh please, don't worry. I didn't come to intrude," Joan said, waving a slim hand in the air. "I just came by to welcome you to the neighborhood and to invite you to our annual Summer party. It's next weekend. There's an invitation in the basket. My husband Stewart is president of the neighborhood association and we host a party every year to kickoff the Summer." She inched closer to Tina.

"That's our way of getting to know all the new rich kids on the block."

"Well, we're hardly that," Brenda said. "Rich, I mean."

"Oh, Brenda's being modest." Tina laughed. "Her family is old money all the way from England."

"And you?" Joan Davis was smiling at Tina.

"Me? I'm just a starving artist Brenda pulled out of poverty." Tina joked. "No, seriously, I teach sculpture at the Newark Institute of Art and work in clay for myself. When I have the time."

"Oh, an artist." Joan's eyes lit up. "I'll have to introduce you to the movers and shakers of the arts community in Tampa."

Tina had definitely made an impression on Joan Davis. But Tina always made a splash in social situations. In a big, bold way. After exchanging goodbyes, Joan got back into her Beemer and drove off.

Brenda slipped her arm through Tina's and kissed her. "As much as I'd like to hassle you about speeding your way here, I'd much rather show you how much I missed you. Follow me inside, little girl."

When they walked in the door, Tina whistled as she looked around.

"Wow, Princess, I leave for a month and you pull a rabbit out of the hat. This is beautiful."

Brenda came up behind her and put her arms around her waist. "Not as beautiful as you."

Tina laughed softly. "Say honey, I know we don't have a bed or anything, but can't we like . . ." She looked up the stairs. "You know, just throw something together and stay here tonight?" Her voice was deep, raspy, and Brenda almost considered it. Almost.

"No, Tina. C'mon, tomorrow night's the big night in our house. I want it to be just right." She broke free of the embrace, grabbed Tina's hand, and led her out the door. "Besides, I've got lots to tell you."

* * *

They say absence makes the heart grow fonder. Brenda could believe that, but they never mentioned the sex part. Distance definitely made that a whole lot better too.

Brenda and Tina spent the rest of the day and evening driving around Tampa. Brenda was particularly proud of her Hyde Park discovery and was quick to introduce Tina to Felice at Teddies in The Park.

They had dinner at a Hyde Park Italian restaurant called Prima Bistro, enjoying their first real night out in Tampa. Brenda shared her discovery in the Malfour attic with Tina. Tina appeared mildly interested, but was more eager in talking about the new projects she wanted to start at Malfour.

Needless to say, there was little time for Brenda to read any of the letters. There had been just too much excitement in the air. And now, the mellow, easy high of the Absolut vodka had all but tucked her in for the night. So much had taken her attention today, that she'd left the book, *The Cigar Kings of Tampa*, in the car. It would have to wait 'till tomorrow.

Chapter 10

The furniture arrived just a mere 30 minutes late. While Brenda busied herself with the movers, Tina unpacked her luggage, set up her supplies, display columns, and clay upstairs in her studio. She also unloaded Brenda's teddy bear supplies into her designated studio.

By the time the movers left, Brenda thought she'd have to down a tranquilizer. She'd been wound up all day. Tina practically flung her on the leather couch in the library. Brenda sank willingly into the soft leather. It was the color of vanilla ice cream. She inhaled deeply. She loved the smell of real leather.

"You stay put," Tina said, pointing a finger. "Don't even lift a hand 'till I get back." Tina almost ran into the kitchen, coming back with two bottles of water.

"Say Princess, you forgot to stock food in our fridge. What's up for dinner?"

Brenda had the bottle in her mouth and practically spit the water out all over herself.

"Oh my God. Tina, tonight. I forgot all about it. I planned a special night for us." She got up and ran to the phone.

* * *

Chef Ron Standau had come highly recommended. Brenda had called Cindy on the chance she might know of a chef who was available for private dinners.

It was their inaugural dinner at Malfour and Brenda wanted to make their first night at home memorable without lifting a finger. Ron Standau earned the asking price for his services. He came prepared with everything but the kitchen sink. Chef Ron even brought along Brenda's favorite vodka, Belvedere. And he hadn't forgotten the champagne either.

The candlelight was still glowing when Chef Ron left. He'd left the kitchen sparkling, his business card sitting atop the German Chocolate cheesecake. It was Brenda and Tina's favorite. Outside, there was the grumbling beginning of a thunderstorm.

"Mmm, this must have cost you a fortune, Princess." Tina was still licking her lips of the cheesecake. She and Brenda were sitting on the Victorian sofa in the living room, two champagne glasses and a bottle of Clicquot Grand Dame on the coffee table. The candles in the room cast orange highlights among the dark shadows of the period furniture. Brenda inhaled the lavender from the candles.

"You never stop worrying about money, do you?" Brenda laid back and rested her head on Tina's lap. "Don't you wish it were cold so we could start up the fireplace?"

"It's too bad we'll never get to use it."

Tina's words sliced into Brenda's magical night. The harsh reality of what Tina meant slapped her hard. They would only be here for the Summer. They'd never be able to use the fireplace. But how could she ever leave Malfour? She sat up quickly.

"Let's open the champagne." She struggled briefly with the cork, spilling a little of it on her skirt.

"Mmm, let me lick some of that off . . ." Tina smiled and tried to grab her, but Brenda laughed and pushed her away.

"Give me your glass. Let's do this right."

Brenda poured the champagne carefully and held up her glass.

"To Malfour House, my darling. And to a brand new start for us." Tina clinked her glass on Brenda's and downed the whole thing in one swallow. She flung the glass at the fireplace. Brenda laughed and did the same.

"Why don't we finish this upstairs?" Champagne bottle in hand, Brenda pulled Tina from the couch slowly and whispered in her ear. "The night is still young and we're just getting started . . ."

* * *

Something woke her up. Brenda's eyes popped open, her heart racing. She listened to the stillness in the room. The air was filled with lavender. It was so quiet, she strained to hear the hum of the air conditioner. So what had wakened her so abruptly?

Then it hit her. The smell of wood burning. Beside her, Tina was fast asleep, rolled up tight in a fetal position, pillow over her head. Brenda didn't want to wake her.

She threw on her terry robe, slipped into her satin flats, and crept quietly out of the room. In the hallway, the smell was overwhelming. She lifted her nose, trying to pin point where it was coming from. The smell was downstairs. She and Tina hadn't left any lights on in the house, but the moonlight coming through some of the windows bathed the house in blue, shimmering highlights.

Brenda was halfway down the stairs when the whispers began. It was more like muffled conversation somewhere very far or like a television left on in another room. Then she heard a door slam. She jumped, looking back up toward their bedroom. But it couldn't be Tina. The door slamming had been downstairs. Was someone in the house? Was it a burglar? Brenda thought of getting Tina, but then changed her mind.

What good would that do?

She continued down the stairs ever so slowly and inched into the dining room, the fear a tight thumping in her chest. Why didn't she just stop, run back upstairs, wake Tina, and call the police? Instinctively, she knew she would keep going. Knew where the smell would lead her. She continued to walk straight into whatever called her down here.

As she approached the kitchen, her blood froze. There was smoke coming from the doors into the kitchen. Malfour House was on fire! Forgetting any danger to herself, Brenda ran and flung the double doors open.

The kitchen was engulfed in swirling smoke. She stopped, confused, wanting to scream. Instead, she plunged head first into the dark wall of smoke. She fumbled her way toward where she thought the range might be. Her hand went out to steady herself but Brenda jumped back in pain. Whatever she touched burned her hand. She screamed.

"Tina! Tina!"

Then the door to the once servants' quarters flew open. Flames erupted in angry orange fingers. A figure stood framed at the door, the fire dancing behind her. The woman stared at Brenda and opened her mouth. Fire spilled from her tongue. She screamed Brenda's name, arms open, beckoning.

And Brenda moved toward her. She couldn't control her legs. Or could she? She wanted to run to the fiery figure, be consumed in the mesmerizing eyes that looked out at her.

"Brenda! Oh my God! Brenda."

Cool hands pulled her away. Away from the kitchen. Away from the fire. Brenda almost wanted to resist the firm grasp. Strong hands brushed her face, her arms, holding her in a loving embrace. Brenda barely focused on Tina's shocked look long enough before the quiet blackness took her away.

* * *

Brenda stood basking in the warm rays of the sun streaming

through her studio windows. She'd worked all morning unpacking bolts of upholstery fabric, ribbons, bags of stuffing, and tray after tray of needles, pins, and scissors. Anything to get her mind off the terrifying images still burning in her brain.

"Need a hand with any of that?" Tina stood at the door with a smile, arms crossed.

"I think I can handle it." Brenda's left hand was bandaged, the pain already a nagging memory. Realizing she may have sounded defensive, she managed a weak smile. "You did such a good job bandaging me up, I'm as good as new."

They'd talked about it 'till the early hours of the morning. Tina had found Brenda dazed and confused in the kitchen. Brenda had somehow managed to turn on the range and burned her hand. She'd been sleepwalking. That was Tina's explanation. Tina had it all figured out and in her own way, was just trying to make Brenda feel better.

Brenda refused to believe Tina's rational explanations. She couldn't have been sleepwalking. She'd never done that in her life. She'd felt the flames. Inhaled the smoke and seen the fear and anger in the fiery woman's face. There was only one problem. There had been no fire. No one had broken into Malfour.

Tina came up behind Brenda and caressed her arms "You know Princess, it isn't that I don't believe you, it's just that . . ."

"You just can't believe what you can't see." Brenda didn't turn, but kept looking out at the rippling water below.

"I'm really sorry you felt I wouldn't understand about your near death experience. I'm sorry I wasn't there for you when you needed to talk. It doesn't make for very open communications between us, does it?" Tina moved in even closer, nuzzling into Brenda's neck. "Maybe we can talk some more tonight?"

Brenda reached up and took Tina's hand. She turned around to face her, trying hard to believe talking would change anything. "If you want to, sweetheart."

Tina took Brenda's face in her hands and kissed her gently.

"I want to."

* * *

Tina and Brenda spent several hours setting up Brenda's workroom. Brenda was feeling the pull again to create her tiny bears. Felice was waiting for her Zodiac Bears line, anxious to start promoting them. Except, Brenda lacked the concentration. She couldn't stop thinking about last night.

Malfour was trying to tell her something. She was convinced. A tiny part of her, that she tried to smother, was screaming the name *Carlotta* over and over in her head.

"Hey Princess. I'm going to the grocery store. We should stock up on some household stuff and I need some things for my studio. Wanna come?"

"No, I think I'm going to stick around here. I feel a nap coming on." She smiled big and wide, hoping the humor could lighten both their moods. There was only one thing Brenda really wanted to do.

* * *

"You're not crazy, Brenda." Mark Demby's laughter wasn't ridicule. "Some people are going to tell you that, but don't believe it. In fact, you're very gifted. There are so few who possess true psychic abilities."

His voice was soft, understanding. The voice of reason. Someone who listened and believed. "Not to stress you out, but your powers are especially interesting to me. You see, when we investigated Malfour, no one on our team saw or heard anything. There was the one who did detect a burning odor. Now you've supplied the missing piece to that puzzle. We didn't know about the fire. You see, this particular member of our group had the ability to smell. Others might be able to see, hear, or feel."

He paused and Brenda could almost hear him exhale deeply.

"But you," he continued, "You're special. You have a very strong link with Malfour. You've experienced a full spectrum sighting. Smell, sight, audio, and touch. Now that last one, that is very uncommon."

"So I'm not imagining all this?"

Mark laughed again loudly on the other end. "Definitely not. You are in tune with real supernatural forces in Malfour. You, my dear, have a direct line to the spirits who live in your house. Open up. Listen to them. Let them show what they need you to see."

His last sentence sent an icy thrill through Brenda. She had come back from the dead but the dead were knocking on her door.

"Brenda, they can see you and you can see them. It isn't uncommon for some who come through the tunnel from a near death experience to come back with psychic hookups to that world. I mean, who knows Brenda, maybe you didn't really want to come back. Maybe a part of you is still back there. By the way, did you get anything out of that book I recommended?"

The book! With so much going on to distract her, not only had she forgotten about the book, but the letters were still in her bag. She thanked Mark Demby, who once again tried his best to get her involved with the Register, and frantically sped down the stairs. This would be a perfect time to look at the book and get into more of the letters. With Tina gone, she would be able to devote all her time reading.

Thank God Tina had taken the Jag. This was one of those rare times when she didn't mind. She unlocked the Jeep and grabbed the bag with the book and her Fendi bag from the front seat. And then she remembered the security box. It had slipped from her memory entirely. She had thrown it on the back seat the day Ed Banners gave it to her. How could she have pushed it so far down her thoughts? The box could contain all the answers to the dark secrets of Malfour. Or nothing at all.

She opened the back door. There was the box. Black with the

dark shadows of a fire decades ago. Brenda just stood there, in the warm, sticky July breeze, staring at the black little box, an unexplained repulsion preventing her from touching it. She didn't have to. Tomorrow or the next day, she would take it to a locksmith and have them crack the lock. She would ask them to clean it off for her too.

She ran back inside, plopped down on the leather sofa in the library and pulled out the book. She flipped quickly to the index page in the back and found *Malfour, page 43*. It was an entire chapter. On the first page was a split photo of the Malfour Cigar Factory, one side dated 1924 and a current one showing the factory as an art gallery.

As Brenda looked closer at the photo, she realized the art gallery was the very same one she passed countless times on 22nd Causeway. Brenda had always been one of those impatient few who loved to look at the pictures first in a book. She turned the page and found a large group photo which took up almost half the page.

To her surprise, this elegant group of people were standing in front of Malfour House! She could barely make out the front door, but it was definitely Malfour. It looked like the entire Malfour household plus staff. She read the caption intently, her eyes hungry for the images revealed before her.

There were four prominent figures standing in the front row, with a tiny dog beside one of the women. Brenda read the names. The old, dour looking man with bushy white moustache in a cap and coat was not listed. Next to him, looking like a young Jay Gatsby, was Albert Malfour.

Brenda strained her eyes. She didn't have her glasses. Albert Malfour was lean, with dark hair swept back off his forehead. He couldn't muster a smile for the camera. He stood very close to the other man, a cold, somber look on his face. His lips were thin and down turned. He had one hand tucked inside his pants.

Beside him was a woman in a wispy, flowing dress, large hat, and fair hair pulled back. A pale, delicate hand held on to the hat. Must have been a blustery day, thought Brenda, trying to capture the moment the photograph was taken. *Carlotta Malfour*. Brenda's eyes froze on the name. The woman whose passionate letters ended up at the bottom of some musty old box. She focused her eyes on Carlotta's face. Pale eyes on a very round, lively face. Not the woman in the flaming doorway.

There was one other woman in the front row. Winifred Malfour. Mrs. Victor Malfour. She stood like a large, dark garbed golem next to Albert, her face stern and unflinching. A wide brimmed hat hid her eyes. On the back row, in dark, uniform clothing, stood what Brenda assumed were the hired help. She took careful inspection of each face. There were only several women among mostly men.

One boy in particular struck Brenda. His face was far too severe for someone his age. He couldn't have been more than fifteen or so. He had shabby little knickers, a cap holding back dark, abundant hair, and a dirty face. One small hand sat on Albert Malfour's shoulder, the other on the older, unnamed man.

Brenda looked closer at the three other women in the back row. A very thin, hollow-cheeked woman wearing the dark outfit and white apron of a maid or house servant called out for her attention. Brenda wished she had her magnifying glass handy, but that could be anywhere in the boxes waiting to be unpacked. The people in the back rows were fuzzy.

But this woman was pale, her face gaunt with high cheekbones. Brenda could only guess she had dark eyes. She wore her hair in a fashion considered rather saucy for the time period, flapper style. Short with bangs and ends that met in points on her cheeks. There was a certain defiance to her stance, a tiny smirk playing with the camera.

The other two women were dressed the same, but their faces were dull and sullen, expressing very little personality. Was no one happy that worked for the Malfours? A tiny shiver went through Brenda. She propped her feet and laid back, eager to read the chapter.

What she read was much of what Mark Demby had already

told her. But there were things about Victor Malfour she hadn't known. He had successfully built a cigar industry in Key West, Florida. At one time, Victor had three Malfour cigar factories in operation. You could say he was the king pin of the industry at that time. That was 1887. In 1889, a fire raged out of control through Key West, devouring most of the city and handing a devastating blow to the cigar industry. Many of the cigar kings left Key West, most of them heading up to Tampa.

Malfour made a fateful decision to stay. Before long, the cigar wars broke out. Cigar factory owners in Tampa were stealing workers from the Key West factories. Accusations and sometimes murder was a common occurrence. The Cuban slave trade was busted when Cubans rebelled and demanded their own terms Everything fell apart in Key West. Victor Malfour was forced to close two of his factories and with tail tucked behind his rear end, high tailed it to Tampa where he built the Malfour Cigar Factory on 22nd Street Causeway. He died of influenza shortly after.

Brenda made a mental note to visit the factory. As soon as possible. She turned the page and there was another photograph. Albert and Carlotta lounged at a table, two tall glasses of a cool drink placed before them. He was dressed in a white long sleeve sweater and light pants and Carlotta, a tight, short sleeve, light colored dress. Her hair hung loose around her shoulders. Brenda recognized the Malfour grounds behind them.

There wasn't much else in the book that she didn't already know. Brenda was so pumped up with Malfour adrenalin that she contemplated getting into more of Carlotta's letters, but her eyes were steadily drooping and she didn't want to fight off the prospect of a nap. After last night, she'd be catching up all week on lost sleep.

Chapter 11

The party at the Davis's was an "informal" formal affair. Brenda was looking forward to the distraction and Tina talked of nothing else the rest of the week. They spent an entire day in Hyde Park Village being picky about everything they tried on. Brenda chose an elegant Armani ankle length dress with a waist jacket in indigo with a hint of shimmery purple. Tina opted for a DKNY pantsuit with a wide shouldered, knee length jacket in chocolate brown.

"How about the orange scarf, Princess?"

"Take the leopard print and let's call it a day." Brenda always had an eye for the accessories.

* * *

The Davis residence was roughly about half a mile from Malfour. Brenda put the top down on the Jag and when they drove into the circle driveway of 102 Peppertree Lane, she momentarily lost touch with reality.

It would have been a sin to call the Davis house just a "house." It was a towering marvel.

"Will you look at that . . ." Tina leaned back in the seat,

taking it all in. "It looks like a Roman temple."

Brenda was hypnotized. Big, fat columns reached up into the pastel sky, dwarfing the large palm trees that were brave enough to stand in the way. Multi-colored outdoor lights washed over the marble. Smaller palm trees formed a circle around the courtyard entrance where a huge fountain pushed a steady flow of water up in the air.

Like sharks in white tuxedos, the valets swarmed her Jag, their faces hungry to be the first behind the seat of the classic.

"Hey, Brenda, should we turn back now?" Tina was wearing a smile and a wink, but Brenda could see the wonder in her dark eyes. The glamour was sucking her in.

Two men in dark uniforms opened the large doors, where they were immediately approached by a young woman carrying a tray.

"Appetizers?"

Tina's hand went up, but Brenda slapped it down with one look. Tina just smiled and watched the leggy blonde bounce away.

"Good evening, ladies. You must be Brenda Strange." The tall, blonde man who looked like a fashion model for the forty-something crowd had snuck up behind them. His black tuxedo hugged a lean frame. He shook Brenda's hand, then glanced briefly toward Tina. "And you must be Tina. I'm Stewart Davis. My wife was right. You arc the spitting image of Princes Di." Hc was looking directly at Brenda, his pale blue eyes darting up and down her body. Although Brenda was getting tired of the comparison, she smiled.

Joan Davis walked up to them, sliding her hand down her husband's arm. She was practically painted into a slinky, crepe dress the color of tangerine. "Brenda. Tina. So glad you could come. The bar is open and in the salon." She pointed back toward the cavernous, sunken room that spread behind them.

"Ladies, why don't I guide you through the house and introductions." Stewart Davis's eyes sparkled, his thin lips almost parted in a smile. Joan had already walked away, disappeared into the sea of black formal wear.

As Stewart guided them from the foyer, the floor to ceiling aquarium immediately grabbed Brenda's attention. It had to be a saltwater tank. The fish, all different sizes, darted lazily among the brightly colored coral and pebbles.

"It's one of my passions." Stewart Davis was standing next to Brenda. "We've dived all over the world."

"So it is saltwater?"

"Oh yes. You can't get the brilliant varieties in fresh water aquariums" His face was almost touching the glass, intent on the beautiful scene that rippled in front of him. "Other than diving, it's one of the few things that can offer me relaxation after a hard day at the office."

"Where do you work, Mr. Davis?" Tina asked.

Stewart led them into the madding crowd. They walked into a sunken room, large and spacious, surrounded by smaller pillars in a carnelian color. Pockets of people collected in every available space.

"Joan didn't tell you, I suppose."

"It wasn't a long visit. She just dropped off a welcome basket."

"Ah, yes. Well, does the name Davross ring a bell?"

A server with a silver tray approached and offered a variety of alcoholic drinks. His white jacket was impeccably clean, black hair brushed back from his forehead.

"Care for a drink, Brenda? Tina?" Stewart urged them to make a selection.

The martinis jumped to attention. "Are these gin or vodka?" Brenda didn't drink Gin.

"Gin, ma'am. I can get you vodka." The young man with the jet black hair snapped his finger and another server jumped beside them, another full tray of martinis.

"It's Absolut, by the way." Stewart leaned close to Brenda. "It always matters to vodka drinkers."

Brenda noticed that he took a traditional martini. She wondered what brand of Gin he liked. She and Tina toasted and they'd barely put lipstick lips to their glasses when a big, brassy woman in a flowing dress grabbed at Stewart Davis's arm.

"Stewart, darling. Did the mayor really say he would come?"

Stewart held his hand out to Brenda and Tina.

"Brenda, Tina, meet Abby Thompson. President of the Junior League and one of our neighbors in the Tides."

Both Brenda and Tina lifted their glasses.

"A pleasure to meet you."

Her eyes fluttered once too many times and she didn't make eye contact. Brenda didn't like her. She was tugging at Stewart's elbow. A large commotion at the front door distracted everyone's attention. The entire room seemed to suddenly shift toward the foyer.

Brenda overhead the word "mayor" in hushed, excited whispers.

"Ladies, if you'll excuse me." With a flash of white teeth, Stewart Davis was gone. Abby Thompson followed him, joining the migration to meet the mayor of Tampa.

Tina leaned closer to Brenda. "Princess, there's so much money in this one room, it would glow green in the dark."

Brenda couldn't control her laughter. Tina was like a little girl sometimes. That's what attracted Brenda to her.

"And look at all the plastic surgery too." Brenda had to whisper that into Tina's ear. They both laughed quietly as they worked their way toward the bar. The martini glasscs on thc trays were dwarf size. Refills were in order.

The bar was black leather with mirror counter and ran almost the entire length of the wall. Two small fountains bubbled forth on each side with tiny palms rising behind them. Two bartenders worked busily behind the bar. One of them approached them.

"What can I get you ladies?"

"Absolut martini, straight up. Two." Brenda pulled out two velvet-covered stools. They'd barely settled into their seats when a short, slender man with graying goatee and thinning hair propped himself next to Brenda and waved to the bartender. He ordered, "My usual," then turned back to Brenda.

"Oh darling, tell me you're not the long lost twin to Princess Diana?"

Tina almost spit out the Absolut. Brenda glared at her, then focused her attention on the thin man.

"No, but I'm beginning to think I should have had a complete facial reconstruction."

He didn't know what to say. She decided to help him out.

"I had to have surgery on part of my face after an accident." It wasn't exactly the thing to discuss at a highbrow party with a total stranger, but the whole Princess Diana thing was starting to get old.

He held up his shot glass. "Well they did a lovely job, my dear."

Brenda looked at Tina and both were in silent agreement. This guy was flaming. He downed the shot and put it gently on the counter. Waved for another.

"I'm Eddy Vandermast." He put out a slender hand. "I do Stewart's books."

"I'm Brenda Strange and this is Tina Marchanti." All of a sudden, he was an extremely interesting guest.

"Ah, word is you two bought the old Malfour house?" He gulped down another shot.

"What are those things?" Tina pointed to the empty shot glass.

"Dewar's, darling. Let me get you one." Eddy motioned to the bartender.

"No thanks," Tina protested, "I'm still a martini girl."

"Oh well, your loss dearie."

"We just moved into Malfour," Brenda said, "Are you familiar with it?"

Eddy smiled, his eyebrows going up. "Uh, am I ever. I'm so glad you bought it. Stewart was going crazy over that blasted property." He rolled his eyes.

"Stewart Davis?" Brenda tried to control her curiosity. Her heart was doing flip-flops. Fortunately for her, Eddy liked to talk.

"Stewart was heavily involved in the development of the Tides. He wanted The Tides to be a premier living space for Tampa's elite. Your property was the one thorn stuck in his side."

Noticing his empty glass, Brenda called for another shot.

"This one's on me, Eddy."

"Good girl. You know all the bar proceeds go to the Humane Charities Fund." His smile was lopsided. How many had he already downed? There was one burning question on Brenda's mind. She waited for the bartender to hand Eddy his scotch.

"Eddy, I see you've met our new neighbors."

Joan Davis stood next to Tina, hand on Tina's shoulder.

"Do you think you can keep Brenda occupied while I whisk Tina away to meet Phil?" She didn't wait for Eddy's answer. Joan pulled Tina by the arm and led her into the party crowd. Tina cast one last, helpless look back at Brenda before she followed Joan's persistent tug.

"I gather Tina is an artist and . . . yours?"

"That obvious?"

"Oh yes, dear, almost as much as I am. My gaydar can pick up signals from as far away as Mars."

Brenda couldn't help but laugh with him.

"Tina's a sculptor and a teacher." Brenda enjoyed the last drop of vodka and popped the two olives in her mouth. They were dessert. "So who's Phil?"

"Oh, Phil? He owns Le Galleria in Ybor. Joan thinks she owns Phil. She's been donating heavily into his gallery's bank account and in exchange, Phil displays her oils. Joan likes to run with the artsy fartsy crowd."

He leaned closer to Brenda. "But between you and me, Joan's not exactly a gifted artist." He winked and rubbed his hands together like a mischievous boy.

"She's also been very distraught lately. Been seeing ghosts."

"Ghosts?" Brenda's ears opened even wider.

"Oh yes, honey. Lost a friend of hers last month. Diving

accident."

"And she's seeing her ghost?"

"So the talk goes."

Joan Davis didn't sound like a very stable person. But Joan Davis wasn't what Brenda wanted to talk about. She found that she liked Eddy Vandermast and could converse easily with him.

"So, Eddy, why was Malfour such a pain for Stewart Davis?"

Eddy didn't drink his shot, but played with the glass.

"Well, it was an eye sore, darling. You bought it. You did renovations, right?"

Brenda nodded.

"Stewart had a picture in his mind of what the Tides should look like. Your old house wasn't part of it." He downed the scotch in several gulps. "He tried forever to buy the property from the Cuencas. Some family dispute stood in the way."

"The Cuencas? Peter Cuenca sold us Malfour."

Eddy shrugged his shoulder. "All I know is Stewart went back and forth with Louis Cuenca. Finally gave up. I think he got an ulcer out of it all." He was holding back a smile.

Louis Cuenca? He wasn't part of the puzzle. Stewart Davis and Davross must have offered him a pretty penny for the property. If Stewart had been so desperate to bulldoze Malfour and put up a concrete mansion, Brenda was willing to bet that he'd put a sweeter offer on the table than she had. Why hadn't Peter Cuenca sold?

"Is this your first time meeting Stewart and Joan?" Eddy broke her thoughts. Good thing, too. They were taking a dangerous turn.

"We just moved into Malfour last month. It's supposed to be our Summer house."

"Supposed? I think not. Why would you want to leave?" Eddy was still looking at her with a question mark on his face.

What could she tell him? She wasn't going to share her growing attachment to the house. Her reluctance to leave Tampa. She hadn't even talked about it with Tina.

"Well, it's hard to give up this weather for Newark."

She wanted to change the conversation back to Stewart Davis.

"What does Stewart do in Davross?"

"Stewart, my dear, is CEO and heart and soul of Davross. He specializes in area revitalization. He buys up large parcels of land in sometimes undesirable sections of a neighborhood, lines up investors, and builds. Once it's up, he's made his money and the investors are left to sink or swim."

Brenda wanted to ask many more questions of Eddy, but was interrupted when two men walked up and greeted him. Eddy introduced her and ordered another round of drinks. Brenda needed another martini. The two men were in the aviation business and completely took over the conversation. Eddy was lost to her.

But the evening had been a revelation. And boring. She never did get to talk to Eddy again. Brenda and Tina met every important person in Tampa's jet set. The mayor. Several City Council members. Judges. Lawyers and doctors. They met all their Tides neighbors, Linda and Sam Becker, Sam being VP of Florida Sun Banking, Henry Bonner, the prominent plastic surgeon and his wife, Silvia, and Lillian Parmelito, widow of pharmaceutical giant Winston Parmelito. Tina seemed to be having a great time and Brenda enjoyed just watching her mingle. She and Joan Davis seemed to have bonded, the arts being the glue.

On the drive home, Brenda couldn't catch her breath. She rattled off all the information she'd found out about Malfour and Stewart Davis. Tina kept interrupting her, boasting about all the contacts she'd made. She seemed especially excited about Phil Brown.

"Phil wants me to bring some of my newer pieces in. I figure I could leave them with him before we leave. He says he can do a show for me and then keep them in the gallery as display pieces."

Brenda smiled inside. It was good to see stars back in Tina's eyes again. The time she spent caring for Brenda had been taxing for Tina. Brenda's news could wait. She would let Tina bask in the moment.

When they stood in the warm glow of the foyer at home, Brenda grabbed for Tina and kissed her hard.

"Mmmm, what's that for?" Tina smiled.

"I love to see you happy. And do I need a reason?" Brenda was teasing her.

"I tell you what, Princess, suppose I go upstairs and turn down the bed. I can be very happy there with you beside me."

She broke away from Brenda and ran up the stairs, looking coyly back down at her half way up the stairs. Brenda was about to take off after her, but noticed a light in the dining room that she didn't remember leaving on.

Nothing seemed suspicious, so chalking it up to a bad memory, she flipped the switch and was on her way up the stairs when Tina's scream made her heart take a tumble. Tina was screaming her name. Brenda never ran so fast up those stairs, taking two steps at the top landing.

Her heart had worked itself up her throat by the time she ran into the bedroom. Tina was standing near the window, hands over her mouth. She looked at Brenda with terrified eyes and pointed to the bed.

Brenda walked slowly, coming to stand at the edge of the bed. Tina had rolled back the comforter. Brenda froze when she saw what had frightened Tina. What looked like two stick figures lay side by side in the center of their bed. As she leaned closer, she realized the figures were made of dirt. Black dirt.

Tina crept up behind her, hugging Brenda close.

"Holy shit, Brenda, what the hell are they?" She whispered.

Brenda didn't answer her. Instead, she put out her hand and swiped at one of the figures. It wasn't dirt. She rubbed the ashes between her fingers. Ashes.

"Brenda, what the hell . . ."

"I don't know, Tina. I don't know."

Tina left Brenda's side and went for the phone. "I'm calling the police."

"No." Brenda's voice stopped her in her tracks.

Tina looked at her, confused. "Brenda, we've got to call the police."

Brenda shook her head, unable to take her eyes off the figures on the bed. On their bed. She felt violated.

"Let's keep our head about this, Tina. Let me think a minute."

Tina walked back to her. "Brenda, please don't tell me you're thinking what I think you're thinking?" She looked incredulously at Brenda.

"Why not, Tina? What would the police do but come in here, tear everything up and do nothing? I can get with Kevin in Newark. He can help us." What she was thinking was that maybe Malfour or Carlotta were trying to communicate.

Tina shook her head, looking from the ashes on the bed, to Brenda. "This is not a game, Brenda. Someone was in the house. We could be in danger." She almost couldn't finish the sentence. Her voice shook with fear. "Brenda, I'm scared."

Brenda wanted desperately for Tina to understand. She didn't want the police or anyone else prowling around Malfour. Yes, she was probably being overprotective, but she could take care of this herself. They would be safe.

"Look, Tina, for the longest time you wanted me to get back into the work force. Get back into the career path. Why not start here? My PI license is valid in any state, as long as it isn't expired."

Tina was afraid, and frustrated. "It's this Goddamn house, isn't it? You don't even want the freaking police in the house, do you?"

She was up close in Brenda's face. "C'mon, tell me, Brenda, it's the house, isn't it?

The figures on the bed taunted Brenda. They sat on her expensive Egyptian cotton sheets and mocked her. Forced her to confront her obsession. She lashed back at Tina.

"Stop it. I need to do this, Tina. It isn't about the house. It's about me." She lied. It was all about the house.

"That's just it, Princess, I can't tell the difference anymore." She turned and walked out.

Chapter 12

"Kevin, I need a good forensics lab here in Tampa. Can you get back to me today with that?"

"Hey, BS. Getting back into the business?"

Brenda hadn't talked to Kevin for months. She remembered the last case the two had worked on together for the firm. A wife beater. The last case before Danny Crane ended her career.

"Not by choice, Kevin. Call me right away, okay?"

"Hey, it sounds serious. Everything okay down there in paradise?"

"Just need ID on something I found."

No need to alarm him. He had his hands full. His agency was the top detective service in Jersey. "Hey Kevin, if I'm not here, leave the info with Tina."

Brenda had intended to head out early this morning. She had a full schedule today. But the morning had gotten away from her. She'd overslept and it was already past ten. She'd spent most of the night making sure Malfour was secure. She hadn't found anything suspicious. Malfour was tight as a drum.

She'd made sure not to touch anything without a glove. A fingerprint kit was top on her list of "things to get" today. She wanted to dust every place someone could have used to get into the house. Although there was no evidence of forced entry, she would dust doorknobs inside the house as well. Her mind kept going back to the light left burning in the dining room last night. She wished now she hadn't touched the switch. She could have dusted for prints.

Tina had not come back to the bed, even after Brenda collected the ashes into a plastic baggie and changed the sheets. Brenda figured she'd slept in the Library or her studio. Brenda had been able to calm Tina down last night, but Tina remained skeptical of Brenda's decision.

Brenda's dilemma at the moment was how long to wait for Kevin's call. Her first stop this morning was The Artists Hub. There was some hope of finding more info on the Malfour family there, since it had been their cigar factory over a century ago. She'd found a locksmith off Bayshore that assured her they could get the lock to the metal security box open. There was no telling what secrets that could reveal.

Then there was the fingerprint kit and finally, she needed to drop off her new Sagittarius bear to Felice. "Saggy," as Brenda called it, was the first in her Zodiac Bear series. He was 3 1/2 inches and sported a two-tone color, brushed velvet look with an archer's cap, a mini bow and arrow, and a quiver full of tiny arrows.

Tina wanted to work on some new pieces for Phil Brown this morning. She was still excited about his offer.

Brenda crept up to the door of her studio. "Hey baby. Think you can pound some sense into that clay?"

Tina was kneading a lump of clay with hard, frantic blows, her face in deep concentration. She looked up at Brenda's voice.

"Got lots of work to do before I can show at Phil's." She smiled, but kept digging at the clay.

Brenda knew only too well that this intensity in her work was a cover for a troubled spirit. Tina was still upset.

"Listen, Tina, Kevin is going to be calling with information. The name of a lab."

Brenda walked up closer to Tina and put a hand on her

shoulder. "I'll find out what last night was about. It won't happen again. We'll get a security system installed."

Tina stopped working and kissed Brenda quickly on the lips. A whisper of a kiss. "I know you will, Princess. Don't worry about me. I'm fine."

She winked at Brenda before going back to work. "Now, get out of here. I've got work to do."

* * *

Brenda took the Jag. Top down. Along the way, she collected stares, thumbs up, and propositions from mostly men who eyed the Jag first, then Brenda sitting behind the wheel. She loved the sunshine and steamy humidity. It was easy to imagine she was on a tropical island out there somewhere.

She decided to pass by The Art Hub and hit it on her way back home. Instead, she headed out to Teddies in the Park. On the passenger seat, was the mysterious security box. That would be her third stop.

Felice loved Saggy. She assured Brenda she could easily sell whatever number of bears Brenda wanted to make. The shop would take a 30% cut. Felice and Brenda agreed on a limited edition of ten for each Zodiac sign. The only thing Brenda had to worry about was finding the time to work on them.

It was a good thing Brenda was good with maps. She'd inherited that from her dad. He was a road freak. Even as a child, she jumped at the chance of going along with him wherever and whenever he offered. That was how she developed her love for the automobile.

The Macy Security for Home and Business was located in north Tampa, on a road named Bryan Dairy. Brenda picked out the deluxe fingerprint kit for professional use. While there, she inquired about a home security system. Anything to make Tina more at ease.

On her way to the locksmith, she wondered if Kevin had

called. Pulling out her cell phone, she dialed Tina. There was no answer. Where could Tina be? Brenda decided to stop for a smoothie lunch at a Smoothie Queen she spotted on the way. She asked about the Guava Delight. It was a tropical fruit, the young man explained. She braved it and it was delicious. She would be back for another one.

Smitty's Locks was located on Bay to Bay, just off Bayshore. It was a small storefront sharing a building with a photographer. Brenda took the blackened metal box from the passenger seat and carried it in both her hands, keeping it away from her white linen blouse. It held an unexplainable fascination for her, the curiosity threatening to overcome all else. What would be inside?

A large man, face almost as red as his golf shirt with the name 'Smitty' embroidered on it, greeted her.

"I'm Brenda Strange. I talked to you about getting this open." She presented him the box, placing it carefully into his hands.

He looked it over and proceeded to plop it unceremoniously on the counter. "Sure, not a problem." He smiled at her. "Be right back." He disappeared through a door behind him.

Brenda eyed the singed little box. She knew it wouldn't be money. Couldn't figure out how she knew this, just knew. She didn't need money. Secrets. She needed answers. She wanted pieces to her puzzle from this little box. Standing there, waiting for Smitty to return, Brenda realized why she'd put off opening the box. It was fear. Fear that instead of clarity, she would find more mysteries. But the curtain was going up. Smitty walked back out holding what looked like a hammer with a rubber head and a screwdriver in his hands.

"This usually does it." He glanced at her briefly, then positioned the flat edge bar on the lock. "This little baby looks pretty old. Been through a fire?" He didn't look at Brenda, just pounded the hammer several times down and the lock broke off, like brittle candy.

He turned to Brenda, a small smile on his big face. "These

old ones cave right in. There you go, Ma'am."

He didn't open the box, just pushed it back toward her. My God, did he expect her to open it right there in front of him? Brenda quivered inside. Tempted, she put out her hand to lift the lid, but drew it back. No. She would wait 'till she got home. Back to Malfour. The box belonged there.

Smitty laid the tools down on the counter and proceeded to write out a receipt. He charged her three dollars. She paid, took the box carefully and put it back on the passenger seat. *Open it*, the little Brenda devil on her left shoulder shrieked.

"No." She said out loud to herself as she put the Jag in reverse and pulled out. She concentrated on getting back to the Crosstown interstate. Brenda was getting very familiar with the streets of South Tampa and Hyde Park. She felt comfortable in that realization.

The old Malfour cigar factory was a large one. Of course, Brenda really didn't have much to compare it to, but it certainly loomed like a giant, red brick dinosaur. Small windows ran the length of the building. Brenda parked her car in a fenced parking lot behind the building.

Wide, steep steps took Brenda to the wooden front double doors, which at one time must have been exquisite, but were now brittle with age. Inside, one huge, open space displayed works of art. There were large, gaudy pieces, photographs and sculptures. The room was stark white with black columns. A hallway stretched ahead of her and an office with drawn blinds was to her right.

A tiny bell jingled when she walked in and from the hallway, a young man came out to greet her, his denim overalls spattered with dried paint. He rubbed his hands on his overalls and reached out for Brenda. Brenda took his hand.

"Hi, I'm Rob Miller. Can I help you with anything?"

"Hi Rob, I'm Brenda Strange. Do you run the gallery?"

He laughed and shook his head. "Oh no, I just rent space. You want Anna. She's the art director. I'll get her for you."

He disappeared back into the hallway. Brenda took the time

to look around more closely. Obviously, The Art Hub was successful. Nothing was out of place. This wasn't like some of the artist's hang outs she and Tina had visited in Jersey. Was this how Florida did the arts?

Brenda was surprised when the short, dark, Asian woman approached her, smiled and shook her hand. She was younger than Brenda expected. Maybe mid-twenties. Dressed in baggy pants and tight shirt, her eyes were bright and black.

"I'm Anna Yin. What can I do for you?"

Brenda introduced herself and told her why she was here.

"Oh yeah, I've heard all about the Malfours. They built this cigar factory." She laughed and touched Brenda's arm. "You've come to the right place then. We have loads of stuff scattered and collected upstairs. Pictures, ledgers, newspapers."

She wrinkled her lips, looking steadily at Brenda. "Now, if I remember correctly, most of the stuff is from the early twenties."

Brenda's mouth was watering. What could possibly be waiting to be found here?

"So, Brenda, wanna see them?" Anna was pointing down the hall. "We've stored most of it upstairs in one of our empty office spaces, but there are some photos in my office too. Feel free to stop on your way out. My office is the room with the mini blinds."

She led Brenda down the narrow hallway, artist's spaces on either side. Winding their way to the back of the building, they walked into a large room that appeared to be mostly storage. Large canvases, tables, dusty fans, even an old, broken window air conditioning unit sat lost in the clutter.

"The elevator is this way." Anna pointed to the right. It was one of those old fashioned, service elevators. This took them up to the third floor.

"How many floors do you have here?" Brenda asked.

"Four. The top floor is my living quarters."

Anna opened the door to the third floor. "Watch your step," she warned, as she and Brenda stepped out and into another long hallway. Anna walked ahead of Brenda.

"Most of the spaces up here aren't rented. The Malfour stuff is in the last office."

The air was stuffy up here. Did they even have air conditioning on this floor? They reached the last door in the hall and Anna pulled out a key chain bursting with keys. She instantly found the right one.

Brenda could swear her knees were going to buckle. She couldn't control the excitement building inside her. Maybe she should go into the private eye business. The way she was acting, uncovering hidden clues was becoming like a powerful drug for her. Trying to figure out the Malfour House mystery had brought out a side of her she'd only meekly tapped into while in Jersey.

Walking inside the room, Brenda noticed how small it was. And the air was even stingier. Anna flipped the light switch and the fluorescent light popped in, casting a harsh glare on the pictures lining the walls.

"We put all the pictures we found of the old factory on the walls. Even talked to the owner about using this room as sort of a Malfour exhibit of sorts."

The idea sounded intelligent to Brenda. "What happened? Owner didn't go for it?"

Anna made a distasteful face. "Davross Industries isn't exactly interested in the past, just what they can build on its foundations."

Davross. Stewart Davis. This was getting very interesting.

"What made them keep this building?" Brenda asked.

Anna Yin made a noise and frowned. "They didn't have a choice. The Preservation Society intervened. This is now a bona fide historic site." She smiled with satisfaction.

"Well Brenda, help yourself to anything here. I can't let you take stuff, but I can let you stay up here . . . as long as you can handle it." She flashed a big smile and walked out, leaving Brenda standing amid a floor littered with boxes.

The silence in the small room screamed. If you tried hard,

you could hear the dust fall. The framed photographs on the wall seemed to beckon to Brenda, so she walked slowly to the first one. It was a shot of the factory dated July 1921. The second photograph was a group of workers sitting on long tables, rolling cigars. The men wore wide brimmed, straw hats. Most of them wore white or light clothing, sleeves rolled up.

She walked through half the room, noticing that most of the photographs were shots of the cigar factory. Then she came across another group photo. This one wasn't a distance shot, but closer, the faces distinguishable. Albert Malfour stood with about ten other men outside the front of the building. Behind them, Brenda could make out the sign that said Malfour Cigars, Tampa Florida.

Standing next to Malfour was the same tall man with long moustache and cap, his arm around a young boy. Brenda looked hard at the boy. Yes, she was sure it was the same young boy who was in her book. The same young man with the haunting eyes. The only caption below the photograph read *Albert Malfour with factory workers, 1924,* written in fading, black ink. Brenda wasn't sure who the big man with the moustache was, but she figured he had to be important. And if the boy was only a factory worker, why did he also appear with the Malfour house staff?

Something Mark Demby told her clicked in her brain. What if this man appearing always at Malfour's side was Roberto Cuenca? And the young boy could be his son, Peter Cuenca.

For some reason, Brenda looked at her watch. It was late. She hoped Kevin had called. She wanted to get those ash samples to the lab today if possible. She wouldn't have much time to spend here. Not today. She pulled out the cell phone and dialed Tina.

After four rings, still no answer. She had to leave now. She could always come back to The Art Hub. She absolutely had to get back home.

She found her way back to the elevator and landed safely back on the first floor. She thanked Anna and headed back to her car. The box still waited on the front seat. Brenda tried not to lift the cover. Tried to fill her mind with anything not connected with the name Malfour.

As she sped past the Gulfbreeze, she thought of Cubbie. She wished she could stop by and say hello, but it was too important to get those ashes analyzed as quickly as possible.

She easily drifted into her Zodiac Bears. Her next one would be "Cappy," for the sign of Capricorn. A mountain climber, to match the true pastime of the real goat.

When Brenda drove up the Malfour driveway, she immediately noticed the Jeep was gone. She hurriedly gathered up the fingerprint kit and the security box, being careful not to drop it. Inside, she called Tina's name, hoping against hope that maybe she would answer. She didn't, of course. She wasn't home.

Brenda went straight to the library, gently dropping the box and fingerprint kit on the large table. She had to get to the answering machine. There were two messages. The first was Kevin. She quickly jotted down the name, address, phone number and contact name of the lab. The second call was Cubbie. She left her number for Brenda to call back.

Brenda reached for the phone and dialed the Blumenthal Lab and Forensics. When she asked the receptionist for John Fulmer and explained why she called, she was quickly told that Blumenthal Lab would be open only for another hour and that only law enforcement agencies would be considered.

Brenda had been brought up in the most brutal of high society's circles. Taught the ABCs of etiquette at an early age, her mother wouldn't have allowed her to even co-habit another room with their wealthy clique without living and breathing proper manners.

So Brenda bit her tongue and dropped Kevin's agency's name. Although the info did little to get her brownie points with the voice on the other end, it did earn her the invitation to visit the lab during business hours which the receptionist volunteered in a rehearsed manner.

Okay, so Brenda had a little over an hour to get to a place called Brandon. She got directions, flung the phone down, ran up the stairs, snatched up the plastic baggie of ashes, and sped back down. As she picked up her handbag, she noticed the small piece of paper she'd somehow managed to bury underneath everything without even noticing it.

It was a note from Tina. She and Joan Davis had gone to Le Galleria. She'd be home soon. Brenda remembered Le Galleria was Phil Brown's gallery. But that didn't smooth over the annoyance that prickled under her skin. Tina had completely disregarded the importance of Kevin's phone call. Brenda distinctly asked for her to take it. And how long had Tina been gone? How soon was soon?

Making sure the map was still tucked in her bag, Brenda shrugged off her feelings about Tina and sped off to Blumenthal Lab.

Chapter 13

"You're jealous." Tina's voice was teasing.

Jealousy was not an emotion Brenda was a stranger to. She'd given in to its nasty results at the law firm. Yes, she'd been jealous of the lawyers who were getting the nod for partnership before her. Jealousy. It was ugly. But with Tina?

"No, not jealous. Confused, maybe."

They were having a good-natured argument. That's what Brenda preferred to call it. She had dropped the ashes into John Fulmer's hands, rushed home, and cooked up her special vegetarian lasagna. It was something both she and Tina enjoyed. It bothered her how much time apart she and Tina were spending.

Tina sat playing with the leftover lasagna on her plate.

"We just went to Le Galleria. Then Phil invited us for a late lunch. He showed us around Centro Ybor." Her hand went out to Brenda.

"And oh my God, Brenda, we'll have to go and try the martini bar at Gameworks."

"Late lunch? More like an early dinner."

Brenda had dinner finished and growing cold before Tina walked through the door. That had been 6:30. "You're not even hungry."

Tina took a sip of red wine.

"Brenda, I couldn't miss the opportunity to meet with Phil." She inched forward on the table. "I mean, this guy is so connected with the arts scene here. And Joan really knows the ins and outs too."

"I just thought you'd be anxious to get this sample thing settled." Brenda was having trouble getting her thoughts out. A helpless feeling was sneaking up, foreign to her.

"I am, honey." Tina leaned back. "It's not like you missed the call." She took another drink of the wine and pushed her plate away.

Brenda knew the conversation was over. But she wasn't done. This was Tina. Her lover. Her companion. They were drifting apart and she wasn't going to let it happen.

"Tina, we have to talk."

Tina dropped the napkin she had in her hand and sat back, arms folded. She looked into Brenda's face, an odd attitude playing in her eyes.

"Yeah, Brenda, we do."

Tina used her name. Brenda knew it was serious when she didn't call her Princess.

"Ever since we moved into Malfour, you've been distant." Tina shook her head. "I mean, it's like I'm in competition with this house for your attention."

Brenda reached over and took her hand. "It's not true. I love you."

She searched for some response in Tina's eyes. It was there. "I do have a deep love for this house and true, I have been very excited over some of the discoveries."

She stopped and remembered the security box. The box that waited with open lid, ready to spill forth it's secrets. Brenda shook her head to shake the persistent thought.

"I just want you to be happy. Here, with me at Malfour." She meant that with all her heart. If only Tina could love Malfour like she did.

Patty Henderson

"I mean, Tina, if that's what's keeping us apart . . ."

Tina squeezed her hand hard and smiled.

"Princess, when you look at me like that, how can I resist you?" She laughed and collapsed back into her chair. "I'm yours. Do with me as you please, my Princess."

Brenda smiled, knowing Tina was merely trying to break the tension.

"Maybe we should spend more time together." Brenda said.

Immediately after she said it, she knew how hard that would be. There was that box waiting for her in the library. A return visit to the Art Hub. And she had yet to get a handle on how to conduct the investigation into the frightening invasion of their home.

Tina got up and started picking up the dishes. She walked up to Brenda and kissed her lightly.

"Dinner was marvelous. Thank you, honey."

Brenda looked back at her as she disappeared into the kitchen.

"Hey Tina, why don't I invite Cubbie for lunch tomorrow? You remember, the waitress I told you about?" She waited for an answer.

Tina came back into the dining room, drying her hands on a dishtowel. "Sure. That would be nice."

"One okay with you?"

"Hmm, unless Joan has other plans . . ." Tina stopped, laughed, and flicked the towel at Brenda's shoulder.

Brenda laughed and ran after her, winding up in Tina's arms.

* * *

Tina had gone upstairs. Brenda, exhausted and somewhat disturbed by the events which unfolded today, had volunteered to put the dishes away. She was wiping the last plate when she heard the hushed whispers.

They rushed into her head like a stir of voices, all jumbled together. She couldn't make out a single word. Until one came through, clear and crisp. *"Help."* Then another, more urgent. *"Carlotta."* It was a woman's voice. But it wasn't the voice she had heard up in the attic.

Brenda dropped the dishtowel, and like a doomed rat, followed the pied piper's chorus of whispers. Followed them through the kitchen door and into the guest room. Into the old servants' quarters. The room that had once been consumed by a great fire. The place where blazing ghosts once beckoned her.

When she opened the door, Brenda realized she hadn't stepped foot in this room since they moved in. It was carpeted. The only room in the house that way. Had she made that odd decision? She couldn't remember. Maybe Benny had asked for the carpeting.

There was a contemporary sleeper sofa, three small bookcases, two chairs, several paintings of Florida scenes and a television up against the brick wall. In anyone's eyes, a very cozy room. But not for Brenda.

Her eyes remained fixed on the brick wall. The image of Ed Banners poking his hand in the burned out wall came flying into her mind. Then she saw the little blackened security box sitting atop the TV.

Brenda knew she hadn't put it there. And Tina didn't get in 'till after she had. So how did it get back here? She was suddenly conscious that the whispering had stopped. In fact, the room was unnaturally quite.

A fluttering of fear tickled her insides. She was called here, alone, for a purpose. The singed box waited for her. Could it be that Malfour wanted it that way? Brenda caught whiff of the all too familiar smell. It was back. Just a faint hint, but she knew it was there.

She walked up and grabbed the box with both hands, no longer caring how black it was. She took it to the sofa and sat down, laying the box neatly on her lap. Then she lifted the lid.

More letters. Inside was a neat bundle of letters, tied together by a red satin ribbon. As Brenda lifted the letters out, a photograph floated to the floor. It landed face up. The two women huddled together stared up at her with smiling faces. Immediately, Brenda knew who they were.

She held the photograph up to the light. It was out of focus and the heat from the fire had tinted the edges brown. It was Carlotta Malfour and another woman, arms locked, faces touching. Brenda struggled with the haunting face of the other woman, and then realized where she'd seen her. The book she bought on the cigar industry in Tampa.

She was the maid throwing attitude. The one with the thin, pale face. Her hand shaking, Brenda turned the photograph over.

Angelique.

The name whispered in her ear was written on the back. Brenda looked around the room. Of course, there was no one there. Brenda smiled a secret little smile. She wondered if Tina was waiting for her upstairs. She focused her attention back on the photograph.

Angelique and Carlotta, South Florida Fair, February, 1926.

The handwriting was large, neat, in green ink. The same handwriting in the letters from the attic. Carlotta. Brenda looked at the photo again. There was a hint of intimacy in their closeness. What could have linked mistress to maid? Was Carlotta Malfour excessively generous to her household staff? Outings to the fair? Where was the rest of the staff?

They wore long coats, Carlotta's trimmed in thick fur. *Tampa must be cold in February.* Carlotta sported a large fur hat to match. Angelique, by contrast, was startling beautiful in her simplicity. No hat, no frills. The Malfours obviously didn't pay lavishly. But at least they got a trip to the fair.

Brenda laid the photo gently on the couch and carefully untied the ribbon. The paper felt brittle, a smoky beige color. The fire. The paper was so fragile, that a piece of letter broke up as she unfolded it.

What would she find? It was obvious that someone had gone to great lengths to hide these from prying eyes. Would they be love letters to Carlotta's mysterious lover captain? What a find that would be. Over a century later, Albert Malfour's suspicions of his wife's adultery would be realized.

One thing was different. There were no holes cut out of these letters. Brenda's hand was shaking again and she realized she'd been holding her breath. As she read the first few lines, a rush of excitement brought a hot flash into her cheeks and her heart stopped for just the smallest second.

March 15, 1925

My Darling Angelique,

> *I am lost in desire for you. I can't count the hours when I shall see your beautiful face again. Will you arrange to prepare my bath today? Oh please say you will? I can almost feel your hands on my body. Please don't worry about him. He will be at the factory until well after supper.*

Do not disappoint me, my sweet.

Carlotta

"Oh my God." Brenda spoke out loud.

She wanted to laugh. Then she wanted to cry. Albert Malfour had been right. His wife was having an affair. With another woman. And a common maid. Carlotta was doomed from the beginning. Not only was she indulging in an adulterous romance, but a lesbian one with a lower class servant.

Brenda could barely control her excitement. What a discovery. As she opened each letter delicately, she went further and further into Carlotta and Angelique's world. So lost was Brenda, that she didn't notice the cold which had crept into the room.

The letters were all love letters from Carlotta to Angelique. Some were embarrassingly personal. They were filled with romantic language and imagery. Brenda longed for the days when people knew how to romance one another.

She felt the chill in her hands first, then shivered. Her whole body was freezing. It was August in Tampa. The high outside had reached 93 today. Why was it cold in the room? Someone called her name. A tiny voice. A little boy.

"Timmy?" Brenda tried to get up, but was almost pushed back into the couch by invisible hands.

"Don't be afraid." Timmy's cheery voice caressed her heart. Brenda wanted to reach out and touch him, but knew there was no one there. At least not Timmy.

There was a woman standing next to the couch, her face just visible over the floor lamp. Brenda recognized the long, blonde curls and oval face. Carlotta Malfour stood frozen, her stare going straight into Brenda's soul.

Brenda remembered Timmy's message. This was what he was preparing her for. No reason to be afraid now. Brenda fought the lump racing up her throat. She had to remain calm.

Carlotta didn't move. She was as still as the quiet in the room. What did she want? Was Brenda supposed to say or do something? Or did she have something to share with her? The apparition remained fixed in her spot, her face, hands and eyes the color of gray porcelain.

Without warning, Carlotta Malfour turned around, away from Brenda. Her blonde hair was the deep maroon of blood, the skull caved in. The violence of the act that created such a wound made Brenda recoil in horror, memories of Danny Crane still too fresh in her life. Carlotta's hands reached up and Brenda cringed at the blackened, burned skin.

This was what Carlotta wanted Brenda to see. She had died a horrible death and it was Brenda's destiny to find out why, who, and when. It was all so very clear now, sitting there in a haunted room, sharing space with the ghost of a woman dead over 70 years ago, why Brenda had been called to Malfour.

She'd never given much thought to destiny, spiritual quests, or the meaning of life and death. It wasn't part of her make up. But ever since Danny Crane pumped those bullets into her, she'd been chosen. If she listened now, she could hear the pleas from the other side. But what were they trying to tell her? Had Carlotta died in that fire? But if so, why was she reported missing?

Time had ceased for Brenda. It didn't seem to exist outside of this room. Carlotta Malfour was turning back around. Brenda got up from the couch and reached out to touch the woman that seemed so real.

"What is going on here?"

"No, not Tina, not now."

"What?"

Brenda didn't realize she had spoken out loud. Hadn't even heard Tina come in. She tried to focus her eyes in her direction.

"I . . . must have . . . lost track of . . . time."

Tina walked over to her, a look of concern on her face.

"Brenda, I've been waiting upstairs for you. I just about fell asleep."

Brenda looked back over the floor lamp. Carlotta was gone.

"Princess, are you going to tell me what you were doing?" Tina looked at the letters and box on the couch. "You were just standing there, reaching into thin air."

Tina picked up one of the letters. "What's all this?"

"No, don't touch it . . . please."

Tina put the letter down quickly, as if she'd been scolded by a parent.

Brenda was confused. "I'm sorry . . . Tina. The paper is very brittle. I had one nearly fall apart in my hands."

She felt all jumbled up inside. She wanted to scream, cry, let the hysteria out. Could she share any of this with Tina?

Tina kept eyeing her every move. "Honey, it's late. Why don't you put all this away and come upstairs?" She moved to Brenda's side and held her close.

Brenda stroked Tina's hand, trying hard to keep the smile

she attempted.

"Tina, honey, why don't we go out to dinner tomorrow? Somewhere special. Talk. Catch up. We haven't had a chance to do that. I mean, we've been caught up in such a whirlwind . . ."

Tina nodded, her mass of black hair falling over her face.

"Yeah, Princess, I'd like that."

When she looked at Brenda, Brenda could see the sleepy circles and red eyes that screamed restless nights. Their relationship was in some kind of limbo and she had to find a way to get it back somehow.

Brenda started putting the letters back in the box, even though she desperately wanted to read more. But now wasn't the time.

"Let me put these away and I'll be right up, okay?"

Tina got up and ran a hand through her hair.

"Sure baby, I'll be waiting."

She was about to leave the room when she turned and looked back at Brenda.

"What are all those letters about, anyway?"

Had she even heard a word Brenda had tried to share with her?

"I'll let you in on all the juicy stuff, okay?"

Tina found her way back upstairs. This was it. Brenda decided that Tina should know about everything she'd discovered so far. Up to a point, that is. Brenda wasn't convinced Tina could understand her communications with the dead of Malfour. Or Timmy. Even though she wanted very much for her lover to share her newfound life, she wasn't ready to allow her. Something prevented her. And until she could put a finger on it, she wasn't about to widen the rift that had already grown wide between them.

Chapter 14

"Scorpion?"

Brenda sat up in bed, trailing the sheet with her. Tina grumbled something and pulled them back.

John Fulmer was on the phone. He was on top of his job early. Too early. Brenda and Tina had made passionate love, slept in late, and weren't in any hurry to end their decadent morning.

Fulmer gave Brenda a quick run down of the lab results. Common Florida scorpion. Pig, dog, and goat excrement. Rooster entrails. Chinese, black, and Guinea peppers. Traces of cooking oil, lemon, salt, and basil root. Brenda fumbled for the pen she kept on the night table.

She thanked Fulmer and hung up. She sat silent, her bare back to Tina.

"Well, Princess, what did he say?"

Brenda looked back at Tina. "Wanted to know if we were conducting cooking classes for the evil dead."

She proceeded to tell Tina of the ingredients Fulmer had found in the ashes.

Tina whistled. "So where does that leave us?"

"With a bigger puzzle than I thought."

Brenda sighed and leaned back into Tina's arms. Thoughts were starting to jump for attention in her head.

"First thought I had when I saw those figures on the bed was voodoo or some kind of scare tactic. A curse, if you will."

She felt Tina tense up.

"Curse? Like, what do you mean, curse? Like some satanic stuff? X-Files?"

"No, no honey. Someone is trying to frighten us." Brenda sat up, looking straight at Tina.

"They had all the opportunity to do whatever they wanted. Steal everything we own. They didn't. They just left those stupid little piles of ashes on the bed."

Tina didn't look convinced. Brenda knew she still would have preferred the police investigate.

Brenda reached out and ran her hand through Tina's hair.

"But that still doesn't explain how they got in without forcing their way." Tina persisted. "Maybe it isn't a real person. Maybe it's one of your ghosts."

Brenda didn't have that answer. But she knew where she could start to find the first clue.

"My sweet darling, I do love you. And I promise to keep us safe here at Malfour." Brenda wanted Tina to believe that.

"Good. Then it's a part-time job for you. At least when we get back home, you'll be able to concentrate on your teddies."

There they were. The words Brenda shunned like unwanted facial hair. It seemed that no matter how much she explained to Tina about her love of Malfour, her enthusiasm for Tampa life, and all the small hints she dropped about Tina's own future here, Tina still had her mindset on Newark. She would have to be brutally honest with Tina. Soon.

"Hey, Princess, what time is your friend due for lunch?"

Tina's eyes were on the alarm clock on the table.

"Oh, my God." Brenda jumped out of bed. "It's eleven already."

She reached over and pulled the covers off Tina. "Come on you . . . you're gonna help me make lunch."

* * *

"I still can't believe what you've done with this place." Cubbie's mouth was full. Brenda had served cucumber sandwiches, biscotte, coffee, and hiding at the end of the serving table, a plate of chocolate-caramel brownies.

"Yeah, Brenda's going to have to find herself a job to pay for it all," Tina said, winking Brenda's way.

"I'd say this is worth whatever you have to do."

Cubbie had taken the grand tour. They sat in the sitting room where Brenda had set out their lunch.

"So you like the Cubs, huh?" asked Tina.

Cubbie looked down at the Chicago Cubs T-shirt she wore. "Not hard to guess, is it?" She reached for a biscotte.

"And you both must be vegetarian, right?"

"We have been for several years." Brenda smiled as she poured her a full cup of hot coffee.

Cubbie took another sandwich. "Well, I love any kind of food." She took a bite and swallowed it in two chews. She laughed and looked at Tina.

"I was born and raised in Tampa. My family was originally from Chicago but left before I was born. But they always considered themselves true blue Chicagoans 'till their death, God bless em."

"Oh Cubbie, I'm sorry about your parents." Brenda sat down next to Tina. "Do you ever feel like you might ever want to go to Chicago?"

Cubbie laughed and waved a big hand in the air. "Oh heavens no. I been married, divorced, work, play, and most likely die here."

Tina reached for a brownie. "You got any kids, Cubbie?"

"Got four. And three grand babies. And I left my baby pictures at home on purpose so I wouldn't pull'em out and bore you two with 'em."

"Don't be silly, you wouldn't bore us," Brenda said.

"All of them are grown up now, so I live alone. Right up off of 50th." Cubbie pointed to her right.

The shrill ring of the phone interrupted them. Tina bounced up. "I'll get it."

When she left, Brenda found the perfect opportunity to ask Cubbie what she wanted.

"Cubbie, what do you know of local religions? Any voodoo or other offbeat religious practices popular here?"

Cubbie eyed her suspiciously. "Mighty strange question coming from you. Doing some kind of research or book?"

Brenda leaned forward. She thought she might get away without having to tell Cubbie what had happened, but it wasn't going to work.

"We found something strange one night when we got back home from a party. Someone had put ashes on our bed in the shape of two stick figures. I took it to mean it was supposed to be Tina and me."

Cubbie was deep in concentration, her eyebrows bunched together. "Did you call the police?"

"No. I wanted to check it out myself."

"Yourself? You some kind of private detective or somethin'?"

Brenda realized that she'd never told her what she did for a living. "You could say that."

Cubbie relaxed, but still seemed perturbed. "Well, personally, I would have called the police, but about your question, I don't know of any kinda voodoo or stuff like that, but there is Santeria."

The word sounded exotic.

"Santeria? What's that all about?"

"I have two friends, Gilda and Hortense, two sisters, who practice it. From what they tell me, it sounds like more of a cult than a religion. I know they dance around and get into trances and they sacrifice animals and stuff."

Brenda was intrigued. She'd heard it mentioned on a TV show she couldn't remember the name of.

"What about curses and things like that? Do you know if they do that?"

"Honey, you sound like you got something scary going on here." Cubbie pointed at Brenda. "You need to get the police involved."

"No, seriously, Cubbie, can you get me in touch with your two friends?" Brenda wasn't going to give up.

"How do you know it isn't some kinda haunting? I mean, hon, this house has that reputation."

Brenda couldn't tell her how she knew it wasn't Malfour. She just did. Neither Carlotta nor Angelique would have done something like that.

"Well, it could be, but I want to check out other possibilities. Now, can you get me their phone numbers?"

Cubbie took a sip of coffee and shook her head. "I don't know. I would love to help, but those two are kinda funny. I'd want to check with them first. See if it's alright."

Brenda realized Tina hadn't returned.

"Would you do that for me, please, Cubbie? I'll give you one of my hand made teddy bears." Brenda smiled.

"Oh honey, you don't have to bribe me. I'll try and call them tonight for ya.

Tina walked back in the room. Brenda leaned over close to Cubbie and whispered in her ear.

"Don't let Tina in on this, okay?"

Cubbie nodded acknowledgment as Tina sat back down next to Brenda.

"Sorry I took so long. That was Joan. We talked about the time frame for my sculptures to be on display at Le Galleria."

She smiled and looked at Brenda. "And your dad called while I was on the phone with Joan. He says he'll call back."

Brenda's heart did flip-flops at the mention of her dad. She loved him dearly and hadn't heard from either of her parents since moving into Malfour. She had sent them an e-mail with her phone number and new address. She thought they'd be dying to get down to Florida and visit Malfour.

Cubbie was still busy working on a cucumber sandwich. "Hey, Cubbie." Brenda laughed. "Leave room for dessert."

* * *

Cubbie had called it Santeria. Brenda entered the word on the computer and waited impatiently for the sites to come up. She caught herself drumming her fingers on the table.

Turns out there were quite a few sites related to Santeria. Brenda scanned down and found one that sounded like it could yield some answers. The site provided background information on Santeria as well as a whole section devoted to the rituals and rites, including curses. Brenda's stomach tightened. She clicked to the prompt for Rituals.

Brenda could not believe what she found. Pages upon pages of spells, rituals, and curses for everything from fertility to the death of one's enemy and the ingredients necessary for their success. She could feel her fingers grow weak as she continued to scroll down the section on curses.

On one page, she came across what she was looking for.

"Bingo," she whispered to herself.

The stark words on the computer screen jumped out into her brain. There were several spells to create unhappiness in a home, cause a tragedy, bring evil to your enemy, and sitting at the bottom, a spell on how to curse your enemy's house. Brenda licked her bottom lip, feeling her heart beating quicker. She went further and read the ingredients.

"I'll be damned." She breathed.

All the ingredients John Fulmer listed in his lab report sat there in front of her. She had one of the answers to her puzzle.

But the bigger ones of why and who remained more disturbing.

Brenda sat back and ran all the possible scenarios in her head. Peter Cuenca had been sole owner of Malfour House. He'd refused to sell his property, leasing it out only once to a restaurant, until he sold it to her. For a much lower price than

Stewart Davis had offered, she suspected.

Stewart Davis was the one thing that didn't make sense. Would talking to Peter Cuenca, or maybe Louis Cuenca, get her any answers? But answers to what? All she had was the scary suspicion that someone could be trying to frighten her and Tina from Malfour. For that suspicion to hold any truth, there had to be a reason why.

And Stewart Davis was the only one she could come up with. He alone had motive. But Davis was a successful businessman. He didn't strike Brenda as stupid or reckless. If he had anything to do with the ashes on their bed, someone else had done the dirty work. Stewart Davis certainly had the money to find the proper professional for the job. But Brenda was having trouble connecting Davis with Santeria.

The religion was one entrenched among blue collar Latinos. Puerto Ricans and Cuban refugees. Stewart didn't belong there. But Brenda wasn't blind to what greed could do to a person. If Stewart Davis wanted Malfour bad enough, he would do whatever it took to get it.

With her and Tina out of the way, Stewart Davis would make an offer they couldn't refuse, tear Malfour down, and build another cookie cutter palace.

Brenda printed out the pages she needed from the site and signed off. Her mind kept working, though. Stewart had been at the party all night. Or at least she assumed. She'd spent most of the night pumping Eddy Vandermast for information. And she was glad she had. But surely, on such an important evening, Stewart Davis wouldn't have had much time to slip away, break into her house without leaving a trace, place the ashes on the bed, and sneak back to his adoring party goers.

No, someone else was involved. Her thoughts went back to Peter Cuenca. She would love to get the figure Davis had put on the Cuenca table. Why had Cuenca turned him down? Had he caught whiff of Stewart Davis's ultimate fate for Malfour? If so, it was obvious Peter Cuenca would rather it have stayed empty than selling out to a land shark like Davis and his company,

Davross.

If Brenda thought Peter would be more talkative, she would have called him. Tried to pick his brain on the matter. Maybe if she rounded up enough courage, she would call anyway. Maybe.

All of a sudden, Brenda felt the lead to her mystery was hot. She could feel the fires of excitement and wanted to turn up the heat. Brenda jumped out of the chair and went in search of Tina.

She found her upstairs at work on a new piece. It appeared to be the beginnings of a bust. An unformed woman.

"Let me guess . . . Joan Davis?" Brenda stood in the doorway, not able to control the smile in her voice.

Tina looked up. "Hardly." She pulled back from the clay bust. "I call it A Gorgon for the New Millennia."

Brenda walked slowly around the bust, coming to stand next to Tina, and put her arm on her shoulder.

"Sounds wicked. What's it going to be?"

Tina looked at her, then back at the sculpture. "A Gorgon for the New Millennia." She was looking at Brenda with amused eyes, egging her on.

Brenda removed her arm from Tina's shoulder and slapped Tina in the rear end. She leaned close to Tina's ear. "Don't you dare make her look like me."

That caused Tina to break out into a roar of laughter. "Princess, I couldn't put your face on anything but an angel."

"Good, that's what I like to hear. Listen, Tina, you got the Davis's phone number?"

Tina arched an eyebrow in question.

"Don't look at me like that." Brenda teased her. "I want to talk to Stewart."

Tina stopped for just a second, then continued to mold and pull on the clay in front of her. "Stewart Davis? What's that all about?"

"I want to talk to Stewart about Eddy Vandermast. I might want Eddy to start up a business account for the Zodiac bears." Brenda lied through her teeth.

Tina remained quiet, putting all her attention on the clay bust.

"Tina, did you know Stewart Davis's company, Davross, made an offer for Malfour?" She had to tell Tina eventually.

"Brenda . . ." Tina had one eyebrow up, a look of disbelief on her face. "You're not going to tell me that in your gorgeous blonde head you suspect Stewart Davis of anything . . . shady?"

Tina kept playing with the clay, her long, slim fingers forming a face. The beginning of a nose was starting to take shape, and a brow above it. A very deformed brow.

Brenda had to give her something. "No, I don't know about Stewart, but I have a hunch that stuff left on our bed was a ritualistic thing of some sort. I asked Cubbie about local religions and checked out the web. Found tons of sites on something called Santeria."

"Santeria?" Tina actually stopped her work and looked at her. "Sounds exotic."

"Well, it is. Kind of. Seems to be a mixed marriage of Catholic ideology and African religions. They do these 'Ebos.' Sacrifices of fruit, trinkets . . ." Her pause caused Tina to move closer, her face bright with curiosity.

"What, Brenda?"

". . . Well, some of the rites call for the sacrifice of animals. Their blood, to be precise." Brenda stopped short of telling Tina about the curse. A curse that could have been placed on Malfour to frighten them. Now wasn't the time.

Tina moved back to her bust in progress. She either lost interest in the secrets of Santeria or was too frightened to know more.

"The invitation with Joan and Stewart's phone number is in the rolodex in the library."

Brenda kissed her quickly and started to walk away, but stopped. "Tina, let's go out to dinner tonight. Let me introduce you to Gulfbreeze."

Tina looked up only briefly from her work. "Sure, Princess. That sounds great."

Brenda worked her way downstairs and dialed the Davis's number from the library.

"Mr. Davis is not in." The woman on the other end was curt. Brenda didn't expect him to be. "May I speak to Mrs. Davis, please? This is Brenda Strange, we're her neighbors."

She could almost see in her mind the picture of the maid with the perfectly ironed dress walk through that palace to discreetly find Joan Davis. It seemed like it took her a long time.

Joan Davis picked up the phone. "Brenda, how are you? I'm sorry, but Stewart isn't here. Is there anything I can do for you? Everything alright with Tina . . . and you?"

There was an odd hesitation in her voice. The words sounded slurred. Was she drinking?

"Everything is fine, Joan. Thanks for asking. I just needed to talk to Stewart about Eddy Vandermast. I was interested in Eddy doing some work for me."

Brenda thought she heard water splashing in the background and hushed whispers. The pool, she remembered, but who was with her?

"Well Stewart would be the one to help you with that, dear. Let me give you his number." She struggled to remember it. Brenda was sure Joan Davis was on something. Joan took forever to give her the seven-digit number.

Brenda thanked her and was ready to hang up, but Joan wasn't done.

"Brenda, will you tell Tina to give me a ring, please?"

Joan was speaking very slowly. Brenda wanted out of the conversation.

"I will. And thanks again." She hung up quickly. Brenda had no interest in waiting for Joan Davis's lethargic response.

She immediately dialed Stewart's work number. The receptionist that answered was cool and professional.

"Hi, I'm Brenda Strange. I'm a friend of Stewart's. Is he in, please?"

"One moment, please."

In seconds, Stewart was on the other end. "Brenda, how very nice to hear from you. How are you and Tina doing?"

"Great, Stewart, thank you. Listen, this isn't entirely a social call, you see, I've been bitten by the history bug and was wondering, since you're in the real estate business, so to speak, if you might have some local history to point out."

"Yes, well, of course I can. I'm rather the history buff myself. Tell you what, Brenda, I'm ready to head out for a business dinner engagement, but why don't you drop by my office around tennish tomorrow morning? That be okay?"

Brenda was willing to cancel everything to meet with Stewart. "Yes, of course."

"Good. I'll switch you back to my receptionist and she can give you the address. I'm in the big glass tower smack in the middle of downtown. You can't miss it."

They said goodbyes and the receptionist politely instructed Brenda on how to get to Davross Industries, Inc. Stewart had sounded enthusiastic enough and Brenda hung up, already going through the questions she was going to slip by Stewart Davis tomorrow morning.

Chapter 15

The Gulfbreeze was so packed, Brenda and Tina had to check in and wait. Cubbie didn't waitress the night shift, so there would be no help there.

When they were finally seated, Brenda was glad they'd gotten a window table. Twilight was creeping in and the sky was a deep shade of purple with streaks of orange. The small candles on the tables cast a quiet, romantic glow.

"Can I get you ladies something to drink before you order?" The waitress was a medium built young woman with an eager smile. Her order pad was open and ready.

"I'd like an Absolut martini, straight up, please." Tina said.

"Make that two, but put an extra olive in mine, please." Brenda knew the chances of getting extra large olives in a restaurant/bar like Gulfbreeze were slim to none.

"Thank you, ladies. My name is Shawna. I'll be right back with your drinks. Menu's on the table."

Shawna left, leaving Brenda admiring the beauty of Tina's face in the candlelight.

"I love it when you look at me like that." Tina was smiling at her.

"How long has it been since I told you how beautiful you

are?" Brenda asked in a soft voice. She wanted very much to lean across the table and kiss her.

Tina's smile widened. "Too long ago."

"Why don't you start keeping a record then, darling," Brenda said, "Starting tonight, I'm never going to let you forget it."

"I've got the memory of an elephant."

They both laughed. Tina sat back in her chair, amused by the decor in the Gulfbreeze. "I can see why you like this place, baby. Kinda . . ."

"Quaint?"

"Yeah, that's it."

They laughed again, until Shawna placed the two martinis gently on the table. They were filled to the brim.

Brenda took the first sip. "Now this is a good martini."

Tina followed her. "Mmm, cold, just how I like them."

It wasn't hard choosing from the menu. Seafood was something they both shared a passion for. Tina ordered the blackened grouper dinner and Brenda decided on the rock shrimp.

The dinners came with a side salad and big chunks of bread and soft whipped butter. Dinner didn't take any longer than most restaurants, but both Tina and Brenda occupied their time by ordering another martini.

Night had fallen and the lights twinkled off the bay waters through the window. The skyline of Tampa came alive with lights in the distance. Brenda finished her salad and reached for her martini when she noticed the far away look in Tina's face.

"I'm almost afraid to say penny for your thoughts." She was smiling as she took a quick sip.

Tina smiled, more with her eyes than her mouth. "I was just thinking that we've been here almost two months and we haven't even hit the beaches."

Brenda put the martini down. "I didn't think you were that interested?" This was the first time Tina had ever mentioned wanting to go to the beach.

"Well, you know, the weather is so good. Almost a shame to waste it."

"Waste what, darling? I thought you had all kinds of gorgons to complete for your gallery show?"

Tina succeeded in a smile. "C'mon, you know what I mean." She reached over and almost grabbed Brenda's hand. "Let's go and stay for a weekend at the most luxurious resort we can find." Her voice was full of enthusiasm.

Brenda looked hard at her over the candles. Tina was really serious. Brenda had honestly not given the beach a single thought. Toasting your skin under ultraviolet sunlight had never appealed to her. "Want to talk it over tonight? In bed?" She had so much to talk to Tina about.

Tina leaned back quickly, just as Shawna started placing their dinner on the table. Brenda kept her eye on Tina. Something was up. Tina's eyes wouldn't meet hers.

"Tina?"

"Okay, okay. I can't keep anything from you, can I?"

Brenda swore there was a tint of frustration.

"Joan and Stewart invited us to their beach house. They have a yacht and several other boats." She stopped and looked at Brenda. "It sounds like fun, Brenda."

She wanted very much for Brenda to say, *Yes, honey, it does*. Brenda could tell. But it didn't. Brenda couldn't think of a more boring time. The only saving grace to a weekend like that would be the chance to dig into Stewart Davis, and maybe the off chance that Eddy Vandermast would be there.

"Why don't you go, honey?" Brenda couldn't believe she said it. It came out without thought.

Tina's eyes widened, a crooked smile forming. "Are you serious? You won't come? You don't mind if I go?"

Brenda lied. "Go, darling. It'll give me time to work on some teddies, catch up on some reading, and dig for information on our puzzle."

Tina seemed to be happy with her lover's decision. She cut up a piece of the blackened grouper and savored it in her mouth.

Brenda was less enthusiastic about her rock shrimp. Not because they weren't good, but because she couldn't get her mind to accept that she was jealous of Tina's relationship with Joan and Stewart Davis. If it came down to pointing fingers at Stewart Davis, it could get sticky. What if Stewart was somehow involved with the strange occurrences at Malfour?

"Brenda, aren't you hungry?" Tina's voice woke her from her dark thoughts.

"I think I'll order another martini." Brenda flagged Shawna down.

"I'm glad I'm driving," Tina said, as she watched Brenda down the last drop of vodka.

* * *

Dinner had been quiet. They both agreed to come back. The three tiny martinis that the Gulfbreeze served up had barely put a dent on Brenda's gloomy mood. The night was too warm, the air stickier than a Honey Bun.

Brenda leaned her head back on the headrest and watched Tina as she drove the SUV onto the bridge. The moon was only a sliver in the sky. It was dark on the bridge, only three light fixtures for the entire length of the bridge. A light mist, an intense marriage of water and the heat, swirled through the beams of the headlights.

Tina looked over at Brenda, smiled, and ran her hand over Brenda's cheek. Brenda kissed it, but her eyes were focused on two approaching pinpoints of light. Another car was speeding toward them.

Brenda squinted. The car had on its bright beams.

"Tina, honey, be careful." She barely got the words out.

The headlights coming toward them swerved directly onto their path, the high beams blinding them.

"Tina, my God, stop."

But Tina didn't stop. She veered to her right. The screaming of metal on concrete pierced the night and Brenda pulled back away from the door. She could almost feel the concrete push inside as the swirling waters of the bay loomed below. The window shattered toward her, raining drops of glass.

The car was suddenly on them, skimming the left side of their car as it bumped against it. Tina finally brought the Jeep to a stop. Brenda turned and watched the car disappear into the dark mist.

"Turn around, Tina. Follow it."

Tina looked at her with disbelief. "Are you crazy? With what just happened, you wanna go on a car chase? Do you have a death wish?" Her eyes were as wide as a cat's in the dark.

Brenda tried to get out of the car. Her door wouldn't budge. Her side was jammed up against the bridge railing.

"What the hell are you doing?" Tina reached for her.

"Let me go, Tina. If you won't do it, I will, even if I have to go on foot."

"What is wrong with you? There's nothing we can do. They're gone." Tina was almost yelling.

Brenda had the crazy thought of jumping over Tina and taking off on foot after the car. "Tina, they just tried to run us into the water. We've got to get back to the guardhouse. They've got the camera."

Tina ran a hand through her hair, trying to catch her breath. "Brenda, honey, let's just settle down, okay." She shook her head, her knuckles white with the intense grip on the steering wheel. "I mean . . . they were probably just drunk. This happens all the time. We'll just call the police and file an accident report."

"No, not the police."

Tina stared unbelieving at Brenda. Without hesitating, she reached in her purse and pulled out the cell phone.

"No, Tina, please, let me handle this."

Tina dialed for an operator. "I'm not listening, Brenda."

* * *

Within fifteen minutes, there were two Tampa Police patrol cars at the scene. One of the officers donned a bright orange vest and stood out in the middle of the lane, flashlight ready to direct any car that might come along.

Brenda told them everything. More than once. She told them the car was a black Toyota Avalon. She knew her cars. Tina contradicted that by saying she wasn't so sure. Whatever Brenda said, Tina cast a doubt. It was too dark, she said. The whole thing happened too quickly, she added. Tina was certain she couldn't be certain of anything.

Brenda suddenly felt she understood what a caged animal must feel like. She paced up and down the bridge, her face turned up to catch the rare breeze that whispered on her face.

The police said they would talk to the guard on duty at the guardhouse. Brenda felt like the whole thing had been taken out of her hands. After the police, the insurance investigators would be snooping around. She wouldn't have any chance at getting quick answers.

The Jeep was damaged, but not so badly that it couldn't run. They rode in silence the rest of the way home, an uncomfortable wall between them.

It was just before ten by the time they walked through the door of Malfour. Tina went straight for the phone. There were messages on the answering machine. Brenda felt lost. She was still very upset with Tina, but afraid of what holding on to that anger could do to their already fragile relationship.

Brenda needed a glass of water. Her mouth felt dry, spongy. When she stepped back out into the foyer, Tina was waiting for her, a serious look on her face.

"Honey, I think you better call your father. He left a message. It's about your mom."

Brenda froze. "What's wrong?"

She didn't wait for Tina's response, but ran right past her and into the library, snatching the phone. She knew there was something wrong. Her heart was beating in her ears. And Brenda suddenly couldn't remember her parent's phone number. Punching the numbers she thought were right, she hungered for her father's voice.

"Hello?"

"Dad? I got your message. What's wrong with mother?" She tried hard to keep her voice calm.

The silence, followed by a long sigh, gouged a hole in Brenda's heart.

"Brenda . . . we got the results of the biopsy your mother had done."

He stopped. Why did he stop? Why hadn't he told her mother was sick?

"Your mother has cancer. It's . . . in the . . . uterus."

Brenda wanted to ask questions, so many questions. As a child, she drove her father, her teachers, her friends, anyone who would listen, crazy with questions. But something held her back. The pain in her father's voice was deep. Too deep to disturb.

"Dad . . ."

"Brenda, she doesn't know yet."

Brenda shivered.

"The doctors say six months . . . uh . . . maybe a year."

Something cold dragged itself into Brenda's heart and sat there. This was her father. And he was talking about her mother. Her mother.

Funny how the oddest memories jump at you at times like these. Brenda clearly saw her mother at her most glamorous, stooped over a sewing machine putting the finishing touches on Brenda's Easter dress. It was always the dress up holidays that Brenda hated.

Brenda grew up too tall and skinny. Her mother could never find the proper dress for her. Every year, she made Brenda an Easter dress. And a Christmas one too.

"Brenda?"

"I'm sorry, dad. I . . . can book a flight tonight. Be there for you and mother."

"No, Brenda. Don't do that. She's talking about us coming

down to visit you and Tina before you have to get back to Newark in September." He paused. "And maybe even stay longer if you don't mind. We could take care of the house for you."

Brenda stiffened. She didn't want to think of leaving Malfour. She didn't want to believe her mother was going to die. And she didn't want to think she could die here.

"Dad, you two come down when you're ready. Just let me know." Brenda thought of her mother. Was she still wearing all her make up? All the gold and diamond jewelry?

"Is mother up?"

"No, no, she's asleep."

Brenda had to ask the inevitable question. "Is she going for chemo?"

Her father sighed again, a long, painful expulsion of grief. "Uh, no. They don't think it will matter. It's too advanced. Besides, I don't want her to go through all that."

Brenda wasn't going to question her father's decision, but she was going to press for her mother's right to know.

"Dad, you've got to tell her."

"I know, but not now, Brenda." His voice was weak.

"Dad, is there anything I can do?" Her knees were ready to buckle.

"Just be there for your mother. I don't . . ." He paused. "I don't know when we'll get down there, but it will have to be soon. There are some things I need to take care of. Make phone calls . . ." His voice trailed off.

Brenda had never heard her father's voice so heavy. She wanted very much to reach out and hold him tight.

"I'll be here, Dad. Call me on my cell phone if you have to."

Brenda told him she loved him, like she always did, then hung up. The room was very still. Brenda reached for the edge of the table for support.

Tina, who had left the room earlier, came up behind Brenda, but didn't touch her. She just waited. Brenda knew she was afraid to make the first move. It had all become so damned fragile.

Brenda turned around, reached out for her, and melted in Tina's arms. She clung to Tina, holding onto the solidity of her body. She never hugged her mother like that.

Brenda felt that she would lose it, spill out the tears she knew were building. But they didn't come.

"It's my mother, Tina. She's been diagnosed with uterine cancer."

Tina hugged tighter, then pulled back, looking deep into Brenda's eyes. "Oh my God, Brenda, I'm so sorry. Are you going to be okay?"

Brenda managed a weak smile. "I've got to be. Dad . . . he's taking it pretty hard." Her father's voice wouldn't leave.

Tina pulled her close again, stroking Brenda's hair. "I'm here for you, baby."

Brenda's whole being shuddered, thankful for Tina's love and devotion. Then her eye caught the names Tina had written on the phone log on the table. Cubbie had called. And Joan Davis.

Right away, her mind shifted. She would be strong for her father and her mother, and when the time came, she would grieve. But Malfour and her life here with Tina were being threatened. It was up to her to find the answers.

"Tina, what did Cubbie say?" She broke the embrace and picked up the paper with the names.

"Um, something about having some phone numbers for you. Friends of hers or something like that. Said you could call her back."

As much as Brenda wanted to speed dial Cubbie's phone number right now, it was too late to make phone calls tonight. They both opted for some warm soymilk and early bed. Just as well for Brenda. She felt deflated of all energy.

In bed that night, with the dark and quiet of Malfour engulfing her, Brenda Strange cried. Not so much because her mother was going to die, but because she'd never been able to love her mother. Hadn't even been able to call her Mom or

Mommy. Mrs. Raymond Strange, the Ice Queen. And the time was now gone.

Was it her mother's fault? Had she been the flawed one? Or was it Brenda? Had she been the one who shut her mother out?

"Princess? . . . Brenda, honey . . . are you crying?"

She'd woken Tina. Without shame, Brenda turned over and buried herself in Tina, her tears falling so hard, she struggled to catch a breath. And somewhere, deep in the walls of Malfour, Brenda heard a distant sigh.

Chapter 16

Brenda awoke to the sound of tapping. She rubbed her eyes and looked at Tina who stood at the bedroom door with a breakfast tray.

"Knock, knock. Hey Princess, wanted to make sure you were awake."

Tina placed the tray over Brenda's lap. She had made a simple but elegant breakfast of bagel, cream cheese, a fresh slice of orange, and a steaming cup of coffee. She stood with arms crossed, a smile tugging at the corner of her mouth.

"And that's strawberry cream cheese, darling."

"Oh my God, Tina, you didn't have to do this for me." Brenda straightened herself up in bed. Inside, she was really glad for Tina's early treat. She was ravenous.

She bit into the bagel and came face to face with last night. It was real. She had talked with her father. Her mother had less than a year to live. She and Tina had been nearly run off the bridge. And she had an appointment with Stewart Davis.

It was nearly eight.

She took a couple of more bites of the bagel and watched Tina move toward the window. The muffled sound of a lawnmower buzzed in the room.

Tina pulled the curtain aside. "Looks like our gardener is back."

Brenda gulped down more coffee and flung herself out of bed.

"I want to talk to him." She practically threw on her blue jeans and short-sleeved blouse and left Tina behind.

When Brenda went out to find Carlos, he was nowhere on the grounds. His riding mower was sitting on the front lawn. Brenda circled out back to the garden and found him on his knees, digging into the shrubs, or what was left of them.

Brenda stopped in her tracks. All of the beautiful red plants and green shrubs that Carlos had worked so diligently at landscaping lay wilted and burned. Brenda touched one of the leaves and it crumbled into tiny pieces.

"Carlos, what the hell happened here?"

Carlos jumped up like a startled cat. "Aye, Senora, this is unexplainable." His voice was agitated, hands waving back and forth in the air. "I planted these myself. They were healthy, good plants."

He reached down and picked up a handful of dirt and brought it up to his nose. "Look, see, Senora," He held out his hand. "Look at this. This is your poison." He pointed to the white, powdery specks sprinkled throughout the dark soil. "It is some kind of poison. See, poison." He held it up for Brenda to sniff.

"Yeah, I see, Carlos." Brenda backed off. She wasn't about to poke her nose into any poison. "Any idea how it got there? Did you find it this morning?"

Carlos nodded his head up and down. "Si, Senora, this morning. I come to do your lawn. I find this poison and dead plants." He looked at Brenda as if Brenda could wave a magic wand and make everything okay.

Brenda looked again at the tainted dirt in the man's hand.

"Would you know what kind of poison that might be?"

Carlos shook his head. "No, Senora. But this was not here when I was here last. Unless, you . . ."

"No, Carlos, we didn't do anything to the garden." Brenda wasn't going to get anything useful out of Carlos. "Wash that dirt off your hands, Carlos, I don't want you getting sick."

He flung the soil back on the ground and ran off to the hose at the garage. Was it just Brenda's imagination, or did the sky take on a dark, angry look? A thunderstorm. Brenda had to get a sample of the dirt to John Fulmer.

Things were getting scary. What would she tell Tina? Maybe nothing at all. No reason to frighten her. But she did need to call Kevin in Newark. Call it fate, destiny, whatever you wanted, but the finger was pointing the way for Brenda. She could no longer deny the excitement she experienced each time danger threatened. The scent of the hunt made her realize it was time to renew her private investigator's license. Hang out the old shingle. Take up that new career Tina had urged her to explore.

"Carlos," she yelled to the dark man still washing poisoned dirt from his hands, "I'll be right back with some baggies. Don't go anywhere."

Brenda literally ran back inside, out to the kitchen pantry, and plucked out a small baggie from the box. When she raced back outside, Carlos was standing like a lost puppy near the dead shrubs, his nose sniffing at the ground.

"Carlos, get up. Let me get this to a lab." She motioned him back and picking up the garden trowel, carefully scooped some of the dirt into the baggie. Standing back up, she sealed the bag and motioned to Carlos.

"Don't touch any of the plants back here. And please, check the other plants on the grounds for the same problem." She left Carlos in a daze, and walked back inside Malfour. Tina was in the library, on the phone. Brenda thought she heard soft laughter. Who was she talking to?

She couldn't worry about that now. She had to get to Stewart's office in less than an hour. Brenda went into the kitchen and slipped the baggie full of poisoned dirt into an old plastic grocery bag. Since her whole day was free after

Stewart's appointment, she could drop the sample at Blumenthal Lab. And there was still so much more to see at The Artists' Hub.

Brenda took a shower, donned a pair of taupe linen pants, tailored blouse, and slipped on her leather sandals. She grabbed her small wallet and practically ran down the stairs.

"Hey, babe, where you off to in such a hurry?" Tina stood in the dining room doorway, munching on an English muffin.

Brenda stopped dead in her tracks. She'd completely forgotten to tell Tina about her appointment with Stewart.

"I've got a meeting with Stewart at ten." She wanted to walk out the door. "I'm sorry, honey, but with everything happening last night and all . . ." Her father's voice was back in her head.

"I understand, Princess, go, go." Tina made a motion with her hands ushering Brenda out the door. "Joan is coming over later today. She wants to see my work. Plus the insurance people called while you were outside. They're coming to look over the Jeep."

Brenda should have been out the door and in her Jag. She would be late if she delayed any longer. But the mention of Joan's name hit her like a bullet. It was true. Joan hadn't seen Tina's work. She had a perfectly legitimate reason for coming to Malfour. But why couldn't she come when Brenda was there?

Tina came up to her, brushed a quick kiss on Brenda's cheek, and took another bite of the muffin. "And don't worry, Princess, if Joan and I go off somewhere, I'll call you on the cell phone and let you know."

As if that made it any better. Brenda faked a smile and walked out the door. She practically ran to the Jag, popped the glove box to make sure the map was there, and backed it out of the garage house.

Davross Industries owned the entire top floor of the Federal Towers building smack in the middle of downtown Tampa. The small glass panes of the thirty-three-story building reflected the gathering dark clouds in muted shades of gray.

Brenda parked the Jag on the private floor the receptionist had suggested. She rode the elevator alone, and when the doors opened, she stood spellbound.

It was like stepping foot into a hotel lobby with plush, darkly-patterned carpeting and rows of huge, bright green tropical plants. Elegant paintings, photographs, and busts lined the walls. To her left, a wall of glass revealed the dark skies and building rooftops.

Brenda noticed some of the paintings as she walked down the lobby. Most of them were abstracts, but she caught several by prominent cubist painters. What she noticed most, though, was how far her sandals sank into the soft carpet.

At the end of the lobby, there was an elegant, waist high desk. A long hallway stretched to the right. The girl behind the desk couldn't have been more than twenty-five, had too much mascara and lips full of collagen.

"May I help you?" Her voice was professional, but she didn't smile.

"I'm Brenda Strange. I have an appointment with Stewart Davis at ten."

The receptionist looked quickly at a large appointment book then up again at Brenda, this time with a smile.

"I'll tell him you're here." She punched a button on the large switchboard and repeated the information. "You can have a seat if you'd like." Her eyes pointed to a row of puffy, velvet chairs down the hallway. Brenda opted to wait at the desk.

Within minutes, Stewart Davis walked up from the hallway, a big smile on his face. His importance was apparent from the expensive double-breasted suit to the cologne he wore.

"Brenda, how very nice to see you again." He extended a hand and Brenda shook it. He motioned her back down the hall where Brenda noticed more cubist art on the walls.

"Susan Zoon is one of my favorites." Brenda had stopped in front of a painting.

Stewart walked up to her and motioned toward another

painting just a few feet away on the wall. He pointed to it.

"I see you admire the art form. Up here is an Arthur Jernukian original."

They both walked toward the painting. Brenda looked at the Jernukian original in awe. "His work goes for astronomical prices."

"It's an indulgence I can thankfully afford. It's the only art that captures my interest." He eyed Brenda more than the painting. "Cubist art makes me work for a meaning." Stewart motioned Brenda into a door to her left.

The room they walked into couldn't have been Stewart Davis's office. There were high back leather chairs scattered throughout a large, open room smothered in smoky grey light from the dark skies outside. The room was a half circle of glass walls. There was a faint aroma of cigar and alcohol.

Against one wall of the room was what appeared to be a small bar.

"Impressive, isn't it?" Stewart was right behind her, his hand on her arm. "Have a seat, Brenda. Can I get you something to drink?" He was walking to the bar. "Martini. Absolut? Correct?"

He pulled out two martini glasses and a silver shaker. "I won't take no for an answer."

"Good memory, Stewart." Brenda walked to one of the heavily padded leather chairs, circling behind to take a better look at the photograph on the wall. It was one of many aerial shots of Tampa in different decades.

Brenda decided she didn't want to sit down before Stewart did. It hinted at weakness. She intended to make a bold statement. Stewart came over, handed Brenda the martini glass.

"Have a seat, Brenda."

They sat across each other, a small glass and iron table between them.

Stewart held the glass out towards Brenda. "Cheers." He took a drink and settled back into the seat.

Brenda took a sip and set her glass down. "This is one hell

of an executive lounge you have here. How do you get any work done?"

"Well, that's easy. I let other people do it for me." His eyes were smiling at her. "Now tell me, Brenda, what got you interested in historical Tampa?"

"Malfour. What do you know about Port of Tampa? Palmetto Beach, in particular?" Brenda took another sip of the Absolut, peeking at Stewart over the rim.

"I take interest in land that I can make mine. Its history becomes a personal advantage for me in dealing with investors. That's how I developed a passion for Tampa history."

"Well, now I understand why you didn't care much about the historical importance of Malfour. You were more interested in the land it sits on."

Stewart sat his martini glass on the table, taking a long, hard look at Brenda. He was trying to unravel her reason for being here.

"I'm a land developer, Brenda. I don't get attached to history. Personally, I don't think there's anything I can tell you that you don't already know about Malfour. Am I right? Tina tells us you've become quite an authority."

Tina. She was spending too much time with the Davis's and not with Brenda. This wasn't going very well. She didn't come here to create hostilities with Stewart, just a lead to fit him into the puzzle at Malfour.

"Stewart, I don't know how you conduct your business. I just happen to know that you put a very attractive offer on the table for Malfour and came up short. And I know why you wanted Malfour."

He chuckled, but it sounded far too serious.

"I'm not an ogre, Brenda. I'm a businessman. I do whatever it takes to get the profits. I had very definite ideas about what kind of community the Tides should be. Malfour House didn't fit the image. And it still doesn't. I hope you don't mind my candor. That, my dear Brenda, is why I was very interested in buying your house." He was brutally honest, but in a cruel manner. He knew how she felt about Malfour.

"So you're a corporate ogre."

"Some think much the same of lawyers." Stewart was going for what he perceived to be Brenda's weak points.

"There were some of my colleagues I thought that of."

"Brenda, let's just say people like you and I simply do our jobs to the best of our abilities. I merely love mine more than most." His smile was too smug.

Her martini was getting warm. He wanted her to admit that because she was a lawyer she was no better than he was. If she condemned him, she'd go down with him.

"I washed my hands of that stink, Stewart. I don't practice law anymore. I don't play those dirty little games."

"I misunderstood then, Brenda. I was under the impression you suffered some kind of . . . breakdown." The blue in his eyes suddenly looked very grey and he wasn't smiling.

Tina again. She was spilling their whole life's story to the Davis'. "I'm afraid you have the advantage over me." Brenda tried to fake a light laugh. "Tina is very talkative. But I'm not here to talk about my past career or yours for that matter." She paused and eyed the opulent room. "You're obviously very good at what you do. I'm just trying to do the same."

Davis cocked his head and arched one blonde eyebrow in a question. "I thought you made teddy bears?"

"Making teddy bears is one of the things I enjoy doing." Now it was Brenda's turn to settle further back into the chair and stare into Davis's face.

"I also happen to be a licensed private investigator." By the look on his face, she had hit the bull's eye with the surprise.

"Well, I had no idea. How very exciting. Are you working on a case?"

"Not exactly."

"Joan will be fascinated. She'll want you to tell her all about it at the beach house. You and Tina are coming, aren't you?" Stewart emptied the martini glass in one swallow.

Brenda remembered the conversation at the Gulfbreeze. She

hadn't realized it had already been planned.

"We have the date written down somewhere." She lied.

"In two weeks. Tina is very excited. We've invited some other friends as well."

Brenda was now even more thankful she wasn't going.

Stewart got up and walked back to the bar with his empty glass. "Brenda, I'd like for us to get to know each other since we're neighbors." He put the glass behind the bar and looked back at her. "You know, I have a large postcard collection of Tampa. It covers just about every period in time from the 20's to the 60's. If you'd like, why don't you come over and take a look."

Brenda really wasn't interested in Tampa, just Malfour. But he was extending a friendly invitation.

"Thank you, Stewart. That sounds interesting. I'll take you up on it." She stood up. It was time to go. He gave her nothing she could use. Maybe he didn't have anything to do with what happened in Malfour. Maybe she was on the wrong track. But she didn't think so. Then she remembered another reason for being here.

"Oh Stewart, would you happen to have Eddy Vandermast's business card? We met at your party and he told me he's your accountant. I might be interested in borrowing him from you."

"That I can help you with. The receptionist has some of Eddy's cards. Tell her I said to hand you one."

They exchanged goodbyes, shook hands, and he once again said how he looked forward to the beach weekend. Brenda would let Tina make up the excuse why she wouldn't be there.

Stewart Davis had been deeply involved in the deal to acquire Malfour. What wasn't he saying? Brenda was willing to play the waiting game. She'd just keep digging until she found his dirty laundry. She remembered to get Eddy's business card from the receptionist on the way out.

As she fired up the Jag, the roll of thunder rumbled through the parking garage. Brenda smiled. Her father always said Mother Nature was a grouchy old woman who always grumbled when she got angry. That was the thunder she always loved as a child.

Brenda put up the top on the Jag and pulled out into downtown traffic. The raindrops splashed thick and wet on her windshield. Driving to every conceivable locale in London and here in America with her father, Brenda had developed an almost uncanny memory with road maps. She remembered the way to Blumenthal Lab without consulting the map.

John Fulmer was there to take the soil sample. He said he could have something for her this afternoon. It was almost noon by the time Brenda left Blumenthal and her hungry stomach was getting increasingly vocal. She had a pasta salad waiting in the fridge back home, but she decided to make one last stop before heading home for lunch.

Chapter 17

As Brenda drove up to the guardhouse, she noticed the guard who stuck his head out to greet her. It was Tony Cutcheon. One of three who worked the shifts. He wasn't Brenda's favorite. She pulled the Jag next to his old Volvo and got out. He walked out to meet her.

"Afternoon, Miss Strange." He tipped his hat to her. Young, tight-lipped, and full of male bravado, Tony Cutcheon acted like a tough cop. He eyed the Jag with unabashed admiration.

"Hi, Tony. Was wondering if you could help me out?" She leaned up against the Jag. Tony looked interested, standing with his hands on his belt.

"Yes, ma'am. I'll do what I can."

Brenda smiled inside. She wondered how long it would take before she'd have to whip out her PI license. Good thing she'd decided to keep it with her.

"Tony, that camera that takes the photos of the cars' plates. How do you store the photos?" She pointed in the direction of the small camera.

His whole attitude changed. His hands went back down to his sides and he stiffened up. He eyed her with suspicion.

"Well, Miss Strange, I'm not at liberty to divulge something like that. You got some kind of problem?" He had a hungry look on his face.

"Can't say for sure." Brenda reached into the Jag and took the leather case out of her purse. It hadn't taken long to come to this. She held up the card certifying her as a licensed private investigator. She noticed the small, gold badge stuck on the other side of the wallet. She'd forgotten Kevin had bought all his operatives "official private investigators" badges. There was nothing official about them. Just eye candy. Something to impress the uninformed.

Tony Cutcheon took the bait. He looked intently at it, his face showing no emotion. He was playing it cool. Brenda put it away slowly, letting the moment sink in.

"You think you can help me out here, Tony?"

This time, it was Brenda who took the cocky stance. She liked this. The whole PI thing was getting under her skin.

"Yes ma'am. I apologize. I didn't know you were with the law."

"Not exactly, but I am conducting an investigation into the accident on the bridge. Your cooperation will help us out." Brenda chose not to correct him. He didn't have to comply with her requests. She was dangerously close to breaking a PI law. Impersonating a police officer or any other official of the law could cost her her license. But Brenda wasn't exactly admitting anything and she was betting Tony Cutcheon wasn't smart enough to question her.

He motioned her into the guardhouse. "We keep binders filled with photo file transfers of the videos. We keep one month's worth here on site. Older files go back to Eagle One Security."

They both stepped into the small guardhouse.

"Tampa Police have already been here. They took photocopies of some of these sheets."

"I'd like to see the binder, please."

"Yes, ma'am." He reached down to a small shelf and pulled out a blue vinyl binder. "Some of them are fuzzy, especially the night shots. And the camera goes on the blink sometimes."

Brenda flipped through the first couple of pages. They were in order according to the date. The photos were small and spaced out across the page. And Tony was right. Some were fuzzy, but with proper magnification, you could read the plate.

She quickly thumbed to last night's date. There were only a handful of photos for that day. The camera appeared to take a fairly tight photo of the license plate and some portions of the rear panel of the cars. She saw the dark red of their Jeep. Tony was right. The night shots were hard to make out. What kind of protection was that if you couldn't see the license plates at night? She noticed a plate that could have been on an old Beetle. That might have been Cubbie's. There were several other daylight shots and then one other night photo.

This one stuck out. The car appeared to be black or very dark. And what was odd was that the license tag numbers were extremely fuzzy. In fact, Brenda couldn't even see any letters or numbers. It had been a black car that nearly ran them off the bridge. A black Toyota Avalon.

"Tony, I'm going to have to make copies of some of these." She looked up and gave him one of her most vulnerable looks. A look that would have melted Tina. "If I promise to bring these back to you before the end of your shift, may I take them?"

When he didn't answer and started to rub his ears in thought, she went in for the kill.

"Of course, if you can't make that kind of decision, I can always talk to your supervisor."

"Oh no, Miss Strange, go right ahead. But you gotta bring them back before I leave." He looked at his watch. "My shift ends at three."

Brenda tucked the binder under her arm and walked out of the guardhouse. "Thanks, Tony. I'll get these scanned and bring them back right away."

She could make a quick lunch of the pasta, scan the photo sheets and have them back to Tony before three. Brenda looked at her watch as she started the Jag. She had a couple of hours.

Brenda was feeling pretty good. The rain had stopped and a pale rainbow was arching across the distant sky. Then her cell phone rang. She was just pulling into Malfour. It was her father.

Her mother was in the hospital. Brenda heard his voice falter. "Dad, do you want me to go up?"

"No, no, honey. She'll be okay. They've given her some medication and are sending her back home tomorrow. You know, they suggested some natural herbs that could help her pain when I get back home." He sounded angry. "Can you believe those quacks?" He continued. "They want me to feed her herbs."

This was going to be hard for both of them. Brenda knew he was going to need her more than he would ever admit.

"Dad, you refused traditional therapy. You've tied their hands. The only thing they could offer her was radiation or chemo. What did you expect them to do for her?"

He wanted a miracle. He wanted his wife free of cancer and back in his life. His pain was evident in the silence on the other end.

"Dad? You sure you don't want me to fly up there? I can catch the next flight out."

"No, Brenda. It's okay. I better go. Your mother is very weak. She needs me there."

In a deep part of Brenda, she wanted to ask if she could talk to her mother. "Dad, you can call whenever you need me."

She cut the engine and flipped the phone shut. This was only the beginning. It was going to get worse. She remembered when Uncle Craig was diagnosed with colon cancer. It took less than one year for it to eat through him. The suffering was intense and the pain ravaged not only her uncle but the entire family. And now they had to do it all over again.

Brenda grabbed the binder and got out of the Jag. She didn't know if it was the lack of food, but her stomach felt sick and she felt deflated. She couldn't get the thoughts of her mother in a hospital bed out of her mind.

When she went to insert the key in the door, she found it

already unlocked. This wasn't like Tina. Was she outside?

"Tina," Brenda called out loud.

There was no answer. Then she noticed the sculptures in the hall. Tina had placed several of her better pieces on black stands throughout the main hall. Brenda needed to scan the photo sheets quickly, so she worked her way to the library where the computer and scanner were.

She found another of Tina's busts there. She'd been busy this morning. Then Brenda remembered. Joan was going to visit. Had they gone off again? And if so, Tina was in serious trouble if she'd left Malfour and not locked the door. But what if she had and someone else opened it?

On impulse, Brenda began a search of the house. Her head pounded with the tension of fear. What if there was someone in Malfour? There were so many places to hide.

With careful moves, Brenda searched all of Malfour. There was no one else in the house. Her anger at Tina mounted. Not only had she left Malfour exposed and unprotected after what had already happened, but she'd put her in danger as well.

Brenda was up in the attic when she happened to glance out the window and noticed the two figures sitting on the bench. Tina and Joan. After she got her blood pressure down, Brenda worked her way back downstairs and out the door.

She was going to confront Tina. Even if she was on the grounds, leaving the front door open to Malfour was stupid and dangerous. *Here I am, trying my best to make it safe, and Tina gets so caught up with Joan Davis that she gives the intruder another easy way in.*

Brenda was still angry when she circled out back and entered the garden. She stopped in her tracks. She had no way of knowing how long Carlos had stayed, but something happened between the time she left and now.

Everything she'd left still green was now an ugly shade of brown, even the grass under her feet. The entire garden was dead. Well, everything except for the circle of vivid, healthy little flowers that surrounded the fountain in the center of the yard. She stood staring at them. Why had these survived the poison? They were like a mirage in the middle of a barren desert.

Brenda crossed over, bent down and took one of the tiny petals in her hand. It was soft and velvety, smooth and warm to the touch. The others danced and played in the light breeze. They seemed oblivious to the death of their sisters around them. Puzzled, Brenda dug in and scooped up some of the soil beneath. Yes, the same white dust was there. The plant murderer had been thorough, but these little beauties survived. Why? Were the colorful Impatiens immune to the poison? Maybe John Fulmer could have an answer for her. She'd make sure to ask him.

She had all intention of speaking to Tina, but now wasn't the time. Let Joan have her for now. Brenda still had to scan the license plate photos and get them back to Tony. And put something in her stomach somewhere in between.

She walked back to the library and started scanning the files. She got the two pages from the night of the accident scanned and was ready to run the binder back to Tony, when a strong feeling stopped her. Brenda always did well playing out her hunches. That's what Kevin loved about her when she got involved in some of their cases.

Tony had said they kept about a month's worth of license tags in the binder. If her memory served her right, the night of the fund raising party at the Davis's wasn't even one month ago. She flipped quickly to the date.

She couldn't stop the smile that formed. The date was there, and as she peeked through the pages, there were more than just two. It was more like five or six pages of cars. Finding her particular black car would be trickier. There were quite a few cars that could have been black and you couldn't tell the make of car.

Brenda chuckled at one plate. Big Shot. Maybe the mayor? When she turned the next page, she stopped. The first photo on top of the page was definitely a black car and the plate was too fuzzy to read. It looked like a match. She fumbled for the page from the accident night and held them side-by-side. They appeared to be identical.

Looking closer, she noticed that this plate wasn't just fuzzy because of a camera problem. No, it wasn't even because the car was moving too fast. This looked more like something she'd seen up in Jersey with several of Kevin's cases. Car thieves or criminals will sometimes spray paint over a car's tag to prevent any kind of I.D. They would then wash off the paint with water. No damage to the plate.

Brenda scanned that page too. When she got back, she would magnify the images and see if there was something else that might be of help. Tina and Joan were still out back. She'd have to tackle that problem later.

Tony Cutcheon was very happy to see her. He was also very willing to be of further service. He was obviously drunk on the possibility of playing out his lifelong fantasy of law enforcement. Maybe he could become Brenda's favorite guard after all.

When she got back to Malfour, Tina and Joan were nowhere in sight. Maybe they'd gone for a walk? Joan's car hadn't been there earlier. Perhaps they'd walked back to the Davis's. Brenda didn't care. She grabbed the bowl of pasta salad and headed to the computer.

She brought up the tag file and clicked on the mag tool. The tiny pictures tripled in size on the screen. Her suspicions had been right. The car that nearly ran them off the bridge had a tag that had been tampered with. No doubt about it.

And the photo right next to it of the car from the party night was the exact same car. She was sure of it. Brenda noticed something else. Something not apparent until she'd magged up the photos. There was a frame around the tag.

Brenda magnified the image again. Bingo. Even though it wasn't real clear, she could see a name on the tag frame. Key Wester Mopeds. The name stuck like fly paper in her head. Why? Then she remembered. Key West. Peter Cuenca. And not just Peter Cuenca. Louis Cuenca owned and operated a moped store in Key West. What had been the name they answered the phone with? She couldn't remember.

She sat very still. Her body was trembling and she needed to calm down. None of these tiny pieces made a whole picture for her yet. If anything, this newfound evidence added to the puzzle.

Brenda looked harder at the photo. The only time she remembered Louis Cuenca visiting Malfour was when he had come with Carlos. He wasn't driving his car. Right now, she had no proof this could even relate to Louis or Peter Cuenca.

But what if the car did belong to either of the Cuencas? What did that prove? Louis Cuenca had had dealings with Stewart Davis. What if he had been at the party? Brenda shook her head. It was hard to rationalize. She hadn't seen him there, but that didn't mean he wasn't. But what about the night of the accident on the bridge? Who was he visiting at the Tides? Stewart? Why?

Nastier thoughts crept in. He could have poisoned the plants that night. He could have placed the ashes on their bed. He could have violated Malfour. But how? Brenda shook her head hard. She wasn't thinking straight. It was an easy question. Louis still had a key to Malfour, of course. That could be how he got in. He just made copies before handing over the keys to Tampa Sun Realty.

The noise behind her made her jump, tripping the plate of pasta to the floor. It splattered everywhere.

"Whoa, Princess, didn't mean to scare you."

It was Tina.

"Oh, my God, you did scare me. I've been working so hard on this." Brenda swiftly closed out the file and the pictures disappeared. She started picking up the pieces of glass off the floor.

"Let me help you, baby." Tina picked up the rest of them. "How long you been home?" She had a big smile for Brenda.

"Not too long."

"Here, let me take those to the trash." She took the rest of the glass shards from Brenda's hand. "I hope you got to eat most of it." She disappeared toward the kitchen.

When she came back, she was holding a letter in hand. She glanced briefly at it, then back at Brenda. Brenda didn't like the look in Tina's eyes.

"I got this today in the mail. It's from the Institute. Classes start in two weeks. They want me there early for teachers orientation." She sat down slowly on the leather couch, her eyes searching Brenda's face.

Brenda could no longer procrastinate. She had to tell Tina she wasn't going back. She wanted to spill everything to her lover. Now was the time.

"Tina, I'm not going back to Newark."

Tina's mouth formed the letter "O" as she sank back into the soft leather of the couch. Nothing came out of her lips. She dropped the letter next to her and started to shake her head.

Brenda had to say something. "You think it's the house, Tina, but it isn't, please. Let me explain."

"You know what, Brenda, don't. I don't care, you know." She made to get up.

"No, please, Tina, I mean it. I need to tell you so much." Brenda reached out to keep her on the couch.

Tina settled back down, her head cocked to one side, looking but not understanding. "Princess, please, don't do this now. I'm not sure I can handle it." There was defeat in her voice.

Brenda had to make her understand. She wasn't trying to hurt Tina. She just wasn't going back to Newark. This was her home now. And she very much wanted Tina here with her.

She got up and snuggled in close to Tina on the couch. When Tina looked at her, the disbelief in her dark brown eyes was like a knife plunged into Brenda's heart. Brenda had to convince her to stay.

Chapter 18

"Stewart? You think Stewart has something to do with all this stuff at Malfour?" Tina looked at Brenda as if she should have her mouth washed out with soap.

Brenda had poured her heart out to Tina, everything from Carlotta and Angelique to the letters and the ghosts. Even her suspicions about Stewart Davis and Louis Cuenca, slim as they were.

"They're just theories I'm working on, Tina, that's all."

"And you're really serious about taking up this PI stuff?"

"Yes, it finally all fell into place after getting involved in all this." Brenda leaned closer to Tina. "Tina, you wanted so badly for me to find something new . . . useful. This is it, darling."

Tina wasn't listening. She'd completely shut down. She shook her head while looking at Brenda.

"I don't know what to say, Brenda. These are freaky things you've told me, but what's even freakier is your answer for all of it."

"I'm not asking you to believe me, Tina. Just keep an open mind to it. Listen. Not to me, but with me."

Tina looked at her hard, searching. When she smiled, it was sad.

"I've been trying, Princess. It's just . . ." She put up her hands in exasperation. "It's just this house." She focused on the floor. "I don't think it's done you any good."

"Honey, it isn't about the house. This is something I've got to do. This is about me. About me and you."

"Oh no, Brenda. It's not about me. It's been you and only you since we walked into this place."

Brenda felt lost. Alone and helpless. If Tina hadn't understood by now, she never would. No amount of effort would fix that. The part of Brenda that was exhausted, defeated, felt angry.

"It wouldn't be so difficult for you to find a good teaching job in the arts here, Tina. I'm not the one closing the door."

Unfortunately, this set Tina off. "Oh, you closed the door the moment we moved into this house."

"That's unfair."

"It's the Goddamn truth." Tina's words were harsh. She looked at Brenda a moment longer. "You don't realize how arrogant and selfish you've become."

Tina got up from the couch in one swift movement. "Joan knows I have to get back in a week, so we're moving up the beach weekend. We're heading out this weekend. And there's also a pool party tonight. We've been invited." She gave a heavy, serious laugh. "I know you won't go."

She started to leave the room. Something stopped her at the doorway. "Will you be okay here?" Her back was turned.

Brenda knew what she meant. She worried about how Brenda was holding up to her mother's cancer. What was there to say?

"I'll be fine."

Tina walked out of the library without another word. The ringing of the phone was like a sudden intrusion.

Brenda picked up the receiver.

"Hey. Got your poison." It was John Fulmer. "It's Kombat Green, just about the most powerful herbicide on the legal market. Enough of it in that small sample you left me to kill a whole field. If you had that poured over your yard, you've got one dead garden there. I suggest you dig it up and re-plant."

"John, are there any plants that are immune to that stuff? I've got a whole row of Impatiens that are still alive and kicking."

"Hmm. That's a mystery. If they were sprinkled with the poison, they should be deader than a doornail. You sure they got the poison?"

Yeah, Brenda was sure. She thanked him and hung up. Her garden had been purposely and maliciously poisoned. Unless Carlos was a trained actor, he had nothing to do with it. Their house had been invaded and some crazy, ritualistic warnings left. Someone was trying to get them out of Malfour. And she was going to find out who and why.

* * *

"Ouch." She'd poked the needle straight into her finger. Brenda sucked up the tiny prick of blood that was oozing out. She was putting the finishing stitch on her tiny archer bear's hat. If she didn't sew it down, it would never stay on.

She was behind on her Saggy bears and Felice had been on her back. Her limited edition had been set at ten and she had only done two. But tonight, with Diana Krall singing on the CD, Tina at the Davis's pool party, and a whole lot of scary things going through her head, Brenda found working on her teddy bears to be the perfect therapy for relief of serious tension. Perhaps when Tina went away for the weekend, she could start work on another teddy.

Unexpectedly, her thoughts drifted to her mother. Her father who was suffering along with her. Alone. As she was alone here tonight. Alone in Malfour.

Without understanding why, she reached for the phone and dialed her father. She asked about her mother. She was sleeping, he said. Hadn't been sleeping well. Anxiety attacks. Depression. Was on anti-depressant medication.

"Dad, you know that gun you always said was mine when I wanted it?"

"The Walther PPK?"

"Yes."

"That's the one I wanted to send you when you started working with Kevin's agency. It's yours, baby. I promised it to you."

"Send it overnight, dad. Can you?"

He was slow to answer. "Brenda, is everything okay? I mean, are you going to be okay with the gun, you know, after . . ."

"Everything's okay, dad. Just FedEx the gun overnight, okay? Malfour is a big house. I would just feel more comfortable if we had a gun in the house. And I've put Danny Crane in the past where he belongs. I can't let him control my future." No way in hell was she going to dump her fears onto her father now.

"Well, you're not going to be there much longer, are you? Don't you want me to just mail it to you at your address in Newark?"

Okay, now what was she supposed to say? Did she want to get into this with her dad now?

"We'll be staying a bit longer, Dad. Just mail it here. You have the address, right?"

"Yeah, sure honey, I've got the address. I'll, uh, send it out tomorrow if you're sure."

Brenda smiled slowly. "Yeah, dad, I'm sure. Give mother my love and kisses and hugs for me, won't you?" How much longer, she wondered, would she have to say that?

Brenda hung up just as Diana Krall finished singing. She put the dandy looking teddy in the finished box with the other one and decided to read more of the letters. So much had been crowding her attention, that Carlotta and Angelique had been pushed back in her thoughts.

Without realizing why, she found herself back in the guestroom. The old servants' quarter. The security box was right where she'd left it. She searched the room with an eye toward the floor lamp next to the couch. The image of Carlotta still haunted her. But Carlotta wasn't there.

Brenda opened the box and made herself comfortable, lying down on the soft ribbed couch. She read every letter in the box. The later dated ones became frantic. It was apparent that Carlotta feared for her life. And for Angelique's as well. These letters were the screams of a woman who expected to pay for her sin. And was willing to sacrifice herself to save Angelique.

July 19, 1926

My Darling Angelique,

It is getting near impossible to spend time with you alone. I believe he suspects us or at the very least, me, of infidelity. Little Petey is like my shadow. He follows me everywhere but to my bath and bedchambers. I'm convinced Alberto has attached him to me to be his pair of spying eyes.

We cannot go on this way. If he finds out, you will be in great danger. I will go to him and tell him I have been unfaithful with another man. He will have to kill me before I give him a name, for I have nothing to give him, but this is the only thing I can think of doing to save you.

I love and desire you more than anything in my life, but we must part for now. I can no longer bear to look at you and not look forward to your sweet lips upon me.

Love,
Carlotta

* * *

Every muscle in Brenda's body tensed. All of a sudden, the stark silence of the house overwhelmed her. It was almost nine and darkness was spreading. She was alone with a letter from a dead woman in her hand. A woman who could very well have been murdered by her husband. Carlotta and Angelique were still here because they more than likely died here. Isn't that why most ghosts remained behind?

Death certificates were easy to track down. She'd contact Kevin in the morning. He wouldn't be able to locate Angelique without a last name, but if Carlotta Malfour died and was buried legally, she should be on record. She remembered Mark Demby had said that Albert filed a missing persons report on his wife, but maybe he hadn't checked into a death certificate for Carlotta. But who was little Petey? A child? Petey. She didn't know why, but she thought of Peter Cuenca. Brenda sat up as if a bolt of lightning had struck her. The possibilities in her head were all dark and dangerous but her heart beat with a rush of adrenalin.

She almost ran to the library where she'd left *The Cigar Kings of Tampa*. She thumbed quickly to the pages she'd marked. The picture with the Malfour family and staff taunted her. There was that young boy. The same young man who also appeared in the photographs at the Art Hub. How old would Peter Cuenca have been in 1926? Could there be a connection? Her whole body tingled. She did the math quickly in her head. Peter Cuenca could be the young boy in the picture. Without all the facts, she couldn't be sure.

Brenda wanted very much for the night to be over so that she could head back to the Art Hub. The answers to her mystery could be there, waiting. And she hadn't ruled out giving Peter Cuenca another phone call.

Then her phone rang. It sounded like an alarm going off in the quiet house. Brenda answered it. Hortensia Gonzalez was on the other end. One of the two sisters Cubbie had spoken of. Brenda had all but forgotten. They practiced Santeria.

Hortensia made it clear that they were hesitant to speak on the phone. Well, at least Hortensia did, and she seemed to speak for Gilda as well. They wanted direct contact. She offered

Brenda an invitation to one of their ceremonies. They held initiations three times a week. Brenda should speak with Papa Chucho, Santero High Priest. Not only could he answer all her questions, but he took great pains to welcome all who expressed an interest in Santeria.

Brenda jumped at the chance. But she made it clear she wasn't interested in being initiated. She just needed some help with several questions. The next initiate night was in two days. Hortensia gave Brenda their address. It was in West Tampa and Brenda was expected at 7 PM sharp.

* * *

Mrs. Tiffy never wanted to have tea with Mrs. Truffle. Brenda sat her little dolls together and offered a teacup to each one. Mrs. Truffle always thought Brenda liked Mrs. Tiffy better.

"It's such a beautiful day, can't we have a lovely tea party without arguments?" Brenda smiled at both of them. Their bright glass eyes smiled back at her, but she knew they resented each other.

Brenda Strange loved hosting her tea parties. She looked forward to the sunny, breezy Sunday mornings. Sunday was the only day she devoted to her ladies. She preferred spending time with cars and trucks and toy soldiers. But today it was Sunday. The backyard became her fancy park where all the rich ladies gathered in fine lace dresses and large brim hats. Mrs. Tiffy and Mrs. Truffle were gifts her father had brought home from England. As corporate manager of overseas production for Jaguar, he traveled extensively. And he always brought her back something. If it wasn't a model car, it was a doll.

It was very hot. Timmy came around back to the yard and tried to grab at one of her teacups with his grubby little hands. He was only three and a half. He wasn't allowed to come to the tea parties. Brenda chased him off and watched him grab his tricycle.

She continued watching as he pedaled erratically down the

driveway toward the street. Brenda dropped the teacup she snatched away from Timmy and yelled a warning to keep away from the street.

Where was her mother? He wasn't supposed to be out without supervision. Timmy didn't listen. He lowered his head and pedaled faster, weaving sideways slowly toward the street. Brenda excused herself from Mrs. Tiffy and Mrs. Truffle and started after her little brother.

He was at the edge of the street. Her father's Jaguar was parked in front of the house. Timmy paused and without looking, pedaled his tricycle into the street from behind the Jaguar.

"Timmy, come back." Brenda screamed.

"Timmy, come back."

"Mother." She screamed again and again.

Brenda caught the bright red car from the corner of her eye. She heard the squealing tires and brakes trying hard to stop. Too late. Brenda saw it all unfold in slow motion. The thud of the bright red car hitting Timmy replayed over and over in her head.

The tricycle crunched under the weight of the car and Timmy's body was flung like a stuffed doll across the street. Brenda wanted to run faster, but her legs had turned to rubber bands and she couldn't go. She kept falling and falling again. Her little brother wasn't moving. He was covered in red. Blood. Everywhere.

"Mother." Brenda screamed. Where was her mother? Her father?

"Mother!"

Brenda sprung up in bed, eyes wide open. The nightmare was back. It was always the same. She woke up with her mother on her lips. Twenty-five years and she still couldn't put Timmy's death behind her. The air conditioner was humming and it was cool, but Brenda felt moist, sweaty. The alarm clock said 2AM. She looked at the empty space on the bed next to her. Tina wasn't home. But someone else was in the room.

Carlotta Malfour sat on the chair near the window, staring silently at Brenda. Silent as the night air. Her clothes, arms, and face burned black and the back of her head a bloody mess. Brenda swallowed hard and made to get out of bed.

"Carlotta?" She inched toward the gray ghostly image.

Carlotta smiled. At the same time, she pointed out the window. Brenda wanted so much to touch her. To feel her pain. She wanted to ask her how this happened. Who had done this to her.

Carlotta was insisting Brenda come to the window with her eyes. They were icy blue, pale, and almost glowing in the dark, singed face.

Brenda inched her way to the window and looked out. Below was the garden. The moon was a pale sliver in the sky. It was too dark for her to see much of anything. When Brenda looked back at Carlotta, she was gone. Brenda reached out and slowly touched the chair where the ghost of Carlotta Malfour had been. It wasn't warm. Nothing solid had been there.

Brenda looked back out and down at the garden. Then she saw the Impatiens around the fountain. The stingy light the moon did give, made the tiny flowers seem alive in the dark shadows. They seemed to glow from within. What did it mean? Was this what Carlotta meant for her to see? If so, why?

Now fully awake, she wondered about Tina. Was the party still going on? Had she decided to stay the night at the Davis'? Either way, they were still a couple. Tina should have called if she was going to be this late. Did she think Brenda didn't care anymore? Had their relationship deteriorated to this level already?

Brenda wasn't going to let Tina off that easy, and she wasn't about to throw in the towel on their relationship. She loved Tina and needed her. Now, more than ever.

Making teddy bears had been what saved her after her brush with death. Tonight was going to be a long one and she was drowning in stress. Her teddy bears beckoned. She was low on her favorite brass jewelry head pins, but she thought she had enough to start on at least one more Saggy.

* * *

In the quiet of the early morning, Brenda found comfort in the soft suede fabrics and the movement of her fingers. *If only Carlotta could be here.*

Chapter 19

Brenda woke to the warm fingers of sunlight playing on her face. As she rubbed the cobwebs off her eyes and tried to focus, she cast a look beside her. Tina had never made it home last night. It had been nearly five before Brenda drifted off to sleep.

It was already 9:45. Way too late for Brenda. Sleeping late always left her feeling drained the rest of the day. She took a quick shower, dressed in jeans and a sleeveless button down shirt, and headed down to the kitchen for a light breakfast before she called Joan Davis.

When she turned into the dining room, Tina was sitting at the table, fork in mouth. She had a lump of scrambled eggs on her plate and more of it in a big bowl beside her. She looked up when Brenda walked in.

"Hey, Princess." She dropped the fork to the plate. "I scrambled us some eggs. There's extra toast too."

Brenda was frozen inside. Part of her was very angry.

"Good morning. What time did you get in?" Brenda didn't feel like a big breakfast. "Thanks for making breakfast." Brenda walked over, took a piece of toast and sat next to Tina. She layered a thin spread of butter on the toast and took a bite.

Tina looked at her, then back at her unfinished eggs on her

plate.

"I should have called, I know, but it got late. Joan and Stewart offered one of their guest rooms"

"Tina, let's just forget about last night." Brenda leaned over and took Tina's hand, then taking her chin, turned Tina so she could look into her face. "Honey, I love you and I want all this ugliness between us to go away. We alone have the power to make it happen."

Tina's eyes were watery, her mouth moving downward. "I love you too, Princess, but you've . . ." She paused and took her gaze from Brenda. "You've changed, Brenda. I mean . . . do you even see me anymore? Hell, Princess, we don't even do things together anymore."

Brenda dropped her own gaze to look down at the lace pattern on the tablecloth. Had she really changed? She loved Tina, but was it different than before?

"I want us to work, Tina. If it means some adjusting, I'm willing to do whatever it takes to make it right again for us. Are you?"

This time, Tina smiled. "Are you willing to leave Malfour, Brenda? To come back home with me?"

Tina would never understand. That was becoming obvious. A deep and heavy feeling of regret settled in Brenda's heart. It wasn't going to work. At least not in this moment and time.

"I can't leave right now, Tina."

Tina's whole body stiffened. She looked away. "Then it's settled."

"No, it isn't. Please, hear me out."

Tina didn't answer.

"Distance doesn't have to be an obstacle for our love, honey. I love you. We have two homes, baby. How many people are lucky enough to have that?"

"Yeah, but we're not suppose to live in them separately." Tina sounded lost.

Brenda laughed lightly, hoping to break the tension. Trying to keep her own heart from breaking. "If we've got love, a time away from each other won't mean an end to our relationship."

Tina turned her head swiftly to meet Brenda. Her eyes were dark, angry, and her fingers nervously tapped the table. "Just so I know, Brenda, you're the one calling it quits, right?"

Brenda shook her head. "I didn't say that, Tina. I'm just not going back to Newark right now. It has nothing to do with our relationship."

"The hell it doesn't." Tina's anger exploded.

Brenda sat stunned at the rage in her lover's face.

"Brenda, we've got problems," Tina continued, her voice more controlled, "Real problems."

"And you think if I go back to Newark with you now that our problems will magically disappear?"

Tina's jawbone betrayed the barely controlled anger. She was crunching down hard on her teeth. "At least we can work on it together."

Brenda was lost. When and how had this happened? "You're not blaming Malfour for this, are you?"

"I think its part of it, yeah."

Brenda felt her own anger build. This wasn't going to take them anywhere constructive.

"You're putting the whole thing on Malfour and on me. It's unfair."

Tina started thumping her fingers on the table again. She leaned closer to Brenda, her other hand waving in the air.

"I have honestly tried understanding all the crazy shit that's been happening to you and I've even tried humoring you in this whole ghosts and beasties thing you got going."

"You stop it right now." Brenda was surprised at the strength in her voice.

Tina backed off, the shock apparent in her face, her mouth open in silence.

"You have your job in Newark. You have to go back. I'm not stopping you. Go."

"You know I can't afford to stay on my own. I can't support myself on just my wages." Tina's voice was a strained whisper with a defeated edge.

Tina had wounded her. Brenda felt weak. She got up from the table. "You never listen, Tina. I never once said I was giving up on our life together. Newark is as much a part of me as you are. I'm not just going to forget that."

Tina wouldn't look up at her.

"Don't worry about the rent. I plan on keeping up my end of it. It's my home too." Brenda started walking out. She needed fresh air. Time to clear her thoughts. "Listen, I have to go back to the Art Hub. Don't know how long I'll be." She was almost out the door.

"I'm leaving next week, Brenda."

Brenda kept walking.

* * *

Anna Yin greeted Brenda with a big smile and a warm touch on the arm.

"I suppose you know how to get back upstairs, right?" She had a sparkle in her eye as she dangled the huge key chain in front of Brenda. "This is the one for the your room." She pulled out one key and handed it to Brenda.

They were in Anna's office and Brenda noticed the photos on the wall. Anna had said they were here. More photos of Albert Malfour's Cigar factory. Anna watched her eyeing the photographs.

"These are just the ones I took from upstairs. Mostly shots of the building."

Brenda walked up to one that showed a group of cigar workers in a large, open room, mostly working, not daring to look up at the camera which sought to capture their souls. But others looked directly at the photographer, a fuzzy look on their faces. Towering above them was the same, older man who appeared in every photograph with Albert Malfour. Brenda pointed to him.

"Do you know who he is?"

Anna looked briefly at the framed photo. "Nope. He sure had to be a big shot, though. He must have been Malfour's right hand man." Anna crunched up her eyebrows in thought. "Come to think of it, I think there's a photo upstairs with names on it."

Brenda's heart did flip-flops. She thanked Anna again, took the keys, and worked her way through the art gallery and up the elevator to the third floor. It was even hotter than before. The dog days of August were nothing to sneeze at here in the Florida humidity. There was definitely no air conditioning up here.

Brenda inserted the key in the lock and opened the door. She flipped the light switch and walked back to the photographs she hadn't had a chance to look at the last time she was here. There was Albert Malfour sitting amid beautifully clad girls on a Gasparilla float. Albert Malfour accepting some award. Albert Malfour with the Chief of Police, a big cigar clamped in his mouth.

The dark thought of Albert fattening the dirty palms of Tampa's police chief chilled Brenda's soul. She walked slowly to a rather large photograph in the back of the room. It was another group shot. Except this one had names scribbled in tiny, barely legible handwriting underneath it on the white border.

Brenda looked at the faces first. It was Albert Malfour and several richly suited gentlemen standing with some less than wealthy workmen. And not far from Albert was the same older man in the other photos. And the haunting young man stood next to him, arms wrapped around the older man's waist.

Brenda let her eyes wander slowly to the names below. She followed the names that started with Albert Malfour. She stopped when she reached a name she recognized. Petey Cuenca. Brenda thought her heart must have stopped beating for a second because the room began to swim and the rush in her ears was like a train speeding through her brain. Then she read the name beside it. The older man. Roberto Cuenca and Petey Cuenca. Peter Cuenca's father.

Brenda thought sure she must have stopped breathing. She

gasped for air and reeled back, leaning against the wall for support. When she recovered, she looked closer at the photograph. It was dated 1926. The same year as the last letter Carlotta had written to Angelique. Brenda looked harder at the small image of Peter Cuenca. He couldn't have been more than fifteen or sixteen years old. His hair was as dark as the scowl on his face. Roberto Cuenca wore the same somber, steely glare in every photograph. A man married to his employer. Driven to duty. Maybe even to keep his master's secrets.

Brenda didn't know why, but she managed to tear herself away from the photograph and dig into one of several boxes that littered the floor. It was labeled Papers and Records. She tore open the flaps and found what appeared to be very old ledgers, papers, and notebooks. Judging from the thick dust on the binders, they'd been stored a long time.

There were some loose papers that proved to be nothing more than newsletters of some sort. Cigar industry chitchat. They were dated from the late 20's, early 30's. Brenda thought that someone somewhere would find these highly collectible. She pulled out the heavy, oversized ledgers. They were of the type where the check writer would have to fill in a small square of the check with the person they wrote the check to, amount and reason, if they so chose. It was the only way of record keeping back then. When they separated the check, the small portion stayed in the ledger.

Brenda noticed that most of the checks were written by Albert Malfour. She leafed through the book, conscious of the history at her fingertips. Checks were written to the First National Bank. Others were for a car dealership, a tobacco farm in Georgia, names of people she didn't know. These must have been the ledgers for Malfour's business expenses. There was nothing that indicated personal use. No grocery stores, department stores, or leisure activities.

At the very end of the first ledger, she found gold. Written in black, fading ink, the name of Roberto Cuenca was still legible. It was a big check. Five hundred dollars in 1926 was mucho cash. She would bet Malfour that this wasn't Cuenca's weekly pay. That exact date was August 29th, 1926. How ironic that the 29th was only four days away. She wondered if there were more checks. Right behind it, was another check written to Roberto Cuenca. This one could have been his paycheck. It was only for twenty-five dollars.

Brenda's gears were turning in her head. She quickly flipped through the last of the checks in the ledger. She found another check for Roberto Cuenca dated one month later for another five hundred dollars. What did Cuenca have on Malfour? Malfour was obviously buying him off. Brenda felt the heat of the room suffocating her. Her heart was ready to fly out of her mouth it was beating so hard.

She dug out another ledger. And another one. There were a total of five ledgers in the box. In each ledger she found payments of five hundred dollars to Roberto Cuenca in addition to his weekly paycheck of twenty-five dollars. It was a safe bet that if the other boxes in the room contained more ledgers, Brenda would find the same payments to Peter Cuenca's father.

Her puzzle was starting to form a picture. An ugly picture. She needed to take these ledgers with her. There were five boxes in the room. She checked and they all contained the same kind of ledgers. With no surviving Malfours, this property now belonged to the owners of this building. She had to speak with Anna.

Her excitement making her quite dizzy, Brenda found her way back down to Anna's office. Anna was speaking with a young woman, but motioned Brenda to come over. The young woman excused herself and walked into the maze of artist spaces.

"Heat finally get to ya?" Anna was smiling.

"Yes, it's pretty hot up there. Thought about putting air conditioning?"

"Not until and if we rent any spaces up there. The owner will have to make that decision."

"Now that you mention that, Anna, I wanted to talk to you

about some of the boxes you have upstairs. Who does it belong to?"

Anna put a hand on her waist and cocked her head. "You know, I don't know. I guess they legally belong to the owner of the building, Stewart Davis. Davross Industries."

Anna frowned. Didn't do a thing for her pretty face. "I'm just the art director. I mean, it's basically an artist co-op. The artists with studio space pay me rent and I turn it over to Davis. I can't make any decisions about anything up in that room, if that's what you're asking."

She looked closely at Brenda and a big smile took over the frown. "It wouldn't take much to convince me to look the other way, though." A mischievous gleam sparkled in her dark eyes.

Brenda liked Anna Yin and found her warm and friendly personality infectious. "Then you're my woman." Brenda hoped Anna didn't catch the red blush in her cheeks as she thought about the double meaning. Anna wasn't going to let her walk out with these historical treasures without some kind of reason and identification. Brenda dug in her purse and pulled out the PI license.

"Anna, I'm going to need to look over the ledgers you have upstairs."

Anna had taken the cardholder and was looking at it intently. She handed it back to Brenda.

"I guess we can't really call you a private dick, huh?" Her eyes looked at Brenda and then she laughed. If Anna thought it was funny, Brenda was going to laugh right along with her. Anything to get those ledgers. And it actually was funny.

"Private eye will do fine." Brenda put the ID back in her purse. "I'll bring them back as soon as I'm done with them."

"You saw that they were all ancient, right? Like from the 1920's. Don't tell me old Malfour's ghost is in financial trouble?"

This time Brenda laughed first. "No, no. Just investigating some historical inaccuracies. These will be a big help."

Anna pulled her hair back with one hand, but the shiny,

black strands spilled back onto her face.

"Sure, you can take them. But I think there's a whole bunch of those boxes up there. They're kinda heavy. You're gonna need help." She opened the door to her office and called someone named Bill. Then she turned back to Brenda. "Bill will help you load them into your car."

"Oh no." Brenda stopped her. "I have my Jag. They'll never fit. I'll have to come back for them with the SUV, maybe later today?"

"Bill, never mind," Anna yelled back out the door. She looked at Brenda and shrugged her shoulders. "No problem. I live here and haven't got any plans for the night. If not Bill, then someone else will help you."

She was smiling again. Brenda found her quite stunning. She broke away from the twinkling eyes of Anna Yin and offered her hand.

"Thanks, Anna, you won't get in trouble, I promise."

"I know." Anna took her hand and winked.

* * *

A picture was starting to take shape in Brenda's mind. Carlotta Malfour disappears. Albert Malfour officially files a missing persons report while at the same time, spreading the rumor that she had run off with some mysterious lover. Carlotta Malfour disappeared without a trace. Meanwhile, Albert Malfour starts writing fat checks to Roberto Cuenca and ultimately hands all his possessions, including Malfour House, to the Cuenca family. It smacked of bribery. The "why" was something Brenda still had to find out.

She could have easily placed a call to Peter Cuenca and possibly gotten all the answers she needed to solve the puzzle, but judging from her conversation with Cuenca before, he wasn't going to volunteer anything easily. Besides, he appeared to be very sick. Would his memory be accurate?

No, Brenda decided to give Kevin a call. Try and have him

trace a death certificate for Carlotta Malfour. And while he was at it, he might try and check into the Malfour will or at the very least, the law firm that handled the estate.

She dialed Kevin's number and started back to Malfour.

"Kevin. I need you to crack some information for me." She loved it when Kevin answered his own phones.

"Hey, BS. Got some action down there in mosquito land?"

"You could say that. I need a death certificate. Write down the name. Carlotta Malfour." She spelled it out for him.

The Gulfbreeze was coming up. She wanted to stop and see Cubbie.

"What state?" Kevin asked.

"Don't know, Kevin. Maybe Florida, but she's a no show for over 70 years. Do I need to have a definite state?"

"Not really, but it would go a lot quicker."

She smiled to herself. "I'm in no hurry." She pulled into the Gulfbreeze parking lot. "Oh, and Kevin, can you also find anything on the last will and testament for an Albert Malfour? Oh, and check out a business by the name of Key Wester Mopeds. Safe bet it's located in Key West, Florida. I need the owner."

"You working on a case, BS? Setting up shop down there?"

"Don't get so excited, okay. It's going to be tough for you. I'm going to be leaning on you real hard for help."

There was broken laughter on the other end. "I can set you up with anything you need. You can link up to my database and the info brokers we use. Even hired help if you want."

"I don't want. I'm a lone wolf on this, Kevin. Thanks, you're a jewel."

"Don't believe all the hype. Does this mean you won't be coming back to work for me?"

"Newark is all yours. If you ever want to vacation in Florida, I'll e-mail you my address."

They both laughed. Brenda thanked him and disconnected. It was the start of the lunch crunch and The Gulfbreeze was packed. There was a line already waiting impatiently for their name to be called.

Brenda spotted Cubbie as she came up to hand in a customer's ticket. Her eyes widened and she smiled wider than Brenda thought it was possible for a human being to smile.

"Hey, sugar, you need a table?"

Brenda walked up to her as Cubbie punched in credit card numbers.

"No, I'm not eating. I just wanted to tell you your friend Hortensia called last night. She invited me to one of their Santeria ceremonies tomorrow night."

Cubbie paused, and grinned even wider. "Well what do you know? Tomorrow is my day off."

Cubbie insisted on coming. She assured Brenda her friends wouldn't mind. Brenda told her to be at Malfour no later than 6:30.

Chapter 20

When Brenda pulled into Malfour, she noticed the new, pewter Grand Cherokee. They must have replaced their old banged up one.

She headed to the library and checked for messages. Nothing.

Upstairs, she found Tina packing in the bedroom. Brenda just stood at the doorway, a look of surprise on her face. Tina stopped and looked at the confusion on her face.

"I'm getting an early start for the beach. Thought I'd pack a few things now." She laughed a short, tight laugh. "You know me, I'll run around at the last minute and still forget something. I figure this way, I'll have a couple of days to remember."

Brenda walked up to her slowly. She noticed Tina's favorite shorts, the bathing suit she'd bought at Westshore Plaza, and her Birkenstock sandals still scattered on the bed.

"When are you leaving?"

"Tomorrow night. We'll be at the beach house 'till Monday." She looked up at Brenda and paused from her packing. "I, uh, left you the number on the night table."

Brenda followed her eyes to the small piece of paper lying on the table.

"Brenda, if you need . . ."

"I know. Thanks." Brenda was straining under the tension in the air.

Tina started packing again, withdrawing her gaze from Brenda. "Your father called." She finished placing everything in the suitcase and slammed it shut. "Said he mailed you the gun this morning." She looked straight into Brenda's face. "What's that all about? You want a gun in the house?"

Brenda was sorry she hadn't been here to take her father's call. "Just for protection."

"Brenda, a gun?" Tina had inched up to face her. "Are you going to be able to even touch a gun?"

It was Danny Crane. That's what she was saying. Brenda Strange wouldn't even be able to see a gun, let alone handle one. And God forbid, fire one. That's what Tina was thinking.

"I'm a licensed private investigator. I have a permit to carry a gun and have awards to prove how capable I am at firing one."

For just a moment, Tina jerked forward. Maybe she wanted to touch Brenda. Or maybe she just wanted to shake some sense into her, Brenda didn't know, because she just stood there, an odd, blank look on her face.

"I guess I've been wrong." When Tina spoke, it was in a soft voice. "I guess we've created one hell of a distance between us."

The look in her eyes said, *How*? How had they become strangers in such a short time? At that moment, Brenda didn't want Tina to leave. She wanted very much to grab her and hold on tight. But she knew now wasn't the time. Tina wasn't going to stay. Oh, if Brenda asked, she would have. But she wouldn't belong to her. She would be with the Davis' somewhere in their enchanted beach house.

"Tina, a gun didn't kill five people, Danny Crane did." How could she explain that Danny Crane blessed her with a gift very few can experience? He allowed her to see the way to God's love and knock on the gate of eternal life. Danny Crane brought

Timmy back to her. And Danny Crane was going to bring justice to Carlotta and Angelique.

Tina made a disgusted look with her face. "You sound like a spokesperson for the NRA."

"You know, Tina, I've really tried to keep us safe after the break in. I've gone out of my way to find who did this and you've done nothing but put roadblocks each step of the way. And you should ask why I want a gun when you go around leaving the door open to the house for any maniac off the street to walk on in? But then you're so busy hanging on every word Joan Davis says I guess you forget little things like that."

Brenda lost it. She'd tried so hard to hold it down. To not throw it into Tina's face. Tina stood, hands on her hips, shaking her head.

"You're jealous. That's it." It was not a pleasant smile on her face. "You won't tear yourself away from this Goddamn house to even do things together, but you don't want me to have friends that do appreciate me and want my time."

Brenda turned away because Tina was right. The road had forked somewhere. They were on separate paths. She was getting exhausted and dangerously close to fatigue. Her heart was beating way too fast and her head felt like it could blow off. She went and sat down slowly on the edge of the bed, head down in her hands. "Tina, I'm sorry. We can't go on like this. We fight every time we see each other."

Tina came up next to her and sat down. "You're right, Princess. Listen, maybe this time away from each other will be good. Distance sometimes clears the airwaves." Tina grabbed Brenda's hand. When Brenda looked at her, for the first time in their relationship, she didn't recognize what she saw in Tina's eyes.

"I don't know what the answer is, Tina, but we've got to want to find it together. Do you?" It was the question she feared to ask.

Tina smiled. "I think I do. I don't know. Like I said, maybe this is a good thing you proposed here. I'll go back, finish my fall term, and you stay. You might need to take care of your mother. Or your father."

The words smacked Brenda hard. She'd wanted to push the reality of it way back into her mind. It wasn't Tina's fault that she was concerned. And she was right.

Brenda smiled back at her. "I do love you."

Tina let go of Brenda's hand and searched her face. "Let's not fight anymore, Princess. I'm sorry I blew up yesterday. We both agree we've been under stress." Her smile was genuine. "And I'm still a bit unsure about this gun thing."

"Don't worry. It's my dad's old gun. He's been waiting for the right time to pass it down. Remember, he insisted I needed it when I was working with Kevin on those cases."

Tina got up and took the suitcase off the bed. "Listen, Phil from Le Galleria wants me to bring a couple of my smaller pieces to him. Joan and I are going to meet him for an early dinner. I didn't know what you . . ."

"Thanks, I have plans too." Brenda couldn't look her in the eyes. "Good luck. Hope he likes your work."

"Oh, by the way, Bertles Jeep came and delivered the new Jeep. I signed, but they need your John Hancock too. They left the contract. Said you needed to hand deliver it to them."

Brenda remembered the boxes at the Art Hub. Thank goodness they had a new SUV. The front wheel on their other one had been severely damaged. It drove with a big thud each time the wheel turned. She was going to need all the room she could use.

"I'm going back to the Art Hub. I'll be bringing some heavy boxes back home. Will you help me carry them in before you go to dinner?" *Dinner with Joan Davis.* Brenda refused to dwell on that.

"Sure. Do you need help getting them here?"

"No, someone is going to load them into the car for me. Thanks, though."

"Have you had lunch?" Tina asked.

Brenda's stomach reminded her that she hadn't. "Actually,

no, and I'm starving."

Tina pulled her off the bed. "How about going to Hyde Park and having something to eat there?"

Was it a peace offering? After the emotional roller coaster ride they'd had these past few days, Brenda was ready to lunge at the invitation.

"I'd love to."

* * *

Brenda sat in the library surrounded by five boxes of dubious historical importance from the Art Hub. These were her "dates" for the evening. Each and every one of them, blind dates. She didn't think Tina would be jealous.

Joan Davis had picked Tina up shortly before four thirty. She was friendly and Brenda thought, already drunk. She could smell the whiskey on her breath. She expressed the proper concern at Brenda for not joining them at the beach but didn't try very hard at convincing her to change her mind. Her curtain of platinum hair was pulled back in a perfect French bun. Brenda thought it made her look older. Joan helped Tina load a couple of Tina's sculptures into the BMW and they were gone.

Brenda had opened all the boxes to get an initial peek at what was there. Seemed to be more of the same thing. She was curious how these insignificant pieces of the Malfour cigar kingdom had ended up like this. It amazed her what survived through history. Albert Malfour's life reduced to boxes of financial ledgers.

Brenda spent most of the night poring over the old ledgers. They gave her another tiny piece for her puzzle. The ledgers seemed to cover the periods between 1925 through 1927. Curious as to when Albert Malfour closed his cigar factory, Brenda pulled down the Cigar Kings of Tampa Bay from the bookshelf. The Malfour Cigar Factory closed its doors in the winter of 1927.

But Albert Malfour didn't start writing fat, five hundred

dollar checks to Roberto Cuenca until August 29th, 1926, one month after Carlotta's last letter to Angelique. Before that, Roberto Cuenca got paid his weekly twenty-five dollars salary.

Something happened in the summer of 1926. Brenda didn't have all the facts to back up the picture she had forming in her head, but she had plenty of signs that led her to color that picture blood red and call it murder.

What if Albert Malfour found out about Carlotta's affair with Angelique, murdered them both in a jealous rage, disposed of their bodies and paid the police to look the other way?

And what about Roberto Cuenca? Where did he fit into the picture? Malfour would have needed help. Who better than his right hand man? Roberto Cuenca could have been an accomplice to the murders of Carlotta and Angelique. For his services and his silence, Albert Malfour paid him handsomely. And for his undying loyalty, Albert gave him Malfour House.

It made sense to Brenda. She shivered with the excitement. It was the perfect set up for Albert Malfour. No one witnessed the murder. He probably killed them both here at the house. No one to finger him except Roberto Cuenca, and five hundred dollars a week took care of him. Malfour then proceeded to shower the police with obscene donations and extra stuffing in the right pockets. Didn't he appear to be the darling of all those politicos and even the Police Chief in those old photos at the Art Hub? There was no doubt. Albert Malfour was plugged in to all the right connections.

But what of the bodies? What would Malfour have done with two bodies? The front door slamming shut dragged Brenda abruptly from her concentration. Tina said goodbye to Joan, who beeped as she drove off. Brenda took a deep breath and looked up at the clock. It was already eleven.

"You've been busy tonight, I see." Tina stood among the boxes, leaning against the doorway. Her face was radiant. "You find anything of value?" She folded her arms on her chest.

"Yes, I did actually. Want to hear it?" Brenda wasn't sure of the answer.

Tina uncrossed her arms and tiptoed through the stacks of ledgers on the floor. "Did you really spend all night looking through all these?" Tina wrinkled her nose. "They really smell dusty." She came and crouched next to Brenda.

"Tina, I think Albert Malfour murdered his wife Carlotta and Angelique. And he had help. Roberto Cuenca." Brenda let the name sink in. She looked at Tina, barely able to control her own excitement.

Tina was slow to catch on, but finally cocked her head to one side and crunched her brows together. "Cuenca? As in Peter Cuenca? They're related, right?"

Brenda nodded her head eagerly. "You bet. Try his father."

"Get outta here. How do you know all this? You got proof in all this?" Tina looked around the scattered ledgers again.

"Well, no, I don't have proof. This murder happened seventy-four years ago, I won't be able to get any proof short of a confession from Albert Malfour or Roberto Cuenca." When she stopped, Brenda distinctly heard a strong whisper in her ear. *Petey . . .*

The word kept repeating over and over.

"Brenda?"

Petey . . .

"Brenda?" Tina shook her shoulder.

Brenda came back to Tina's questioning face.

"Tina, the last letter Carlotta wrote to Angelique said something about someone named Petey tagging her everywhere she went. Petey was a child, a boy, I'm sure."

"Yeah, so?"

"The name, Tina. What if Peter Cuenca is Carlotta's Petey? He could be. And if he is, then he could know what happened that night." Brenda was so focused on her thoughts, she almost couldn't see straight.

Tina had half a grin spreading on her face. "Yeah, but I still don't see why any of this is such a big deal, Princess. I mean, you said you couldn't prove anything. And even if Peter Cuenca does know, what of it? Princess, this is ancient history. These guys are all dead. Who are you going to punish? I mean, who really cares? Nobody left to sit in a jail cell, Brenda."

Brenda couldn't stop the tears that pooled at the tip of her eyes. Of course Tina couldn't see it. This wasn't about punishing anyone. This was about justice. For Carlotta and Angelique. No one deserved to be brutally murdered and disposed of like an animal. Carlotta and Angelique demanded their rest. Their dignity.

"I care, Tina. I need to talk to Peter Cuenca."

Tina got up. "Don't go getting crazy with this, Brenda."

Brenda wasn't going to do anything until she had more information. A good PI never went in with guns blazing until they had a clear target. She had to hear from Kevin.

Chapter 21

Brenda had just hung up with Maid for Today when the doorbell rang. She made arrangements for weekly maid service. The realization that Malfour was more house than she wanted to handle on her own had sunk in fast. She had never bought into the mental brainwashing of the American housewife that there was joy in housekeeping.

"I'll get it, Tina." She called upstairs.

Before Brenda got to the door, there were two solid knocks. The hairy guy in the blue FedEx shorts stood with two packages under his arm. She signed for them and practically closed the door in his face. She was that excited.

The heavier package was the gun. Her father's bold handwriting gave that away. The other box was so light she could have held it up with her pinky. She'd been waiting for this one. She couldn't make another teddy without her brass head jewelry pins. She'd also bought some extra honey tan-colored upholstery fabric. She worked hard networking with other teddy bear makers to find upholstery fabric and when her favorite color was available, she bought it all out.

Brenda rushed upstairs to her studio and gently placed the light box of pins and upholstery on her supply shelf. She was looking forward to making more bears with her free time. As she walked by the bedroom, she peeked inside and found Tina standing very still looking out the window, her face wistful.

"Tina?" Brenda walked in quietly, tucking the gun box under her arm.

Tina jumped at the sound of Brenda's voice. She smiled shyly. "Oh, Princess, I didn't hear you come in." She looked at Brenda a moment then nodded toward the window. "I never took the time to admire the view from up here. It's beautiful."

Not as beautiful as you, Brenda wanted to say, but smiled at her instead. "Are you all packed up? If you're going to forget something, now is the time to do it so you can remember it while you're still here."

"I think I've actually got everything I'm going to need, clothes wise, anyway." She sighed and clapped her hands on her legs.

You could stay here. Enjoy this beautiful view with me everyday of our lives, Brenda thought. That was something else Brenda wanted to say. She didn't.

"What time are they coming for you?" Time had run away from Brenda. It was already Thursday afternoon.

"Five thirty."

"That's only two and a half hours from now."

The way Tina looked at her made Brenda want to kiss her. She put the box on the bed and went up to Tina, touching her arm, then bringing her closer.

"You're not upset about me not going? You understand, right?" Brenda asked.

Tina held Brenda tight and studied every inch of her face. "This is a whole new side of you, Princess, that I don't know." She grinned wickedly. "But isn't it exciting to be in love with a new you."

Brenda kissed her then. The taste of Tina was just as good as when they first met, and now, here and in this moment, nothing mattered more than Tina's lips.

Until the very low, persistent sound of a phone ringing

reached her ear. Tina pulled back and strained to listen. "Princess, that's your cell phone, isn't it?"

Brenda tore herself away from Tina and made a dash down the stairs and into the library where she'd left her handbag with the phone tucked inside.

Fumbling through her handbag was never an easy matter, so she emptied the whole contents onto the floor. Her phone kept ringing. Was it her father? Kevin?

"Hello?" She found herself out of breath.

"Hey, BS, this is Kevin. Sorry it took so long to get back to you, but I got some hits for you."

Brenda held her breath. She didn't know what she wanted to hear first. "Thanks, Kevin. I knew you'd come through."

"Yeah, well, save your thanks. I couldn't find proof this Carlotta Malfour of yours ever went to see her maker. Got a birth certificate. Born in Cuba, 1902 to one Alfonso and Christina Moreno. Married off to Albert Malfour in 1919, and then dropped off the face of the earth." He paused for a second. "Now, you want Louis or Peter Cuenca next?"

Brenda was still with Carlotta. It was strange having dates to go with the mangled corpse of Carlotta Malfour. This beautiful woman had been born and had led a life before she was murdered.

"Hey, BS, you with me?"

"Yes, I'm sorry, Kevin." Brenda focused on Louis. "I hope we got luckier with them. Tell me about Louis."

"Oh, we got'em both."

She could almost see Kevin smile.

"You were on the right track, BS. Off to a good start, I'd say. Louis Cuenca is the sole owner of Key Wester Mopeds. Small business on Harris Street, Key West, Florida. Mr. Peter Cuenca gave it to his son for his twentieth birthday. Been downhill ever since."

"Downhill? How exactly?" Brenda's hand tightened on the cell phone.

"This guy's running the business in the red line. He owes

more debt than I do. Credit card check shows maxed out accounts. My guess is he owes Uncle Sam big time."

The song Kevin was singing was the music Brenda wanted to hear. What she was seeing in her mind was starting to make sense. And it was also dangerous. She'd ended up with two puzzles, and pieces for both were snapping into place.

"Anything criminal on file for Louis?" Brenda asked.

"The only thing on the guy is an arrest twenty years ago. Got charged with assault at a local bar. Punched a guy out. Clean other than that. Got a wife, Edna and three kids, two girls, Lucy and Maria. The eldest, Maria, is married and lives in Cleveland with a husband and one kid. As far as I can tell, the other daughter and son, Christopher, still live in Key West, but I have lots of addresses for the boy, so that one might be a drifter."

Brenda was willing to bet that it was Maria and her family who'd lived for a short time at Malfour.

"His son? Do you think he might be draining dad's bank account?" It was a possibility, and she had to explore every one that might lead somewhere.

"Not if he were my kid, but who knows."

"Thanks, Kevin. What about Peter?"

Kevin took a deep breath on the other end. "This guy is clean as a whistle. Lived at the same address since 1927. Didn't seem to hold down any kind of job since then. This guy get an inheritance or something?"

"I'm working on that, Kevin. Tell me more."

"Well, Peter Cuenca was responsible for two kids, one you know, Louis, who's the youngest and another daughter, Miriam. She's retired and lives with her husband in Miami. Peter's wife died in 1995. This guy lived a very low profile."

Maybe Brenda knew why. "Anything on the Malfour will? Attorney's name, address?"

"Hey, what kind of operation do you think I run here?"

They laughed like they often did together.

"Looks like Rogers, Haney, and Lucas did the original will.

Rogers is gone and Haney and Lucas have taken on Humberto and Gibbons. But you should know, BS, that if you've got a living member mentioned in that will, which your Peter Cuenca fits the bill, it's off limits. Even if your Mr. Albert Malfour is dust in his maker's eyes, you can't take a peek until all parties in the will have taken their trip to the beyond. You still want the address?"

Brenda was disappointed but not deterred. *Why had Albert Malfour left his home to Peter Cuenca? He had paid Roberto Cuenca handsomely as long as he lived. Why did Peter get Malfour House?*

"No thanks, Kevin. I appreciate the help. I couldn't have done this without you."

"But you're going to."

Brenda smiled into the phone.

"I'm going to set you up with everything you'll need to run this kind of investigation. You know, I've been meaning to take a vacation in Florida, didn't I tell you?"

Brenda laughed again and watched Tina come into the room.

"How much longer you and Tina going to be enjoying the leisure life down there before heading back up?" Kevin asked.

He hit the raw nerve without even aiming for it.

"Umm, why don't I call you after I wrap this up. I'll make sure you get the proper welcome." Brenda turned away nonchalantly from Tina's questioning gaze.

"If you don't call, I'll just show up at your door, you know," Kevin said.

She exchanged her goodbyes with Kevin and disconnected. Tina carefully pushed aside Brenda's empty handbag and made room on the couch, stretching out.

"Changing purses again?" Tina picked up one of Brenda's lipstick cases from the floor and eyed it with interest.

"It's always so hard getting the cell phone when I need it. I think I just need a bigger handbag." Brenda started picking up everything she'd emptied on the floor and put it back in the bag.

Tina laughed lightly. "Oh, I don't know, that bag could be a perfect private eye accessory. I mean, Princess, well packed, that thing could be a lethal weapon."

Brenda gave her one of her warning looks: chin down, eyes intently pointed at her. Tina put her hands up in a stop signal as Brenda slunk toward her with loaded handbag swinging.

"Stop. Stop. I give up."

They couldn't stop laughing as Brenda finished stuffing everything into the Donna Karen canvas bag. Tina's whole face changed into a serious question.

"I saw the box upstairs from your dad." She started shaking her head. "Princess, if you feel so unsafe here that you need a gun, why stay?"

While Brenda understood Tina's concern, she didn't particularly welcome it. And time was running short. The information Kevin gave her was sizzling like hot oil in her head and she didn't want to throw cold water on it.

"Tina, let's please not bring that up. I'm okay with Malfour and I wanted the gun. I didn't feel I needed it."

Tina looked at her hard, unconvinced. A small smile finally formed. "Okay, no more negative talk." She put her hands on her hips. "Listen, I've still got the small bag to pack with stuff like suntan lotion, toothpaste, things like that. You'll be here before I leave, right?"

"I'll be here."

Tina went back upstairs, leaving Brenda alone with two mysteries threatening to split open and reveal the ugly secrets underneath. Suspecting Stewart Davis of having dirty hands in dealings with Malfour House may not have been off base, but his greed didn't warrant desperation. No, Stewart Davis didn't need Malfour that bad. But Louis Cuenca did.

With his business in the red and his finances in ruin, Cuenca would be desperate enough to do anything for money. What if Stewart Davis offered Louis Cuenca an amount too rich for him to turn down to make sure Malfour House was sold to Davross Industries? Would such a desperate man have given up just because his father refused and sold to someone else?

Brenda grabbed her bag and keys, and started out the door. She had less than an hour to catch Stewart at home before they set out with Tina to their Baywatch weekend. She didn't want to face Tina. She would have too many questions and delay her.

"Tina, I've got to catch up with Stewart on something before you all take off. Be right back." She called up to her.

Brenda heard a loud "What?" from upstairs as she walked out the door.

* * *

Stewart had on the most ridiculous looking Hawaiian shirt Brenda had ever seen. It was gaudy and *sooo* high tack. *Just goes to show you, money doesn't buy taste.*

He was very surprised to see Brenda and strained when she requested they speak privately. She didn't see Joan anywhere. Maybe she was upstairs getting all her suitcases ready. Stewart asked hesitantly if everything was okay. Brenda assured him that Tina was at this very moment doing some last minute packing. This seemed to set him at ease.

"Brenda, can I get you a drink?" He urged her toward the bar.

"No, Stewart, I only drink on social occasions."

He stopped in his tracks as his eyes immediately narrowed and his smile faltered.

"Well, that sounds rather ominous." He ushered Brenda into a large entertainment room filled with state of the art audio and video equipment, a television the size of one wall, and a small in-ground Jacuzzi.

Brenda was momentarily distracted by the excess in the room, but focused back on Stewart Davis who stood hands in pocket searching her face for some clues on why she was here.

"Somehow, I don't think you're here for those Tampa postcards. Am I right?" He was trying his best to distract her.

"You could say this is a professional visit. Can I expect you to be honest? You do conduct your private affairs as professionally as your business ones?" Brenda looked at him seriously.

He nodded slowly. "Especially a new neighbor. Professional, you say? Teddy bears or private eye?"

His wit was on the mark and Brenda found him non-defensive.

"Malfour business, Stewart. I know you put an offer on the table for Malfour House. Peter Cuenca turned you down. I also know you worked closely with Louis Cuenca, Peter's son."

Stewart actually wanted to break a smile. "Brenda, I wanted to buy Malfour because I intended to bring it down completely and build a custom home on the site. We had the contract pre-drawn and the builder lined up." He stopped, raised an eyebrow and challenged Brenda for more. "But we've already been through all this."

Brenda smiled back. "I'm sorry you didn't get what you wanted, but as much as this might disappoint you, I'm not interested in you."

He seemed at a lost for words. She liked that.

"You know how difficult it can be to keep a business afloat in today's economy," Brenda continued. "How easy it might be for a desperate man to make a deal with the devil." Brenda stopped and smiled ever so politely at Stewart. "Louis Cuenca isn't doing so well with Key Wester Mopeds. Did he offer to bring you Malfour for a price, Stewart?"

Brenda could tell he wanted very much to lie. He fidgeted and shifted his feet.

"I haven't seen Louis Cuenca in some time."

"How long? Was he at your party last month?"

"He most certainly was not at the party. He wasn't on the guest list and I can't remember exactly when it was I saw him last." He averted her gaze. "I'd say at least four months."

"What about Peter Cuenca?" Brenda was going to reel him in.

"What the devil are you doing here? I feel as if I'm being

questioned for some crime?"

Brenda decided to back off. After all, he hadn't committed a crime, unless you counted corporate greed mongering.

"I'm sorry, Stewart, it's just that there have been some very strange things happening at our house and I suspect someone is trying to scare us into leaving."

"I am sorry to hear that, but I certainly hope you don't suspect me?" He was insulted, his body language more feminine than masculine. Brenda was surprised at his lack of fortitude. Stewart Davis was a fluff. And completely confused.

"No, of course I don't." She softened her voice. "But you did have dealings with Louis Cuenca?"

"Brenda, despite what you think, I am not this scoundrel you've obviously made up your mind I am." He took his hands out of his pockets and raised one up when he spoke. "I flew out a couple of times to Key West and he showed me around his shop. He also visited here once or twice. What I offered Louis Cuenca was not an illegal proposition. Hell, some even call it a bargaining tool. I offered him five hundred thousand dollars if he could get me Malfour House." Stewart ran a hand through his wavy blond hair. "What I did wasn't wrong, Brenda."

All of a sudden, he looked more like a vulnerable little boy playing a big, tough business tycoon. Brenda wanted to go up and give him a big hug, but restrained herself. That would only have confused him further.

He'd just given Brenda the reason for Louis Cuenca breaking and entering Malfour, violating their privacy, and poisoning their plants. With her and Tina out of the way, Brenda was betting Cuenca would somehow make sure Stewart Davis and his half-a-million were the winners. But the how was still the missing piece.

"I didn't say it was."

"You don't really think he would do something crazy, would you? For half-a-million?"

"Stewart, think like the majority of the population and then answer that question. There are many that would kill for that kind of money."

He seemed genuinely perplexed. His face was stuck between a frown and a smile. "Brenda, you certainly don't think I would put Louis Cuenca up to murder just to get my greedy little hands on Malfour, do you?"

Brenda raised an eyebrow. "You have no dealings with Cuenca now?"

He looked at her first in surprise, then in defense. "I am not the big boogey man sending Louis Cuenca out on missions of evictions by any means, Brenda. I am not the brain behind his operations. As a matter of fact, I can help you and Tina. I know a great securities company with top of the line security guards." He made a move for his wallet in his back pocket.

"Stewart?" Joan Davis's voice echoed somewhere in the house.

Brenda decided it was time to leave. She didn't particularly want to encounter Joan Davis.

"No, no, thank you Stewart, but I don't need a security guard." She started to thank Stewart for his candor and honesty, and to walk out the door, but stopped.

"Oh, by the way Stewart, does Louis Cuenca drive a black car?"

Stewart thought a moment. "Why yes, a Toyota, I believe."

Bingo. Brenda couldn't suppress a smile as she walked out the door. "Say hello to Joan for me. Have a lovely time."

She scooted out the front door, escaping the walking curtain of hair.

Chapter 22

Tina didn't prod Brenda with too many questions. She was so busy making sure she'd be ready when Stewart and Joan came for her, Brenda's hasty visit to Stewart didn't seem important. Brenda was thankful for that.

Stewart and Joan arrived promptly at five thirty. They both popped in, marveled at what Brenda and Tina had done with Malfour, and were on their way with Tina in tow.

Brenda didn't have much time to miss Tina because Cubbie arrived on time at six thirty. She wore a denim shirt, jeans and a Chicago Bulls baseball cap.

"You have an entire closet for your collection?" Brenda teased her as she eyed the new hat.

"Oh yeah, I have this contraption that hangs behind my door, and I store all my hats on that."

"So these are part of your wardrobe, huh?" Brenda touched the brim of Cubbie's hat."

Cubbie grinned shyly. "Yeah, I'm not hard to shop for, you know. Everybody knows what to get me for Christmas and birthdays." She laughed, "My kids even get me new hats for Mother's day."

Brenda laughed with her, grabbed her purse, and they were

off to Hortensia and Gilda's house. Cubbie guided Brenda to what she called "New West Tampa," an area not too far from Raymond James Stadium, home of the Tampa Bay Buccaneers.

"Gomez is the next right." Cubbie pointed and Brenda made the turn.

"So Cubbie, where is Old West Tampa?"

"Further east." Cubbie pointed again. "West Tampa just kept expanding. The new families wanted newer homes and the neighborhoods in West Tampa were mostly older, unkempt. And then it got crime infested, so the incoming Hispanic population just spread out into New West Tampa."

Brenda pulled the Jeep to a stop in front of a small, modest house the color of coffee with black trim. Cubbie was excited as they walked up to the door.

"They just painted the house. It was the most horrendous color of yellow." She knocked hard, then looked back at Brenda. "Now I gotta warn you, Hortensia and Gilda are kinda weird, but loveable once you get to know them."

"Cubbie, you're the one freaking me out. I mean, these women are your friends, right?"

"Course they are, silly." Cubbie laughed.

The door opened and a woman with bushy, salt and pepper hair poked her head out. Brenda noticed her prominent nose.

"Ah, Cubbie," she said in a deep voice Brenda recognized. It was Hortensia. The woman smiled wide at Cubbie. Her smile faded just slightly as she turned to Brenda. "And you must be Brenda."

She didn't move an inch, but stayed hidden behind the door.

Brenda nodded and smiled. "Yes, I'm Brenda. Nice to meet you." Hortensia offered no hand to shake.

"Gilda and I will be right out." Hortensia slammed the door shut, leaving Brenda and Cubbie on the porch.

"Is this how they treat all their friends, Cubbie?" Brenda couldn't help the amused smile on her lips.

Cubbie leaned closer. "That's just 'cause you're with me," she whispered. "I warned you, honey, they're a bit squirrelly, but both of 'em are good folks and give you the shirt off their backs."

"Well, they can keep their shirts, Cubbie, I just want their cooperation."

The door popped open and two middle-aged women shuffled out hurriedly, Hortensia nearly pushing Gilda into Cubbie. Locking the door behind her, she turned and looked at Brenda.

"I'm sorry, Brenda, but we don't allow people we don't know into our home, please forgive us. But next time, you are welcome to visit." She turned to her sister. "This is my sister, Gilda." Hortensia grabbed Gilda and practically flung the meek, thin woman at Brenda. Gilda was a small woman whose clothes were too big for her tiny frame. She smiled up at Brenda.

"Hello, Brenda."

Brenda liked the innocent, childlike look in the woman's face. "Well, shall we get going?" Brenda pointed toward the Jeep.

Hortensia and Gilda settled comfortably in the back seat. Hortensia wrapped a black shawl over her shoulders even though it was over ninety degrees out. Looking at them through the rear view mirror, they looked like characters from a Grimm's fairy tale.

"Take Columbus to Armenia and I'll guide you from there," Hortensia told Brenda.

Brenda, of course, didn't know what or where Columbus or Armenia were. Cubbie provided the directions as Brenda drove away from Gomez Street.

"Brenda, Cubbie told us a little bit about you. You and your roommate moved into the haunted house."

Brenda wanted to laugh at the roommate bit. She cast a look at Cubbie next to her. Cubbie formed a crooked smile and gave a slight shrug of the shoulder. But it was Hortensia's reference to Malfour as "the haunted house" that immediately struck her.

"Well, it isn't about Malfour that I'm attending your ceremonies tonight." Brenda had no intention of getting into her case with these women.

"Why do you want to know about Santeria, then? You know, Peter's son, Louis could help you. He comes every once in awhile to ask favors of Papa Chucho and the Orishas. We were very surprised when Cubbie told us you had bought his house."

Brenda almost brought the SUV to a screeching halt. She pulled into a gas station, stopped the Jeep, and turned back to Hortensia.

"What is wrong? Why did you stop?" Gilda asked meekly, looking as if Brenda was some maniac sure to do them in right here and now.

"You know Louis Cuenca?" Brenda had her eyes on Hortensia. "He's been to this, Papa Chucho?"

Hortensia nodded her head quickly. "Yes, yes. We have seen him at least twice. He comes to Papa Chucho whenever he is in Tampa. He said you bought his house. The one with ghosts."

Brenda was beside herself. If this Papa Chucho was in any way connected to those ritual ashes on her bed and to Louis Cuenca, then she had enough to hit Louis Cuenca with.

Brenda apologized to Hortensia and Gilda and merely gave a reassuring smile to Cubbie who had been looking at her in amused confusion.

The address on Chestnut was only a ten-minute ride from the sisters' house. Brenda saw why many had fled Old West Tampa. Economically, it was starving. Old, shabby houses lay huddled among dirt lots and empty storefronts.

It was at one of these houses that Hortensia directed Brenda toward. There were cars jammed fender to fender on the large yard, a sprawling Oak hanging over the whole property.

Brenda opted to park across the street in an abandoned cement lot. She locked all the doors and engaged the car alarm. Her insides were jumping like popcorn in a microwave. Cubbie was talking to her friends. She was a Santeria virgin too.

Gilda huddled close to her sister, both of them eager to go

inside. Brenda distinctly caught the low thumping of bongo drums from inside as they stepped on the porch. Hortensia didn't even knock, she just turned the knob and she and Gilda shuffled in, leaving Brenda and Cubbie behind.

The room Brenda entered was a large living room, surrounded by oddball chairs, floor pillows, and a long table in the center of the room that was literally covered with fruit and vegetables and loaves of bread. Several people sat on the floor.

Up against the wall opposite the door was a makeshift altar. Brenda guessed it was a table with a colorful tablecloth. Large figurines sat fighting for space with candles and food on the altar. Brenda couldn't tell from this distance, but the statues could have been Catholic saints.

She lifted her nose slightly to catch the odd smell wafting through the room. It was mildly scented, yet heavy, organic, like someone was cooking in the kitchen.

Brenda noticed a doorway hidden by black curtains next to the altar.

"Tell me again what we're doing here?" Cubbie leaned over and whispered to Brenda.

Before Brenda could answer her, the curtains in the doorway parted and several men walked into the room. One was a young man in white, a red scarf around his neck. But it was the older man that caught Brenda's attention. He was tall and bony with dark skin and shockingly white, bushy hair.

As soon as Hortensia and Gilda saw him, they bolted. Cubbie started after them, but Brenda grabbed her back.

"Let's just wait, okay?"

Brenda didn't take her eyes off the small group of the two sisters and the older man. She saw Hortensia say something and point their way, and watched as the old man turned his gaze on her and Cubbie. Gilda, meanwhile, had walked slowly to the altar and placed a small, dark bottle among the clutter already there.

What was Hortensia saying? Was she telling him all about Brenda and Malfour? If this man had anything to do with Louis

Cuenca's attempt to frighten her and Tina out of Malfour, he would already be preparing himself for the questions he knew were coming.

The leathery man lifted his hand and motioned for Brenda and Cubbie. Hortensia had a big grin on her face.

"You promise me this isn't going to give me nightmares tonight, right?" Cubbie asked. "I don't even like scary movies."

"You can stay with me if you want."

"That's not the answer I was looking for."

Hortensia touched the older man's arm. "Brenda, Cubbie, this is Papa Chucho."

Papa Chucho took Brenda's hand and cupped it with both of his. He did the same with Cubbie. When he smiled, it was rather frightening. His leathery skin was stretched so thin across his face, his teeth seemed to jump out at you.

"Hortensia has told me you seek to know the ways of Santeria. I will try to be of help." He looked directly at Brenda. "Please, let's go where we can talk." He pointed back toward the curtains.

Cubbie started to walk beside Brenda, but Brenda blocked her way.

"I've got to go alone. Wait here, okay. Have some fruit or something to eat." She nodded in the direction of the table stuffed with food.

The room behind the curtains was more like a den. A very crowded den. There was a small couch, a rusty desk and old chair, and a tiny television that must have been at least twenty years old. Pictures and posters of religious icons, saints, and Jesus covered every available wall space. And taking up space on every tabletop or shelf were statues and figurines, big and small, of what Brenda recognized as Catholic saints.

Papa Chucho walked to the desk and leaned back against it. He eyed Brenda with interest, a strange smile on his lips.

"You are not here because you are interested in Santeria, so what exactly is it you think I can do for you?"

"You're right. I'm not looking to join your religion, but I do need your help in answering some questions that might relate to it."

He let out a sigh. "Please remember that it is not in the best interest of my people or my religion to be open to strangers. Much harm has been done to the image of Santeria from people like you. Hortensia and Gilda are very special to me, that is the only reason why you are here in this room speaking with me"

"And I do appreciate you making the time to speak with me and I respect your religious faith. But your answers to my questions could be important to the welfare and safety of my loved ones."

Brenda pulled the printed-paper from her handbag and handed it to Papa Chucho.

"It's a recipe I got from a Santeria site on the web. And below that, I've sketched the figures left on our bed. It's a curse, isn't it? An Ebos to cause harm in someone's house?"

He barely looked at it, handing it back to Brenda. He was shutting her out.

"Papa Chucho, someone broke into my home and left the remains of these ingredients on our bed. I have reason to believe that someone is trying to frighten us out of our home. Our house has been invaded, our garden poisoned and who knows what could be the next step if we don't leave. Now, have you been involved with a curse of this type recently?"

Papa Chucho squared his tiny shoulders and crossed his hands on his chest. Every move he made was deliberate and slow.

"There are many who come to me for help. They all seek different things from the Orishas. Wealth, health, love . . . pain. It matters little to me why or what their desires are. I am only their oracle to the Orishas."

He wasn't going to answer her questions. But Brenda wasn't leaving without something.

"Did Louis Cuenca come to you for an ebos like this? Did you put a curse on my house?"

The old man narrowed his eyes into tiny slits and grinned. "I can help you against such a curse, if that is what you seek."

"I don't need your magic. What I need is the truth. Does Louis Cuenca want us out of Malfour House?"

Papa Chucho didn't speak. In fact, he didn't even look at her. He closed his eyes and leaned his head back slightly. Outside, the drumbeats became more frenzied and loud. She had to keep pushing him.

"Look, I can't prove it, but Hortensia has already told me that Louis Cuenca visited here. My guess is he came to you for this." She tapped the paper in her hand.

The old man could very well have been in a trance. He hadn't moved, opened his eyes, or uttered a word. Was he blowing her off? She didn't know, but she wasn't done.

"I wanted to ask for your help. I'm not interested in getting the police involved, but if I call in a breaking and entering, they'll be talking to you in less friendly terms"

Papa Chucho opened his eyes slowly and grinned at her like a ghoul. "I have never had problems here. We are a peaceful religious group." Was there just an edge of menace in his voice?

Brenda didn't want to back down now. "Are you familiar with the phrase "accessory to a crime?"

"I don't deal with criminals or crime."

"An accessory is someone who knowingly and willingly cooperates in aiding another in criminal activities."

He unfolded his arms and placed them by his side on the desk. "I have committed no crime. What my people do after they leave here is beyond my control. I am a Santero, high priest and voice of the Orishas. I do not condone or encourage criminal behavior."

"A jury might be interested in hearing about your curses and rituals. They might understand your position. And then, they might not." Brenda fixed him with one of her steely stares. Tina always said she could scare the bejeesus out of anybody with her ice blue eyes if she wanted to.

Papa Chucho, while not running in fear of her, did stand up straight, a milder look in his eyes.

"I cannot speak the names of those who come to me with needs. I am their channel to the Orishas. It is a sacred act. Would you ask a Catholic priest to divulge the confessor and his sin?" He put his hands together in front of him. "I can offer you an ebos to remove any curse that has been put on you or your house. That is all I can do for you, Brenda Strange."

He was done, and the meeting over. Brenda held out her hand.

"I can take care of myself and my home. Thank you for your offer and your time."

Even though he had not cooperated with her, Hortensia had unwittingly done the work for him. Brenda knew now that Louis Cuenca had come here. More than likely, he came asking Papa Chucho for his help to put a curse on Malfour. Or maybe he cursed Tina and herself, she wasn't sure. He then proceeded to carry out the necessary steps to make sure the curse worked, like sneaking into Malfour and placing the stick figures on her bed. When it didn't, he took another step toward its success. He poisoned the garden. But something must have intensified his desperation. Perhaps he got deeper into debt or something darker, but whatever it was, it drove him to ram his car into their SUV on the Tides bridge. Brenda didn't believe he would stop there.

* * *

"I hope you got what you needed, honey, cause that was one weird trip." Cubbie blurted out, settling into the front seat.

Brenda pulled out onto Chestnut and tried to remember how they got to "la casa del los gallos."

"You remember how to get back home?" Cubbie asked.

Brenda was very good with directions. All she needed was to notice a few of the street names and the way home clicked in her head. She was so lost in thought that she didn't even notice Cubbie leaning over and staring in her face.

"Hello, you there, honey?"

"Oh, I'm sorry, Cubbie, I'm still back at the House of Roosters."

"Tell me about it. And didn't I tell you my friends were a little different? Hope they didn't freak you out or anything."

Brenda cast a quick glance at Cubbie and smiled. "I don't get freaked that easily. But I was surprised they were going to stay the night. Is it something Papa Chucho encourages?"

"Oh who knows," Cubbie waved a hand in the air. "That's a strange bunch. You're not going back, are you?"

"He wasn't interested in talking. I think he's hiding something."

Brenda pulled up at the guardhouse, flashed her pass, and sped onto the bridge. It was 9 PM and the full moon had nestled itself in the black sky.

"Say Brenda, honey, you gonna be alright tonight, I mean, with Tina gone and all?"

"That's very sweet of you, Cubbie, but I'm a big girl. I've got tons of stuff I've got to catch up on. This time alone will be good for me." Brenda looked at the woman beside her with the silly baseball cap and smiled.

Cubbie smiled back and patted Brenda's shoulder. "Okay, but if you need anything . . ."

"I'll call. I know."

Brenda watched as Cubbie's beat up VW drove off. When she opened the door to Malfour and walked in, she immediately felt the great silence. Malfour was deep in silence. Brenda breathed in the smell of Malfour. She was home. It was as if a pair of arms embraced her. She opened her mouth but didn't speak.

Honey, I'm home, she wanted to say. But would Carlotta have heard?

Chapter 23

It was going to be a busy Friday. Despite missing Tina, Brenda had gotten a good night's rest. She'd booked a couple of hours of target practice at Cotter's Aim and Fire. It had been a long time since Brenda had held a gun in her hand, let alone fired one. And frankly, she was unsure how she would feel when she did. Would the anger on Danny Crane's face haunt her? Would the crack of the gun send shivers up her spine? She didn't know, but she was going to find out.

Brenda was trying hard not to jump the gun with the Louis Cuenca thing. There was too much to sort out. She felt she had enough circumstantial evidence to prove Louis Cuenca invaded their home, more than likely poisoned their garden, and tried to run them off the bridge.

On top of that, the past was coming alive and peeling away the layers to a dark secret. The puzzle to Carlotta Malfour's disappearance seventy-four years ago was nearly complete. Something horrible happened in Malfour. There had been a fire and there had been a murder. Brenda was convinced Albert Malfour murdered his wife and probably her lover as well. She just didn't know how. She suspected Peter Cuenca might hold that last, missing puzzle piece.

* * *

Cotter's Aim and Fire turned out to be a large indoor firing range south of Raymond James Stadium. Brenda was getting to know her way around Tampa pretty well.

Her father had sent several boxes of bullets with the gun. His thoughtfulness always amazed Brenda. It was one of the things that made him a special dad. Her thoughts stuck on her father. And then her mother. She realized she hadn't heard anything from her father and made a mental note to call him this weekend.

After two hours of firing the Walther PPK, Brenda realized how woefully out of practice she was in firing a gun. But at least Danny Crane wasn't still lurking in her brain. She was hoping he was gone for good. She bonded with the small PPK and she felt pretty good about her ability to hit a non-moving object, but beyond that, she'd need more hours with the gun to insure pinpoint accuracy.

After leaving Cotter's Aim and Fire, she decided to make a short stop at Teddies in the Park. Felice was behind the counter.

"Brenda, how good to see you. Got any more bears?" She almost jumped from behind the counter with an eager look on her face.

"No bears, just wanted to stop and say hello."

Felice pointed to the spot where Brenda had left her first Zodiac bear. "You can see it's gone. I sold it several weeks ago. Mini bears have a very loyal following and each time the teddy bear magazines do their annual miniature bear issues, the mini's fly out of here like hotcakes." There was genuine glee in Felice's eyes. The woman loved what she did.

"Felice, I apologize for not getting back to you. I do have more Saggys for you, though, and I have the whole weekend to make more."

"You think you can work on a deadline? Remember that show I told you about? The one in Disney you said you couldn't go to 'cause you weren't going to be here? Well, it is *THE* teddy bear show of the year. It'll be a great place to showcase your zodiac bear line." Felice smiled big and wide and winked. "You think you can get me enough by November?"

"I'm going with you. If that's okay, that is."

Felice looked at her with genuine surprise. "I thought you were heading back to Newark for the rest of the year?"

"Well, I was, but decided to make this my home. I love it here."

"That is wonderful news." Felice clapped her hands. "I can certainly use the help at the show. But I've got to warn you, this year's theme is miniature bears, so you think you can have the entire edition of ten done in time for the show? If my guess is right, they'll sell out." Felice seemed to be talking non-stop.

Brenda smiled. "Well, I doubt that they'll sell out . . ."

"Oh they will, Brenda, I know. I've been in the teddy bear hobby for ten years and in the business for four. Believe me, your bears are pretty special."

They're for Timmy, Brenda wanted to say. "Well, they come from my heart," she said instead.

A customer walked in and Felice made a move to greet her. "Looks like you've got your work cut out for you, Brenda. We'll talk before the show."

Brenda waved goodbye and left Hyde Park. Making her miniature bears would be the salve for her exhausted nerves. A day didn't go by without thoughts of her father. The pain her mother was going through. And every time she walked into Malfour, the inevitable confrontation with Louis Cuenca and Peter Cuenca loomed like a shadow ready to pounce. And then there was Tina.

Her life had definitely taken a dramatic turn since moving into Malfour. The bullets that tore into her body had led her to the truth. Death was life and the light of love was the path to eternity.

But had these changes made her a better person? Tina didn't think so. Had she really become as obsessive and selfish as Tina pictured her? And what part was Malfour playing in her transformation? The forces that still lived there had become as important to her as reality itself.

When Brenda got back to Malfour, she went straight to the answering machine. She missed Tina more than she thought she would. The scent of her on the bed beside her. The way the stubborn curls dripped down her forehead. But there were no messages. Why hadn't Tina called?

"Silly, you. You should ask?" Brenda said out loud to Malfour. Tina was probably having the time of her life with Stewart and Joan and their friends. Brenda shook her head to chase out the ugly thoughts that threatened to creep in.

It was late afternoon and clouds were trying to crowd out the sun. A perfect time to call Peter Cuenca. There was no reason to put it off any longer. Brenda figured Louis Cuenca would still be at the shop and therefore avoid two confrontations simultaneously. She was still unsure how to handle Louis Cuenca.

The dangerous idea of baiting him had crossed her mind. But with Tina out of the house, it was risky. She could intimate that she and Tina would be away for the weekend. Make him think Malfour was sitting here empty, waiting for him. But what if he took her bait and came after her? She'd be alone. She could always call Cubbie, but she didn't want to put her friend in that kind danger. What if he had a gun? She felt for the Walther PPK on her waist. She had one too.

Getting him to come after her would prove his guilt once and for all. She shrugged it off. That kind of stunt only happened in books and movies. With her luck, Tina would come home to a corpse. She had to get to Peter Cuenca first.

She looked up the number on the Rolodex and dialed. It rang three times before anyone picked up.

"Yes, hello?"

Brenda recognized the voice. Her stomach tightened.

"Hello, Louis?" She wasn't expecting him. "I would like to speak with your father if he's in, please." She could almost picture the man on the other end.

"Well, yes." There was hesitation. "Is everything alright at Malfour?"

He initiated the game and it was now up to Brenda to choose how to play.

"Sure, everything is great. We love it. Come and visit again when you're in town." She paused, considering her next choice of words carefully. "I understand you come to Tampa often." If she was going to go into the PI business, she had to trust her instincts and take the chances that came with the job. She could hear Tina's voice in her head. She wouldn't like this at all.

There was the silence of unexpected surprise on the other end.

"Well, I . . . don't really go that often . . ." His voice betrayed his confusion. Brenda had broadsided him.

"May I speak with your father, please?"

"Is there anything I can help you with?" His voice was slow, deliberate, the tone guarded.

"No, thank you, I really need your father."

"Sure, I'll get him, but may I remind you that he is a very old man. He isn't well."

"I'll only keep him a moment."

Louis left the phone and there was nothing for a very long time. Brenda remembered the last time she had spoken with Peter Cuenca. It had certainly been a lesson in patience. Her thoughts went back to Louis. Would he listen in on another phone?

"Yes?" It was Peter.

"Mr. Cuenca, this is Brenda Strange. Tina and I bought your house, Malfour, in Tampa."

"Yes?"

Damn, thought Brenda, *does this man have a vocabulary that includes more than one or two words?*

"Mr. Cuenca, I don't quite know how to ask this, but let me be brief. When I moved into Malfour, I found a box with some clothing that appeared very old, and mysterious letters with pieces of them cut out. They were written by Carlotta Malfour."

Peter Cuenca burst into an intense coughing fit. She waited for the coughing to stop.

"Mr. Cuenca, does that name mean anything to you?"

"What do you want? Why are you calling, Brenda?" His question was like a gasp into the phone.

"Mr. Cuenca, I've been doing some research into the Malfour history and I'm conducting an investigation into the disappearance of Carlotta Malfour. Now, I've discovered photographs from the twenties of the Malfour family." She paused, waiting for her own heart to settle down. "There are also photographs of a man I believe to be your father, Roberto Cuenca and a young boy I think is you."

"Why? Why are you asking me these things?"

"Mr. Cuenca, was Roberto your father?"

"What business is this of yours?" His raspy voice was defensive.

"Mr. Cuenca, when the contractors tore down walls in Malfour, they found an old securities box. Inside were love letters from Carlotta Malfour to a maid named Angelique. There was also a picture of the both of them. I believe Carlotta was murdered because of her affair with Angelique." Brenda waited for Cuenca to speak. But there was nothing. "Please, Mr. Cuenca, I need your help. You were a young man at the time of Carlotta's disappearance. If you have information you can give me, I would appreciate it."

Brenda stopped again, waiting desperately for Peter Cuenca to open up and spill forth all the answers she was looking for. Instead, all she heard was a heavy breathing in her ear.

"Mr. Cuenca?"

He started to cough into the phone. She was afraid he was going to choke or have a stroke. The coughing stopped, replaced by the sound of a man trying hard to breathe.

"I can no longer speak to you, Ms Strange."

"No, no, Mr. Cuenca, please don't hang up." Brenda was desperate. If she lost him now, he wouldn't talk to her again.

"I have ledgers, Mr. Cuenca. Albert paid your father large sums of money for something. Please tell me what you know."

"I am very ill, Ms Strange. Goodbye." Peter Cuenca's voice was like a whimper. Then the line went dead.

Chapter 24

The phone was ringing in Brenda's ear. She fumbled for the receiver, rubbing her eyes from the sun streaming through the window.

"Hello?"

"Hey, sleepy head. What are you doing?" It was Tina.

Brenda sat up in bed, flipping the sheet out of her way. The alarm clock said 10 AM. She'd overslept again.

"Well, it took you long enough to think of me," Brenda said with a groggy voice.

"Wish you were here."

"Don't be so corny." Brenda laughed. "Are you having a good time?"

"Been drinking too much. Languishing on the deck of a yacht, and talking to all kinds of really groovy people."

Brenda was glad she wasn't there.

"How are you doing, Princess?" Tina's voice showed concern. "I mean . . . have you heard from your dad? Your mom?"

"No, no. I'm calling dad today. Thanks for asking."

"You doing okay there, Princess?"

Brenda knew what she meant. Are you okay without me?

"I've got seven bears to do before November. I have more work than I have time for. I'm fine, honey." She smiled into the phone and hoped Tina saw it.

"We're heading off to a private island today. Joan says you can only get to it by boat."

Brenda could hear the excitement in her voice. No way was she going to steal that from Tina by telling her about the conversation with Peter Cuenca and the invitation to Louis. There were already enough hard bumps on their road still left to smooth over. No use worrying Tina.

"Well, my schedule doesn't sound half as exciting as yours, sweetie. Don't drink too much where you'll fall off the yacht, okay? Remember, you can't swim."

Tina laughed hard on the other end. Brenda shivered. She hadn't realized how much she wanted Tina's touch.

"Don't worry, Princess, Joan and Stewart both swim like the little fish they collect. Listen, baby, I better run."

"Yeah, you go on. Have a good time."

"You've got my number. If you need anything . . ."

"Yeah, yeah," Brenda said. "I'll see you Monday."

The truth of the matter was that while she missed Tina like crazy, she didn't feel alone. Or afraid. She wasn't alone. Carlotta and Angelique were here. She knew it. She felt them all around her. There was a certain electricity in the air. Malfour was as alive today as it had been centuries ago.

Brenda got up, showered, fixed herself a bowl of corn flakes with soymilk and diced bananas, and decided to start work on a new Saggy bear. Brenda figured that if she worked all day Saturday and Sunday with no distractions, she could easily get several bears finished. But not before she called her father.

She waited the five rings before the answering machine picked up. They weren't home. Her mother must have been feeling well enough to go out. She left a short message and hung up. Brenda was aware of the sudden pang of pain building inside her chest. She couldn't let it overwhelm her. There was too much going on right here in her life. Her very life was being threatened again. This time, she had control. Brenda Strange wasn't going to be a victim. Carlotta and Angelique had been victims also. Justice had now placed the sword in her hand and she would be the avenger.

* * *

Thunderstorms rolled in early evening. The downpour lasted almost two hours. Brenda lay in bed, the picture of Carlotta and Angelique beside her.

She'd spent an exhausting day in her workroom, getting one bear nearly finished. Her fingers were sore. She didn't like wearing a thimble. The miniature size of the bears made the needlework especially painful. Bear buyers often questioned the high price for such a tiny bear, but in truth, the work and craftsmanship that went into the making of a miniature required the same skills, if not more than a common sized bear.

Brenda had just finished her dinner of Fiesta Chicken salad when the thundershowers began. Her father hadn't returned her phone call so she tried him again. Still no answer. She left another message.

She had to chase her concern away. She couldn't panic every time her mother and father weren't home. So she went to the little black security box and pulled the photograph out.

Lying in bed, she studied every inch of the photograph. Now that she knew more of Carlotta and Angelique, it was obvious in the photograph that the two women were happy in an intimate way.

The two were too close. Were they holding hands in the folds of those coats? Did they go to a secret place and make love all afternoon after they left the fair?

Brenda's eyelids refused to stay open and her thoughts were getting foggy. After late nights and then sleeping too far into the morning, Brenda welcomed the rest.

* * *

Brenda woke up gasping in fear as the sheets were ripped from her. She sat up in bed, naked, heart ready to leap out of her chest. The sheets lay crumpled on the floor.

She forced her eyes to adjust to the darkness in the room as she scanned the dark corners. She was still groggy. Brenda fully expected to find some maniac lunging at her with a knife. But there was no one there.

"*Beware.*" The whisper was strong in her ear. A woman's urgent message.

"*Get up.*" A different woman urged.

Brenda groped for her robe, wrapped it tightly around her waist, and looked around the room again.

"Carlotta? Angelique?"

There was no answer. She shook her head in the dark. Did she expect ghosts to be at her beck and call? She started for the door.

"*The window.*"

Brenda almost jumped at the intensity of the voice. She took a couple of hesitant steps to the window, pulled the drapes aside, and peered out into the night. The garden lay below, bathed in the muted, silvery color of a nearly full moon. And walking along the path to the back door was a man, his dark clothes and hair hidden in the shadows.

Brenda beat down the fear gathering in her stomach. Louis Cuenca? Had he decided to take up her invite so soon? If he was that desperate, then he was also dangerous. She watched him reach the back of the house and disappear from her sight. *He must have gotten into the house.*

Brenda tore the robe off and grabbed her sweat pants and tank top from the chair. She dug out the Walther PPK from her underwear drawer. She had just tucked the small gun into her pants when she heard a door creak. He was downstairs.

Brenda swallowed hard, stepped quietly to the door, and peeked out. The hallway was awash in the pastel orange light of the nightlight she'd plugged in the wall.

She pulled out the gun and crept into the hallway, gun held with both hands and pointed in front of her. Brenda hugged the wall all the way down the stairs. When she hit the bottom of the stairs, she stopped cold and listened.

It sounded like a can or something metallic hitting the floor. Then the smell hit her. Gasoline. The son of bitch was going to torch Malfour.

"No, not again."

Brenda fought down the wave of nausea that rippled through her. What was she supposed to do? She couldn't barge in on him. What if he had a gun? The library. She would wait for him there and trap him. She would be in control of the situation.

The adrenalin shot through her as she moved quietly toward the library. She could call 911 from there. If she'd been thinking straight, she would have grabbed the cell phone. It was of no use upstairs in her purse.

Brenda had a clear path down the hallway. If it was Louis, he was doing a thorough job in the kitchen and dining area. Brenda had to shove the painful image of Malfour being defiled in this manner out of her head. She couldn't let anger take control.

Looking back once to make sure she hadn't been seen, she made a dart for the library. The darkness downstairs was like a solid wall. She was halfway down the hall when she ran into the sculpture. The bust came crashing down, making a loud "thunk" as it hit the floor. It was Tina's Medusa. The stand wobbled and threatened to tip over as well, until Brenda grabbed it and held onto it for dear life as if it were a lifesaver. She listened.

The noise in the kitchen stopped. The silence was deafening. Brenda took off running without looking back until she was in the library. She pulled the double doors shut and latched them. She was surprisingly calm, considering Louis Cuenca would come crashing through them at any moment.

She fumbled for the phone and dialed 911. Nothing. The line was dead. He'd thought of everything. He'd cut the line. She really wished she had her cell phone now. Brenda didn't know which was worse, the pitch black of the room or the silence.

Where was he? As her eyes adjusted to the dark, she was thankful that there was at least some shimmer of light from the moon outside coming through the window. Thank God she'd forgotten to close the drapes.

Brenda looked around the room for the best place to hide. She had to have the upper hand when he came through those doors.

She circled behind the desk that sat near the wall to the left. That whole part of the room was in shadows. Deep shadows. He wouldn't see her there. Not until it was too late for him. Brenda had a direct line of view to the doors. The click of the doorknob turning, interrupted the stillness. After one try, he stopped. Brenda was afraid the sound of her heart beating in her chest would blow her cover.

The loud crack of gunfire made Brenda jump, and she tightened her grip on the Walther PPK to where she could see her knuckles blanching of all color. The doors still held. There was another burst of gunfire and Brenda saw the door splinter and the knob fly off. The doors flew open as Louis Cuenca walked into the room.

She watched from the shadows as he stood like a panther in the dim light of the moon. He scanned the room slowly. He held what appeared to be a semi-automatic in one hand and in the other, a red gas can. He stood in the room for what seemed like forever to Brenda without moving.

"Hello, Brenda," he said into the darkness. "I know you're here. Is this any way to treat an invited guest?" He taunted her with his voice. He started to splash the gasoline on the floor, the couch, even the bookcases. The bookcases full of antique books. He was going to torch Malfour. Brenda held her breath and the pain building into rage inside her.

"You don't mind if I just continue my work while you watch, do you?" The bastard was enjoying this. He kept the gun pointed where he could fire if he caught sight of her. The gasoline fumes in the room were making Brenda dizzy and she feared she would have to cough and throw up.

He emptied the can, flung it against the wall and started to walk toward the desk. To Brenda. His black clothes made him hard to make out. He blended too well with the other shadows. Brenda had to stop him now. He was going to find her eventually.

"Stop right there. Drop the gun. I've got a gun pointed at your head. I can see you and I can fire it." Would she be able to shoot a man? Danny Crane laughed in her head.

Louis Cuenca stopped, his face grim, threatening. He pointed the gun into the darkness. If he fired, he had a fifty-fifty chance of hitting her. Shooting duckies in the dark.

"Don't even try it, Louis. I swear if you just make a move to fire the gun, I will shoot you."

He stood there, gun aimed in her direction for seconds before he slowly lowered the gun.

"Put it on the floor in front of you."

Louis bent down carefully and laid the semi-automatic on the floor. Crouched like a tiger ready to pounce, he looked up and grinned. "Where do you want it now, Brenda?"

"Get up. Now. Kick the gun this way, toward the desk."

"Sure. Sure. Anything you say." With one swift move, his gun came sliding toward her.

She wasn't about to go for it. She wanted the gun out of his hands. But before she even had time to move, Louis Cuenca had reached inside his pants and held up something in his hand. His lips twisted in a wicked grin.

"Guess what this is, Brenda?" He held it out for her to see, waving it in the air. It was a match. "All I gotta do is drop this match and your gun isn't going to mean shit." He took a glance at the doors behind him. "How much you wanna bet I can barricade those doors behind me before you can get out?"

Brenda was breathing so hard she thought she might be hyperventilating.

"I'm not going to play games with you, Louis. Drop the

match or I will shoot." *Please God, make him drop the match.*

"Oh, I'll definitely drop the match. After I light it."

Brenda had to stop him. Why didn't she just shoot?

"Why, Louis? Why make it murder?"

He laughed out loud. "You're a smart bitch. This house means jack shit to me standing. And you mean even less. You probably know I stand to gain a considerable amount of money once you, your bitch girlfriend, and this house are gone. My father will have no choice but to sell the lot to the highest bidder." He stopped and grinned even wider. "And you know who that would be, don't you, Brenda." He inched a few steps her way.

"Stop right there. Don't come any closer." If she kept talking, he would figure out exactly where she was hiding in the shadows. On the other hand, each minute he talked allowed her to get a better lead on the hand holding the match.

"All I have to do is holler for Tina upstairs."

Louis laughed out loud. "I know we're alone. I've been watching the house all afternoon. I know what you did, when, and how. It's just you and me, kid."

He looked so much like Danny Crane.

Please, God, make him drop the match.

Brenda's thoughts were racing. If he got too cocky, he might just make a mistake. Louis Cuenca raised the hand with the match again. He was going to strike it. If she didn't stop him now, it would be too late. Too late for Carlotta, Angelique, and Malfour. She wasn't going to let that happen.

A sudden rush of cold air entered the room. Was it a draft? Then Brenda saw them moving. The library doors were slowly closing behind Louis Cuenca. He wasn't aware. The sound they made when they slammed shut wiped the evil grin off his face. He whirled around, a frightened look on his face.

"You fucking bitch," he roared at her. "Who's out there?" he screamed at the doors.

"Drop the match, Louis, and we can end this peacefully."

Please God, make him drop the match.

He moved like a caged animal toward the windows. "You're gonna burn, baby." He was going to jump out the window once he set the fire.

Every bone in her body resisted the command to move, but she inched slowly out of the shadowy corner, gun pointed at Louis Cuenca.

He looked at her and smiled, eyeing the barrel of the gun aimed at him. "You won't shoot." He struck the match with his thumbnail. The match didn't strike.

Brenda felt the rage Danny Crane must have felt. She fired the PPK. Danny Crane's face exploded in her mind. Louis Cuenca grabbed one of his legs as he went down on both knees.

"Goddamn you." He screamed as he attempted to light the match still clutched in his hand.

Brenda fired again. His body lurched backwards, toppling over, his head making a hard sound as it hit the floor. Brenda inched her way across the room, but not before she flipped on the lamp on the desk. Louis Cuenca wasn't moving. He lay sprawled in an awkward position, hands spread out. Brenda plucked the match from beside him where it had fallen.

She approached the doors, eyeing the hole where the doorknob had once been. The door had splintered above the knob. She slowly opened them, trying to figure out how they had closed shut. Was it a draft? She swung the door back and forth. The only thing that made sense to her wouldn't to anyone else. She looked around the library. Was Carlotta here? Fresh air circulated into the room. Just in time, because Brenda couldn't hold the nausea any longer. She threw up all over Louis Cuenca.

She walked over to the windows and flung them wide open. The muggy night almost made her feel woozy again, but the fresh air felt good in her lungs. It smelled of sweet, damp grass.

Brenda took Louis Cuenca's pulse. He wasn't dead, but he was bleeding all over the place. She had to call an ambulance. She worked her way as quickly as she could manage up the stairs to her room for the cell phone. Dialing 911, she calmly explained what had happened.

When she came back downstairs, she realized she still held the Walther PPK in her hand.

Chapter 25

"Sugar, you have got to be the most courageous woman I know or the craziest. Haven't figured it out yet." Cubbie made her way out of the kitchen holding a serving plate with two large omelets, enough toast for two, and butter. She set them on the table in front of Brenda.

Cubbie had called for Brenda early with an invitation to a movie. Brenda told her what had happened and Cubbie rushed over quicker than Brenda thought she could move. She raided the kitchen and prepared breakfast.

"These omelets are my specialty. Jalapeños, cheese, onions and mushrooms. I normally toss bacon in the mix, but you being vegetarian and all, I couldn't find a trace of meat in there."

She flopped the oversized omelet on Brenda's plate and did the same for herself. She reached for the toast as she sat down across from Brenda.

"Cubbie, you're not my slave. This looks marvelous and you're very sweet to do this, but I can cook for myself."

Cubbie stopped in the middle of buttering her toast and eyed Brenda with one eyebrow up high. "Listen, honey, you look like dirt. You haven't slept all night and your insides are probably doing flip-flops. Now sit back and let Cubbie take care of you."

There was no way Brenda was going to win with her. Besides, she really did feel like dirt, whether she looked like it or not.

"Now, do you want butter on your toast?"

"Light, please."

Cubbie spread just the right amount of butter and passed it to Brenda.

"I don't think I could've kept my cool like you," Cubbie continued where she'd left off as she stuffed a forkful of omelet in her mouth. "You say he's going to live, huh? Too bad."

"Cubbie, I wasn't shooting to kill."

"Well, I would've."

"I'm just glad it's all over with." Brenda finally tasted the omelet. It was delicious. She took another bite. She was ravenous.

Cubbie took a sip of coffee. "Are you gonna have to spend a lot of money replacing the stuff he messed up in there?"

"We'll be okay. Thankfully, when I fell over Tina's sculpture, I must have interrupted him. He hadn't even gotten started. The only damage is in the library." She painfully remembered the books the gasoline destroyed. Tina had brought them from Newark and they would be nearly impossible to replace.

"You're not gonna have to see this bastard again, are you?"

"The police want to ask me more questions and there will be depositions and then court."

"Now, Brenda, honey, tell me again why you haven't called Tina and told her."

"Cubbie, it'll just ruin her last chance at a nice vacation before she has to head back to school. A rather selfish thing for me to do, don't you think? Besides, it was no big thing."

Cubbie laughed. "Sugar, this is a big thing, believe me. I hate to think what you consider big."

Brenda thought a moment. "Losing one's soul."

"Don't you go getting all metaphysical on me, now."

"Cubbie, do you think I should call his father? I mean, I shot his son."

Cubbie was making quick work of the omelet. The woman made love to food. She swallowed another forkful and shook her head.

"I wouldn't want nothin' to do with that brood, honey. Just let sleeping dogs lie."

Brenda laughed. She marveled at Cubbie's simple, country ways. Cubbie was right, but she hadn't been able to get the thought out of her head. She couldn't help feeling she owed the old man an explanation.

Cubbie had almost inhaled the omelet. Brenda was taking her time, enjoying each bite.

"Why don't we take in that movie after all?" Cubbie asked Brenda. "It'll get your mind off of things."

"I've got a deadline for my bears, Cubbie. I should be working right now."

"Deadlines can be broken. When we get back from the movie, I'll help you do some sprucin' up around here. How's that for a deal you can't refuse?"

Brenda took another bite of the omelet and thought about it.

"Okay, that settles it. Movie it is." Cubbie picked up her plate and started towards the kitchen.

"Hey now, wait a minute, I didn't say yes."

"I heard you loud and clear." Cubbie winked and disappeared into the kitchen.

* * *

It was a very strange Monday. Brenda caught up on much needed sleep, waking up refreshed and ready to tackle the new day. Except she forgot it was Monday.

Maid for Today showed up at ten. It was the time Brenda had set up. She'd forgotten. And then her parents were still missing. She'd dialed them earlier and their answering machine picked up again. Her next step would be to call her Aunt

Miriam and Uncle George. Sometimes her mother and dad would spend weeks at their mansion in Tarryton. She had to keep telling herself that no news was good news. Her mother was doing fine.

Then, at around 2 PM, Tina came home. It was a real surprise for Brenda, but more so for Tina. She didn't expect to find the heavy-duty-cleaning going on in the library. Brenda didn't even hear her come in. The sound of the floor stripper drowned out everything else.

Brenda felt a pair of arms circle her waist tightly.

"Honey, I'm home," Tina whispered in her ear.

Tina smelled of the sea and suntan lotion. When Brenda turned to hug her, she noticed how dark Tina looked.

"Hey, you look sexy with that tan, honey. Welcome back."

"I had a great time, Princess." Tina kissed Brenda lightly on the lips. "Wish you'd been there."

"I'm glad you had a good time, honey." Brenda was happy she'd made the right decision not to call Tina.

"So, anything exciting happen around here while I was gone?" Tina was eyeing the crew working on the hardwood floor and the splintered door.

Brenda took her hand and led her away to the living room. She closed the double doors behind her.

"Princess, everything okay? Is your mother . . ."

"It's not my mother, honey." Brenda watched the concern grow on Tina's face. "Listen, I think you should sit down." Brenda ran a hand through her hair.

Tina and Brenda sat side by side on the Victorian couch.

"Princess, you're scaring me. What happened?"

"I shot Louis Cuenca."

Tina's mouth looked like the letter "O." "You what?"

"He came here to kill us and burn Malfour down. He poured gasoline all over the library." Brenda inched closer to Tina. "You might want to take a look at some of your books."

"Oh my God, Princess, forget the books. Are you alright?" Tina touched Brenda's arm and began rubbing her neck.

"I'm okay, honey, but remember my theory that Stewart was somehow involved with the Malfour problems?"

"Brenda, I'm not going to let you bring Stewart into this."

"Listen to me, baby. It wasn't Stewart who was responsible." Brenda stopped and shook her head. "Well, not directly anyway."

"Brenda, c'mon, this isn't a courtroom. Tell me what happened, please."

"Stewart Davis offered Louis Cuenca half-a-million if he made sure Davross Industries signed the dotted line on the contract for Malfour. Tina, Stewart admitted that to me. He wanted this property bad. Malfour doesn't fit in with the rest of the Tides."

"Yeah, so?" Tina looked perplexed and somewhat defensive.

"Louis Cuenca was involved with Santeria. You remember that freaky religion I told you about. He put a curse on us, Malfour, or maybe both. He had keys made, that's how he got inside. He put those ashes on our bed. He poisoned the garden. I got Kevin to check him out. Tina, Louis Cuenca was desperate for that money. His business is almost belly up. He's broke. The way he saw it, he had nothing to lose."

Tina was shaking her head in disbelief. She put one hand in the air. "I just can't believe he came here. Did he have a gun? How did you shoot him?"

Should Brenda tell her that it was Carlotta and Angelique who woke her from sleep to see Louis entering the house? No, Tina would never believe it.

"He had a gun, but I had mine too." Brenda stopped. She knew what would come next.

"I can't believe you shot him, Brenda."

"I fired the gun." Brenda paused. "Twice, Tina. I'm past Danny Crane."

Tina shook her head, dismay in her eyes. "I just can't believe he would come here and do this."

"Well, I think I helped him out a bit." Brenda had to tell her.

Tina looked at her hard. "You what?"

"I talked to him. I invited him to visit."

Tina stayed for a few seconds looking at her, then turned away and fell back on the sofa, her eyes closed.

"Brenda, you've got a freaking death wish." Tina ran a hand over her face as she slowly looked back at Brenda. "I don't know whether to be angry or worried."

Tina's words grabbed on in Brenda's head and wouldn't let go. Did she have a death wish? Was she seeking the final trip through that tunnel? Was her desire to reach the light stronger than her wish to remain in this real world? A world where her mother was being eaten alive by a ruthless disease. A dark place where children suffered at the hands of parents and died before understanding hate.

"Princess, I'm afraid. Afraid you'll rush headstrong at the dragons you want to slay. I'm afraid I'm going to get a phone call in the middle of the night from the police telling me something I don't want to hear." Tina's eyes were aimed at the floor and there was a whimper in her voice.

Brenda needed to see her face. She pulled up close to Tina and lifted her face to meet hers. The pain in Tina's eyes stunned her. Brenda grabbed her and held tight.

"My darling, I don't intend to get myself killed. Please tell me you won't worry about me." Brenda could see a tiny trickle of a tear forming in Tina's eyes.

Tina attempted a smile. "You know I love you, don't you? Why do you make it so hard? I'm so afraid . . . for us."

Brenda dried the tears off her lover's cheek and kissed her softly, then harder as Tina responded.

"Don't be afraid, baby," Brenda whispered. She got up and pulled Tina with her. "Let's go upstairs. I really missed you." She nibbled on Tina's ear.

"Now?" Tina looked at the doors. "With those guys down here?"

"Now." Brenda yanked her by the hand and they bolted upstairs, latched the bedroom door, and made love, stifling the screams of their passion with pillows.

Chapter 26

Brenda found her parents the following morning. It was just as she suspected. She'd gotten a hold of them at her Aunt Miriam and Uncle George's. She talked to her mother for a few minutes. She said she was feeling much better. But Brenda knew the words were meaningless. Her mother never expressed her true emotions. Brenda had always depended on her father for that. They were staying there for another week and then heading back home. Her father mentioned Malfour again and Brenda agreed to let him know when would be best for her.

Brenda was upstairs in her workroom when she heard the doorbell. It was early afternoon. She continued folding the tiny hat for her newest Saggy.

She stopped in mid-stitch when the sound of muted voices reached her. Someone was downstairs. She got up just as Tina practically flew into the room.

"You better come down. You won't believe who's downstairs."

Before Tina even finished the sentence, Brenda knew. She knew who waited for her. They both went downstairs. There was a young man with long, dark hair and moustache and an old man in a wheelchair with different tanks and tubes attached to it.

The man who sat in the wheelchair looked like a piece of crumpled paper. The young man with him looked to be in his early twenties. But it was the older man who held Brenda's attention. His head bent so low, it almost touched his sunken chest.

"Mr. Cuenca?" Brenda stooped down to look at him.

Peter Cuenca lifted his red-rimmed eyes, and Brenda was surprised at the wetness in them. He was crying. He didn't focus on her right away, looking past her down the hall. He didn't speak or acknowledge her.

Brenda looked up at the young man. He shrugged his shoulders.

"He's okay. He's just slow."

"I'm Brenda Strange."

"Hi, I'm Manuel. This is my great grandfather." He shook her hand. "You two know each other?"

"We've only spoken on the phone," Brenda said, her eyes on Peter Cuenca.

Cuenca slowly shifted his gaze to her and let his head drop back on the headrest. Brenda looked into eyes still moist with tears.

"Mr. Cuenca, I've tried contacting you at home. I wanted to talk to you about your son." This wasn't exactly the way she had in mind to discuss Louis Cuenca with his father.

"Miss Strange, I have come a long way." His voice was like a hard gurgle. He paused, putting a hand to his chest. "I have come a long way to see you. I don't wish to discuss my son." When he finished, his whole body jerked back into the chair, and he gripped the arms so hard, his bony knuckles were turning white.

Brenda looked at Manuel with concern.

"Just let him calm down," he said. He put a hand on his great grandfather's shoulder.

Brenda was trying hard to control the thumping of her heart. It felt like it was going to do an Alien number out of her chest.

She looked back down at the frail old man.

"Please don't rush, Mr. Cuenca. Take your time. Would you care for something to drink?" Brenda looked back at Tina.

"No," the old man said with difficulty. "I won't be staying that long. I must speak to you in private."

Brenda left Tina and Manuel in the hall and wheeled Peter Cuenca into the library. She shut the newly replaced doors behind her. She came around to face him, back to the windows.

"Mr. Cuenca, why are you here?" Way down deep in the most sacred place of her heart, she knew the answer.

That's when he started to cry. Deep, heart wrenching sounds that sent his tiny shoulders trembling. His mouth opened in sobs as he looked helplessly at Brenda. Then he stopped. It was as though his voice had been taken from him. He was staring straight ahead, but not at Brenda. There was something behind her.

Brenda turned and held her breath when she saw them. Carlotta and Angelique stood side by side in front of the window. But they were radiant, beautiful and full of life, much like the photograph taken seventy-four years ago. Gone were the monstrous wounds that had taken their lives.

Brenda tore her gaze from them to look back at Cuenca. He was still focused on the windows. Dear God, did he see them too?

"Mr. Cuenca?" Brenda reached out to touch him.

"Forgive me," he said. It was more like a gasp.

Brenda looked back toward the window, but Carlotta and Angelique were gone. The tears were streaming down Peter Cuenca's face. It was time for him to make his peace.

"Mr. Cuenca, I don't need your forgiveness, but they do. Carlotta and Angelique. You know what happened here, don't you? Albert Malfour murdered his wife and her lover, Angelique, here. Tell me how, Mr. Cuenca. Tell them."

Peter Cuenca shook his head. "I have lived in Hell for over seventy-four years. When I leave here today, I pray Heaven will be my next stop."

It was time for Brenda to remain silent. The past was here to listen. To forgive or condemn. Peter Cuenca finally looked directly at Brenda.

"May God have mercy on Albert Malfour's soul. He was a powerful man. And he was a jealous one. He treated everyone like dirt, but especially his wife." Cuenca stopped, his chest heaving violently.

"Take your time, Mr. Cuenca," Brenda said.

He rubbed his eyes with a shaking hand.

"Many of us knew about her affair. He was the last to know."

"How did he find out? Who told him?"

Peter Cuenca burst into tears again. "My father," he sobbed. "My father helped him murder both of them." His hands went up and covered his face.

A surge of anger, relief, and pity swept over Brenda. She could almost feel something heavy lifting from her soul. And did the room brighten or had the sun peeked out from the clouds?

"How did it happen, Mr. Cuenca? Were you there?"

With his face still buried in his hands, Cuenca shook his head. "My sin is not murder." He slowly raised his face to her. The pain that poured from his eyes struck Brenda like the bullet his son never fired at her. Brenda had to control the sudden urge to cry with him.

She bent down and took both his shoulders. "I know it's painful, but you have to tell us."

He gave her a puzzled look, his mouth open in an agonizing grimace. He cried as he spoke.

"Albert, he locked them both in the servants' quarters. My father . . . my father . . ." He sobbed uncontrollably. "He had poured kerosene all over the room. Albert threw a torch into the room as he locked the door behind him."

Brenda could no longer stop the tears. Angelique had burned. She was the fiery figure in the servants' room.

"They both died in the fire?" She held on tighter to the old man's shoulders. "Tell me, did they both die in the fire?"

He shook his head slowly. "No. Carlotta tried to escape." He started shaking his head in anger, trying to chase the demons of those memories out of his mind. "He bludgeoned her to death outside. She couldn't run."

Brenda let go of him and stood up. The horror of what happened in Malfour House was slowly being chased back into the hell where Albert Malfour occupied. But there were still unanswered pieces to the puzzle.

"The letters upstairs. Who cut the pieces and why?"

Peter Cuenca was having trouble catching his breath.

"Do you need help, Mr. Cuenca? Should I get Manuel?"

He put a weak hand in the air. "No. My confession is not yet finished." He swallowed hard and continued. "I gave him those letters. He made me spy on her. When he read them, he was so enraged, he couldn't stand to read Angelique's name on the letters, so he painstakingly cut them out. He was like a madman. He kept the letters hoping to blackmail his wife into prostituting herself for his rich clients who kept his business afloat. But his ego and jealousy led him to murder instead."

Angelique must have hidden the rest of the letters in the security box so Albert wouldn't find them. They survived the fire that she couldn't. The room began to spin for Brenda. She thought she might have to sit down. It felt as though a giant hand was squeezing hard on her heart. She could almost feel the pain Carlotta and Angelique must have gone through.

"The fire. How was it contained? The only evidence of fire in Malfour is in the servant's quarter." Brenda asked. But did she really expect a 94-year-old man to recollect memories from so long ago accurately? Yes, any human being with a heart would never forget the sight, sound, and smell of another human being burning alive.

Peter Cuenca could barely shake his head. "He owned half the police department and the fire department as well. He paid several off duty firemen extra to be there. He even hired builders to come in and add an extra wall to the servant's quarters. He'd become possessed with his monstrous act."

"I understand now why he died a penniless derelict," Brenda said. "It took all his money to bury the murders." Brenda felt the urge to cry, strike out at Peter Cuenca. Except it wasn't Cuenca she wanted to hurt, but a man already long dead.

"Where are they? What did they do with the bodies?" Brenda's voice was a controlled whisper.

Peter Cuenca opened his mouth to speak, but a violent cough erupted instead. Brenda rushed toward the door.

"Let me get you some water."

"No. I have to tell you now." He turned and looked out the windows behind Brenda. "They are still here, Brenda."

Brenda looked back to where Carlotta and Angelique had been only moments ago. Directly in her sight was the water fountain in the backyard, the Impatiens blooming in all their bright colors. Brenda knew then where the bodies of Angelique and Carlotta were. And why the poison couldn't kill the Impatiens.

She looked back at Peter Cuenca. "You buried them?"

He looked at her and sighed, his eyes pleading forgiveness.

"God forgive me. My father forced me to help him. We dug that hole well into the night, then poured cement over the bodies. Albert left his scorched and bloodied clothes for me to dispose of, but I panicked. I just stuffed them in a box with the letters."

"Oh, my God," Brenda said, "The clothes in the attic."

Brenda had to sit down. She sank into the leather couch.

"So that's why your father got those checks from Albert Malfour. He got paid for murder and for his silence."

"He promised our family that we would have everything we ever wanted and needed for as long as he lived."

The past had spoken and Brenda listened. "And that's why you held on to this property. If a developer came in and built on this site, the bodies would be discovered."

Peter Cuenca dried the tears from his eyes. "I could not let my children take possession of this house. Louis needed money.

He squandered everything I gave him and then got furious when I left him nothing in the will. All I had was this house and he wanted to sell to a developer. If you had not bought Malfour, when I died, this house would have gone to the preservation society. It would be forever protected from the land sharks that wanted to tear it down."

Brenda walked slowly to stand in front of the window. The garden outside was still dead, the grass and plants brown with poison. She kept her eye on the water fountain. On Carlotta and Angelique's grave.

"Mr. Cuenca, seventy-four years ago you were an accessory to a murder. Do you know what that means?" She let the words out slowly, not really sure where she wanted them to go. "An accessory bears responsibility in a crime."

She waited and when he didn't answer, turned back toward him. Peter Cuenca's head had dropped back down onto his chest. Was he alive? She walked quickly to his side. When she bent down, he opened his eyes and propped his head to look at her. She noticed the thick film of cataracts that covered most of his eyes.

"Look at me, Brenda, I am near death. I can only put myself at your mercy. The dead I wronged can no longer forgive me."

Forgive.

Brenda heard the voice in her ear and smiled. She crouched down and looked at Peter Cuenca. "Maybe they can hear you, Mr. Cuenca, if you speak from the heart." She got up, took his wheelchair, and moved to the doors.

Tina and Manuel were in the living room waiting. When they heard the doors to the library open, they met them in the hallway. Brenda stepped from behind the wheelchair to face Peter Cuenca.

"I'm going to press charges against your son, Mr. Cuenca. There has to be a balance to justice."

Peter Cuenca looked at her long and hard. He didn't speak, but grabbed her hand swiftly and squeezed.

He turned to his great grandson. "Manuelito, take me

home."

Brenda stood, her back to Tina, and watched Manuel close the front door behind him. She felt Tina come up and put a hand on her shoulder.

Forgive. The house whispered.

"What the hell was all that about, Princess?"

Brenda didn't answer, she just fell into Tina's arms

Chapter 27

Nights came and went too quickly. They found Brenda preoccupied, staring at the garden below from the bedroom window. Tina would be leaving tomorrow. The Art Institute waited in Newark. She already had invites to "Welcome Home" parties. She would sleep in their bed alone. Without her.

Tina had been supportive of Brenda's decision not to expose Peter Cuenca's involvement in the murder of Carlotta Malfour and her lover, Angelique. She didn't understand, but she allowed Brenda her reason, whatever it was.

They hadn't spoken much of Tina's impending departure. Tina seemed to have somehow stuffed her worries and frustration over Brenda staying behind at Malfour somewhere deep inside her. Each time Brenda caught her packing in the bedroom, she avoided the room and found somewhere else to hide her own feelings.

Brenda was in the library, laptop perched on her lap, when she saw Tina come down the stairs lugging two huge suitcases and a small carry-on tucked under her arm. She placed them near the front door. Brenda held her breath as she told her heart to settle down. Tina was walking toward her.

"Listen, Princess, I need to talk to you about the sculptures."

She came and sat down next to Brenda on the couch. Her skin was still a lovely shade of cocoa and the hip hugger jeans and short blouse she wore so well jumbled Brenda's feelings inside.

"Joan will be coming for the pieces Phil is going to feature at his gallery. Everything is all taken care of." Tina stopped and stared deep into Brenda's face.

Brenda couldn't stand the heat of Tina's eyes. She glanced quickly across the hallway at the three pieces of luggage.

"Planning on taking an early flight?" She had to lighten the mood.

"No, still leaving at ten tomorrow morning." Tina didn't take her eyes off her. "You know I can't let you take me to the airport, right?" It was a sad smile that formed on her mouth. She started to shake her head.

"Tina, you don't have to go."

"Do you have to stay?" Tina shook her mass of black hair. "See, this isn't going to get us anywhere."

Brenda snapped the laptop shut. She broke their eye contact. "Will you visit on weekends?" She had to look back at Tina. "I want you to."

"You know I can't afford that."

Brenda opened her mouth.

"No, I won't let you pay for it. Too extravagant. It's not my style. We made a pact, remember? Your money wasn't ever, ever going to play a part in our relationship."

Tina stopped and eyed everything in the room. "Guess what, Princess, this whole house is your money."

Brenda remembered the night they made that silly pact. Tina was so damned adamant that just because Brenda and her family were wealthy, their love, their relationship, was going to be neutral ground. Two people giving equal parts. And it had worked.

Brenda swallowed hard, pushing down the lump that formed in her throat. "Tina, I can't . . ."

Tina put a finger over Brenda's lips. "I know, Princess. I know." She put her head down on Brenda's shoulder and sank deeper into Brenda's body.

* * *

The birds chirping outside nudged Brenda awake. She rubbed her eyes, and waited for the early morning grogginess to clear.

Immediately, her eyes went to the alarm clock. It was nine-thirty. Tina. She wasn't in bed, but there was a note on her pillow.

Brenda took it in her hand slowly, her heart sinking.

Princess,

You know I can't say goodbye, and that's the only word I know to describe how I'm feeling.

I love you,
Tina

It was nine thirty. Tina could still be downstairs. Brenda threw on her leggings and oversized shirt and ran down the stairs.

Please let her be here. She ran into the kitchen, the library, even the guestroom. She worked her way back into the hallway and noticed that the suitcases Tina had placed near the door yesterday were gone. Tina was gone.

* * *

Brenda tried working on a new Saggy bear but couldn't get her mind off Tina. Cubbie called and made a futile attempt to get Brenda out to a Devil Rays baseball game. The Chicago White Sox were in town and she had two tickets.

Brenda politely declined, being honest by telling her baseball wasn't her favorite sport. In reality, Brenda didn't care for sports at all. There was bonding to do with Malfour. This was her home and now her solitary companion.

She ordered a cheese pizza, ate a couple of pieces, and took the first step in making herself part of Malfour. Upstairs in the attic, she took the box with the pants, shirt, and shoes out into the back garden, stuffed the clothes in the oversized garbage bag, and walked to the edge of the channel wall.

Brenda flung the bag as far as she could into the bay waters. The black bag bobbled on the surface and slowly crept away. A monster had worn those clothes, and the evil he committed in the past deserved no place in the present.

She walked back into Malfour and, with purpose, went into each room and closed the drapes on all the windows. Daylight was just a candle burning outside, and dark shadows were seeping into every part of Malfour.

Brenda went into the pantry and located as many candles as she could find. She and Tina had gone crazy at Pier One and bought close to a hundred candles of different shapes and sizes, scented and unscented. She placed the candles upstairs in the bedroom and downstairs in the library, living room, dining room, kitchen, and guestroom.

Malfour seemed to come alive in the glow of candlelight. The shadows that danced and swayed among the walls looked like living things.

As Brenda walked through each room lighting the candles, she could feel the house watching. And to her ears, she could swear its heart was racing along with hers.

It was in the guestroom that she lit the last candle. She wanted to spend time here. This was where Carlotta and Angelique had died. Brenda sat on the couch, right next to the floor lamp where Carlotta had stood behind. She had the security box in her lap and opened it carefully, taking out the photograph of Carlotta and Angelique.

"I hope you don't mind me leaving you in your resting place," Brenda said out loud into the room. "The flowers seem to love you."

She was disappointed when only silence answered her. Brenda looked at the photograph and the two smiling women who on that day in the past had lived and loved for the moment. Those thoughts inevitably brought Tina racing back into her heart.

So much had changed since Danny Crane burst into that office. In less than one year, Brenda had died, seen the face of God, and came back. She had gained much, but lost too much. Was she ready to take on her new career? Would she be successful? Could she face the reality of Tina's absence from her life? And would she be able to grieve for her mother when cancer took her from her?

Brenda didn't stop the tears that tumbled down her cheeks. She put her head back and cried out loud into the flickering shadows. Something touched her hair. Brenda jumped and looked all around her.

In the corner, standing in front of the brick wall, was Carlotta. The radiant, beautiful Carlotta. She was smiling. Brenda got up and carefully walked to her, hands outstretched. She wanted very much to touch her.

We are still here.

The voice from behind her stopped Brenda cold. She turned quickly around to see Angelique standing on the other end of the room.

Always.

This time, it was Carlotta's whisper in Brenda's ear. When Brenda looked back at Carlotta, she was gone.

Always.

Brenda looked back for Angelique, but she also had disappeared. A cold wave of fatigue hit Brenda and she had to run back to the couch and sit down. Her tears led into sobs, except this time, they were tears of joy.

She wasn't alone. She wasn't alone at all.

Epilogue

Even the phone ringing, sounded cranky to Brenda. She was trying to enter her data on the Albert Malfour case and Louis Cuenca into her laptop. If she was going to make a business of this, she'd better start keeping a journal. She had a good mind to let the answering machine pick up, but then thought of her mother . . . Tina . . . It had been a while since she'd talked to either one.

"Hello."

"Hey BS, how's my lone wolf making out down there?"

Brenda smiled immediately. "Kevin, what a nice surprise. Or is it?"

"When will you ever learn that I am always a surprise, even to myself."

They both laughed out loud.

"I got something for you, Brenda. You gotta take it."

"I can be selective."

"Not with this one. I need you to jog your memory up for me. Back in July, Tampa Police pulled a stiff from the bay. They couldn't come up with much so the case is in limbo land. Still have it open but stuck with a diving accident label. You remember anything by any chance? I mean, you two were down there at that time?"

Brenda remembered very clearly that morning in the hotel room. Tina had teased her with the bad state of crime in Tampa.

"I saw a news clip. They'd just found her. What's up?"

"Well, seems she's got a sis up here in Jersey town who's convinced her sister was murdered. She isn't buying the accident angle. Swears her sister never did any diving."

"I don't know, Kevin. I'm still trying to enjoy myself and I've got a teddy bear convention in less than a month. I have to put the finishing touches on my bears. Besides, everything is cold by now. What could I dig up that the police haven't?" Brenda really *was* pressed for time.

"I'm asking more as a favor than anything else. I mean, the fee will be yours, but . . ."

"I don't care about the money."

"Well, that's your problem. Mine is that my man on the case, Rick, had a minor heart attack while working it. Needs a new ticker. I can't take the case. Too much on my plate as it is. I figured this might be a good first one for you to hit a home run with."

"I've already hit several home runs, Kevin."

"Yeah, but this is in the land of the living, BS. And c'mon, it's right there in your back yard."

Brenda reconsidered. Yes, she had some minor things she still needed to get done to make her bears ready for the convention next month, but getting into the deep and dirty of a new case thrilled her.

"This one is a favor for you, Kevin. What do you have so far?"

"That's my gal."

"Not if you keep referring to me as that."

"Okay, white flag. Listen, Rick got a copy of the police report, but you might want to check in with our connection in Tampa. Did you get all the files I sent you?"

"They're downloaded."

"Good, look up Detective Lisa Chambliss. She'll be extra

kind to our PIs. I'll fax you the police report and anything else Rick had on the case."

"Kevin, this isn't going to be a common thing, will it?

"Specify common."

"I'm going to choose my own cases, okay?"

"You're the boss, lady." He chuckled. "Thanks, okay?"

She hung up with Kevin and within minutes, the fax machine beeped. As Brenda Strange watched the sheets of paper roll off the fax machine, she couldn't help but wonder if she was fully prepared for a new case. For a new beginning.

The End

A Spectral Visions Imprint
Riverwatch by Joseph Nassise

When his construction team finds the tunnel hidden beneath the cellar floor in the old Blake family mansion in Harrington Falls, Jake Caruso is excited by the possibility of what he might find hidden there. Exploring its depths, he discovers an even greater mystery: a sealed stone chamber at the end of that tunnel.

When the seal on that long forgotten chamber is broken, a reign of terror and death comes unbidden to the residents of the small mountain community. Something is stalking its citizens; something that comes in the dark of night on silent wings and strikes without warning, leaving a trail of blood in its wake. Something that should never have been released from the prison the Guardian had fashioned for it years before.

Now Jake, with the help of his friends Sam Travers and Katelynn Riley, will be forced to confront this ancient evil in an effort to stop the creature's rampage. The Nightshade, however, has other plans. **ISBN: 1-931402-19-1**
NOW AVAILABLE

* * *

A Spectral Visions Imprint
Night Terrors by Drew Williams

He came to them in summer, while everyone slept . . .

For Detective Steve Wyckoff, the summer brought four suicides and a grisly murder to his hometown. Deaths that would haunt his dreams and lead him to the brink of madness.

For David Cavanaugh, the summer brought back long forgotten dreams of childhood. Dreams that became nightmares for which there would be no escape.

For Nathan Espy, the summer brought freedom from a life of abuse. Freedom purchased at the cost of his own soul.

From an abyss of darkness, he came to their dreams and whispered his name.

"Dust" **ISBN: 1-931402-24-8**
NOW AVAILABLE
Published By Barclay Books, LLC
http://www.barclaybooks.com

A Spectral Visions Imprint
Third Ring by Phillip Tomasso III

Private Investigator, Nicholas Tartaglia, is back . . .

Two men burglarize the home of the city's most prominent CEO, searching for a mystical book. They are discovered in the midst of the crime by a family member and in the chaos, one of the burglars winds up dead. So does the CEO's only son.

When Tartaglia receives a call defense attorney Lynn Scannella, an old friend, he learns that she has just been assigned to represent the man accused of the burglary and murder. With time being of the essence, Scannella needs Tartaglia's help investigating the circumstances in order to establish a defense for her client.

In a desperate search for answers, Tartaglia finds himself submerged in a raging river of deception and witchcraft. It quickly becomes apparent that getting a man out of jail might be the least of Tartaglia's concerns as he uncovers an underworld consumed by the use of black magic . . . and a plot that scares the hell out of him.

ISBN: 1931402-11-6

NOW AVAILABLE

* * *

A Spectral Visions Imprint
Island Life by William Meikle

On a small, sparsely populated island in the Scottish Outer Hebrides, a group of archeology students are opening what seems to be an early Neolithic burial mound. Marine biologist Duncan McKenzie is also working on the island, staying with the lighthouse caretakers, Dick and Tom, while he completes his studies of the local water supply.

One afternoon the three men are disturbed in their work by the appearance of a dazed female student from the excavation, who is badly traumatized. She tells of the slaughter of the rest of her party by something released from the mound.
Soon everyone Duncan knows is either missing or dead and there are things moving in the fog.

Large, hulking, unholy things.

Things with a taste for human flesh.

NOW AVAILABLE
Published By Barclay Books, LLC
http://www.barclaybooks.com

A Spectral Visions Imprint
The Apostate by Paul Lonardo

An invasive evil is spreading through Caldera, a burgeoning desert metropolis that has been heralded as the gateway of the new millennium. However, as the malevolent shadow spreads across the land, the prospects for the 21st century begin to look bleak.

Then three seemingly ordinary people are brought together:
Julian, an environmentalist, is sent to Caldera to investigate bizarre ecological occurrences.

Saney, a relocated psychiatrist, is trying to understand why the city's inhabitants are experiencing an unusually high frequency of mental disorders.

Finally, Chris, a runaway teenage boy, happens along and the three of them quickly discover that they are the only people who can defeat the true source of the region's evil, which may or may not be the Devil himself.

When a man claiming to work for a mysterious global organization informs the trio that Satan has, in fact, chosen Caldera as the site of the final battle between good and evil, only one question remains . . . Is it too late for humanity? **ISBN: 1-931402-13-2**
NOW AVAILABLE

* * *

A Spectral Visions Imprint
Phantom Feast by Diana Barron

A haunted antique circus wagon . . .
A murderous dwarf . . .
A disappearing town under siege . . .

The citizens of sleepy little Hester, New York are plunged into unimaginable terror when their town is transformed into snowy old-growth forests, lush, steamy jungles, and grassy, golden savannas by a powerful, supernatural force determined to live . . . again.

Danger and death stalk two handsome young cops, a retired couple and their dog, the town 'bad girl', her younger sister's boyfriend, and three members of the local motorcycle gang.

They find themselves battling the elements, restless spirits, and each other on a perilous journey into the unknown, where nothing is familiar, and people are not what they at first appear to be. Who, or what, are the real monsters? **ISBN: 1-931402-21-3**
NOW AVAILABLE

Published By Barclay Books, LLC
http://www.barclaybooks.com

A Spectral Visions Imprint
Spirit Of Independence by Keith Rommel

Travis Winter, the Spirit of Independence, was viciously murdered in World War II. Soon after his untimely death, he discovers he is a chosen celestial knight—a new breed of Angel destined to fight the age-old war between Heaven and Hell. Yet, confusion reigns for Travis when he is pulled into Hell and is confronted by the Devil himself, somewhat disguised as a saddened creature who begs only to be heard.

Freed by a band of Angels sent to rescue him, Travis rejects the Devil's plea and begins a fifty-year-long odyssey to uncover the true reasons why Heaven and Hell war.

Now, in this, the present day, Travis comes to you, the reader, to share recent and extraordinary revelations that will no doubt change the way you view the Kingdom of Heaven and Hell. And what is revealed will change your own afterlife in ways you could never imagine! **ISBN: 1-931402-07-8**
NOW AVAILABLE

* * *

A Spectral Visions Imprint
Psyclone by Roger Sharp

Dr. David Brooks is a front-runner in the cloning realm and a renowned Geneticist. He is a highly successful scientist who seems to stumble into one discovery after another. However, Dr. Brooks cannot find anyone close to him that shares his views on the cloning of humans.

Therefore he works in secrecy on a cloning project and has hidden his most recent discovery, the ability to clone beyond infancy. It is a clone of himself that this successful and secret experiment has rendered. The goal he has in mind is to recreate, in this clone, his twin brother, who had been abducted over twenty years ago.

Though the clone grows rapidly and is identical to David in appearance, a major question remains: Can anyone really clone a soul? Or is the clone an open vessel to an opportunistic spirit . . . a demon? The answer comes to Dr. Brooks soon, and at a cost . . . that of material destruction and the slaughter of innocent lives.
ISBN: 1-931402-01-9
NOW AVAILABLE

Published By Barclay Books, LLC
http://www.barclaybooks.com

A Spectral Visions Imprint
Dark Resurrection by John Karr

When Victor Galloway, a prominent surgeon and family man, suffers a heart attack while home alone, he claws his way to the phone and manages to dial 911. The paramedics arrive, smile down at him, and, to his horror, give him a lethal injection.

As Victor's life is ending, his nightmare begins. Rushed to the Holy Evangelical Lady of the Lake Medical Center, he is met in the emergency room by Randolph Tobias, CEO of H.E. L.L. "I need your skills as a surgeon to harvest the living and feed my people," says Tobias. "Join us and you may remain with your family. Join us and you will never die again."

Despite his refusal of Tobias' offer, Victor is pressed into the ranks of the undead. Like Tobias and his people, Victor begins to crave human flesh. His humanity, however, refuses to be vanquished. Risking the lives of his wife and son, Victor wages a battle against Tobias in an attempt to stop him and his people from preying further upon the living. **ISBN: 1-931402-23-X**
NOW AVAILABLE

* * *

Suspense
The Institut by John Warmus

LaRochelle, France: 1938: "Gently," Inspector Edmund Defont ordered the body to be cut down. Those who did not know him would suspect he feared he might hurt the dead girl—or wake her. The two policemen who worked silently under his command knew his sole intent was to preserve the crime scene. Thus, begins Edmond Defont's police investigation into the nightmares of David Proust, a young, affable priest who dreams and women die. When Defont's prime suspect and best friend both disappear in the middle of the night, his search takes him to the *Institut d'Infantiles*: an ancient Roman fortress in the middle of the Carpathian Mountains in the wilds of Poland: a place that conceals the mysteries of centuries. **ISBN: 1-931402-09-4**
NOW AVAILABLE

Published By Barclay Books, LLC
http://www.barclaybooks.com

Sci-Fi Suspense
Memory Bank by Sandi Marchetti

A planetary crisis has pulled the world's leaders together in a most deadly period in history. Virus after virus has attacked the earth leaving only a small remaining human population. Even those who have been working on a cure for these organisms have succumbed to them.

What can a planet do to survive? The answer, after careful consideration, came from a scientist in the Mid East. Regression. This theory had been proven in 2010. Now, all the great minds of the past could be brought back and have them forward the planet once again. Greats such as Einstein, Edison, Bell, and hundreds of thousands of others who were instrumental in promoting the prosperity of our earth could return.

Microchips were placed in every newborn child and were to be activated on the child's 18th birthday. Persons already living had these chips implanted behind their ears with activation set for one year after implant. Regression centers were set up in every large city with prominent leaders, expert hypnotherapists, and psychologists in attendance, all practicing a standard protocol. Except for one, in New York City; the August Webster Center wasn't playing by the rules. Unlike the other centers, Dr. Webster wasn't eradicating past memory after he regressed his subjects. They were left holding horrific memories of past lives. Soon, rapists, murderers, and villains of the past were on the streets again. The suicide rate increased astronomically in New York City, and those with new souls did not seem to live more than six months after their regression session.

Upon the initiation of the Webster Center psychologist in session, three professionals take on the task of investigating Webster. A frustrating road they travel, with death as a stumbling block along the way. It is not until they reach the very end that they discover an astonishing motivating past-life factor behind the demise of so many.   **ISBN: 1-931402-12-4**
NOW AVAILABLE

* * *

Suspense
The Institut by John Warmus

LaRochelle, France: 1938: "Gently," Inspector Edmund Defont ordered the body to be cut down. Those who did not know him would suspect he feared he might hurt the dead girl—or wake her. The two policemen who worked silently under his command knew his sole intent was to preserve the crime scene. Thus, begins Edmond Defont's police investigation into the nightmares of David Proust, a young, affable priest who dreams and women die. When Defont's prime suspect and best friend both disappear in the middle of the night, his search takes him to the *Institut d'Infantiles*: an ancient Roman fortress in the middle of the Carpathian Mountains in the wilds of Poland: a place that conceals the mysteries of centuries.   **ISBN: 1-931402-09-4**
NOW AVAILABLE

Published By Barclay Books, LLC
http://www.barclaybooks.com

Mystery\Suspense
Soft Case by John Misak

New York City homicide detective John Keegan wants nothing more than a dose of excitement. After nine years on the job and countless cases, his life has fallen into a series of routines. He no longer sees purpose in his job or his life, and with each day that passes, he tries to think of another way to break the monotony. It would take a miracle case to restore his faith and enthusiasm. A miracle case he wants, a disastrous one he receives. Excitement he gets in droves.

When software giant Ronald Mullins is apparently murdered, the case falls on his desk, thanks to his eager partner. At first reluctant to take on the high profile murder, Keegan dives in head first, only to find that there is a lot more to it than any one could have imagined. Along the way he will not only have to examine the clouded facts of the case, but the facts of his own life as well. To investigate the case of his life, he'll have to fend off the media, handle his over-zealous partner, and confront conspiracy and corruption which go to the top of the city government.

When the entire police organization turns against him, Keegan is forced to handle the case alone. Armed with a sardonic wit and a distrust of everyone around him, Keegan must risk his job, his friendships, and even his life to solve the biggest case the city has seen in decades.
ISBN: 1-931402-10-8

NOW AVAILABLE

* * *

Mystery\Fantasy
The House On The Bluff by
Elena Dorothy Bowman

A deserted house in New England contains a secret reaching back to the Crusades.

In a White Stone Abbey, situated in a dense English forest, a scroll, which held the secret to the present day Pierce House on the opposite side of the Atlantic, lay hidden in a chamber behind an alter, protected down thru the ages by brown robed monks until the 18th Century. On the quill scripted parchment were words that foretold the future of a dwelling, its surrounding properties, and, through the generations, to its final location in consecrated grounds to a distant land across the seas. It also foretold of the horrendous trials set before it, and who the true owner would ultimately be.

To the day she entered her ancestral home, with its promise of terror or fulfillment, The House On The Bluff maintained its enchantment and its ageless elegance, standing as a silent sentinel waiting for the one long destined to enter with her Consort, to claim ownership.

ISBN: 1-931402-00-0   **NOW AVAILABLE**

Published By Barclay Books, LLC
http://www.barclaybooks.com

Mystery
Death On The Hill by James R. Snedden

As a favor to an old friend, a vacationing Chicago investigative reporter is pressed into action to cover the story. Due to the nature of the killing, it soon becomes obvious that standard police investigative procedures won't be enough to solve the crime.

After the murdered woman's identity is established, it becomes apparent that things aren't what they appear to be. During a visit to the dead woman's office, the reporter notices a picture of the woman and two Chinese men. He recognizes one as the key figure in the Democratic National Committee fundraising scandal, and the other turns out to be a Triad leader wanted in Hong Kong.

Calling on his contacts in Washington, he is put in touch with three local Asian sources in the Los Angeles area to help him dig out information. Enlisting the help of influential members of the local Chinese community and two tenacious detectives from Hong Kong, the mystery is solved . . . but in the most bizarre way imaginable!

ISBN: 1-931402-05-1

NOW AVAILABLE

* * *

Nonfiction Health\Fitness
The Workout Notebook by Karen Madrid

Karen has always had an interest in staying in shape. After the latest fad diet on the market left her with acne and exhaustion, she decided to develop her own plan and devise easy methods that work for weight control. She decided that she didn't want any more suffering from diet plans that were concocted by people who were just plain CRAZY! Her goal is to have *The Workout Notebook* all medical doctors as a natural way to help their patients manage weight control and good health; it is already being used by many with positive results. **ISBN: 1-931402-06-X**

NOW AVAILABLE

Published By Barclay Books, LLC
http://www.barclaybooks.com

Action\Adventure
Vultures In The Sky by Shields McTavish

Lieutenant-Colonel Douglas Mark White, a fighter squadron commander stationed on Vancouver Island, analyzes evidence surrounding the crash of an Arcturus maritime patrol plane: he concludes that the aircraft was shot down by a hostile fighter.

Aggressively, Doug pushes for authorities to investigate the incident. Subsequently, large-scale air activity in Canadian air space is detected involving unregistered jet transports and fighters. The armed aircraft are marked with the insignia of the United States Air Force.

Doug attempts to solve the mystery despite the resistance of the Wing Commander, the seeming disinterest of authorities at higher HQ, and a lack of resources. Accidental damage to his eyes, which places his position as a flyer and squadron commander in jeopardy, complicates his quest. Ultimately, he discovers that there is a large-scale drug-smuggling operation flying from Mexico and Columbia to a fake USAF air base in British Columbia.

Doug, despite eyesight difficulties and self-doubt related to the death of a squadron pilot, struggles to defeat the smugglers. His fight to destroy the 'Vultures' culminates in an air battle and personal clash for survival with their detestable leader.
ISBN: 1-931402-02-7

NOW AVAILABLE

* * *

Action\Adventure\Suspense
Appointment In Samara by Clive Warner

A part time job with the CIA is fun. That's what Martin Conley thinks until one day a dying KGB agent gives him information that changes his life. Conley sets off for the Wadi Hadhramout to retrieve the codes to a biological weapon that can wipe out America. A beautiful Lebanese girl, Alia, acts as his guide. A storm wrecks their boat on the Yemen shore, leaving them to struggle on, and Alia is abducted by tribesmen.

Realizing he has fallen in love with her, Conley rescues Alia, and is drawn into a civil war between North and South Yemen.

Conley delivers the codes to his masters but new evidence makes him wonder if the weapon will neutralized —or used against China?

There is only one thing to be done: destroy the weapon himself. Defying his CIA masters, Conley and Alia set off on a mission to find and destroy it—but time has run out. **ISBN: 1-931402-25-6**

NOW AVAILABLE

Published By Barclay Books, LLC
http://www.barclaybooks.com

Drama
Do No Harm by James R. Snedden

Three young men with totally different aspirations meet in medical school where they form a lasting friendship. The author follows their lives, cleverly weaving their stories of intrigue and sex, probing the events influencing their lives, ambitions, and career:

Charles, poor boy from up state New York, whose goal is wealth and social status. He sets up practice in the City of New York; however, when legitimate means don't produce financial rewards quickly enough, he resorts to criminal activity, consorting with members of the underworld and making himself vulnerable to blackmail.

Abner, a farm boy from rural Illinois, inspired by the doctor who cared for his family. His altruistic motives turn to disappointment when reality replaces dreams. Returning to his hometown, he is met with resentment and hostility and must decide to leave or stay and fight.

David, the rich boy from San Francisco. The only son of a wealthy businessman, he chooses medical school to escape his parents and their plans for him to carry on the family business. An adventurer and ladies man, tragedy strikes just as he finds purpose in his life.
ISBN: 1-931402-27-2

NOW AVAILABLE

* * *

A Spectral Visions Imprint
Monstrosity by Paul Lonardo

A prominent New England university is slowly falling under the influence of an alien cult that promises to deliver an elixir of immortality to its followers. Jack McRae is the only person in town who suspects that the cult may not be delivering exactly what it has promised. But he is a young outcast whose only connection to Bister University is his girlfriend, Katie. However, after a string of disappearances, Katie falls prey to the Second Chance Cult and its charismatic leader, and it is now up to Jack to rescue her from its greedy clutches. His suspicions lead him on a perilous journey into the inner sanctum of one of the Nation's oldest private institutions. As Jack closes in on the truth behind the alien mystery, he witnesses cult members undergoing bizarre transformations, discovers grotesque insect/rodent creatures hiding in the walls and floors all around the university, and then uncovers the possible plotting of a mass suicide ritual. All the evidence leads Jack to affirm his belief that an alien intelligence may not exist. But Jack soon finds out that what's really going on involves something even more sinister, though very much terrestrial.   **ISBN: 1-931402-14-0**

NOW AVAILABLE
Published By Barclay Books, LLC
http://www.barclaybooks.com